Brother's Revenge

By Amber Fawn

ISBN: 978-1-3999-9940-3

Readers note: 'Brother's Revenge' is book 3 in the 'Orchid's children' series. This book is not a standalone. I highly suggest reading book 1 'Consequences' and book 2 'Saving Sweet Sienna' first, in order for the storyline to make sense.

To you all - I'm sorry.

CHAPTER 1:

WHO IS MY BROTHER?

Marcus

Meeting your mother for the first time after being given up as a child is one thing, but discovering in the same breath that you have a brother you never knew existed, is a revelation so overwhelming that it recalibrates your entire existence. A discovery so profound that it redefines your very identity, leaving you to reconcile the fragmented pieces of your past and reframe your understanding of who you are and where you belong.

Unveiling the truth that an entire life has been intertwined with yours, yet hidden in shadow, is like staring at a mirror that reflects a reality that's not your own; like I'm a stranger in my own story.

As I struggle to process this bombshell, my mother's face crumples with worry, her hands trembling as they reach for mine.

"Of course you have a brother." She whispers urgently, shaking her head in disbelief. I shrug, and yes I know that's a pretty pathetic response to such a huge disclosure, but I'm not sure how else I should respond.

How exactly are you supposed to react to finding out you have a sibling you never knew existed?

It's like I'm trapped in a vivid hallucination, where each moment bends and stretches, too strange to be real but too visceral to be dismissed as a dream.

My mother's eyes fill with tears as she takes a deep breath.

"Noah," she says in a defeated sigh, "your brother, sweet. Noah?" The name echoes in my mind, stirring up a whirlpool of confusion and curiosity. The ground beneath me feels shaky, unsteady.

Noah.
I have a brother named Noah.
Noted.

And he's Somewhere out there, living his own life, possibly wondering the same things I've always wondered.

"I don't know him." I state, the words feeling inadequate. My mother's sobs begin softly but quickly escalate, her body wracked with grief. She covers her face with her hands, and her whole frame shakes as the weight of the past crashes over her. Instinctively, though it feels foreign and awkward, I step forward and pull her into a hug.

The act feels strange, like wearing clothes that don't fit. Comforting a woman who is biologically my mother, yet whom I've never known, is deeply disorientating.

Her pain is tangible, a raw wound laid bare.

"Hey," I say softly. "It's okay." She looks up at me, her eyes red and glistening with tears, searching my face for something, perhaps a sign that I don't hate her. As she looks at me, I begin to notice our shared features for the first time. I'm struck by the unmistakable resemblance between us.

The curve of her lips, the shape of her nose, even the colour and texture of her hair; all mirroring my own. The recognition is complex, grounding me in the reality of our connection in a way that words alone could never achieve.

This woman, this stranger, is my fucking *mother*.
My flesh and blood.

"I just.. I'm sorry, sweet. I don't understand how this could've happened," she says, her voice quivering. "All the years I spent down there, I kept one sliver of hope that at the very least, my children would have had each other." Her words hit me hard, and I can see the depth of her regret.

"It's okay, mum." I interrupt, though it's not. Nothing about this situation is okay. "We'll figure this out. I'll find him. I'll find Noah, okay?" Her sobbing quiets a little, and she takes a shuddering breath, nodding slowly.

I nod back, more to myself than to her. I've just promised to find a brother I've never met, a person whose existence I only learned about minutes ago. The enormity of the task ahead doesn't fully register, but one thing is clear; I need answers. For myself, for her, and for Noah, wherever he may be.

I start thinking more about him. Would he be taller than me? Shorter? Do we have the same mannerisms, the same laugh? It's fun to envision a brother who might share my quirks and idiosyncrasies. Someone who, despite the years and distance, may feel an inexplicable bond with me simply because we share the same blood.

Though, admittedly, I haven't had the best luck with that concept so far.

I wonder what kind of person he is. Is he funny? Does he know about me? The thought that he might have spent years wondering, as I did, if he had a sibling out there somewhere tugs at my heart. What has his life been like? Has he been happy? The questions multiply, each one bringing with it a new layer of curiosity. The prospect of finding Noah is no longer just about answers; it's about the possibility of forging a bond that was meant to be there all along.

I refuse to let my father's actions set the tone for what family is. After all, I've experienced firsthand the warmth and solidarity of family through Skylar's. I know what family can be.

As I mull over the myriad of questions swirling in my mind, another peculiar realisation dawns on me; I don't even know my own mother's name.

"Uh, mum," I start, "what's your name?" I ask tentatively. She looks up at me, her tear-streaked face momentarily frozen.

"Charlotte." Sienna interjects softly, her voice carrying a mixture of empathy and understanding. I glance back at Sienna to see her smiling. "We met already."

My stomach churns, and I feel a wave of nausea. The way they look at each other, the pain and regret in their eyes. They clearly share an unspoken bond, born of their mutual suffering, and in their gazes, I see the reflection of what they must have endured in that basement.

My mother's eyes are red and swollen, but there's a glimmer of hope and gratitude as she looks at Sienna.

"I never imagined I'd meet my son's girlfriend in such a way," she says, her voice laced with a hint of sadness. "But I'm very happy that my son has such a beautiful angel in his life." Sienna blushes and glances up to me.

"Thank you, but I'm not his girlfriend," she says, with a cheeky smile. "Marcus doesn't really *do* labels." I roll my eyes, a small smile tugging at the corners of my mouth.

"*Oh*, I see. You're too cool for that are you, Marcus Bear?" My mother chips in, crossing her arms and giving me a look that feels very stereotypically motherly. I blink, taken aback. "Hm?" She adds. Sienna stifles a laugh beside me, clearly enjoying this. I raise my hands in mock surrender.

"Alright, alright. How about we hold off on the lectures for a little while?" I suggest with a smile,

"I wanna know more about Noah. When did you last see him?"

"The same evening that I last saw you, my sweet." She replies softly, as if it's obvious. "You went into that house *together*."

"That makes no sense." I blurt out instinctively. "I would know him, or at least vaguely remember him." She takes a deep breath, gathering her thoughts before speaking again.

"You were both so young," she begins, her voice trembling. "If somebody had come to collect him early on, you probably *wouldn't* remember."

"I guess." I nod slowly, feeling a slow, simmering rage beneath my skin. The question that has been burning inside me for as long as I can remember, and now it bursts forth like a wildfire.

"Why did you give us up?" The words hang in the air like a challenge, heavy with accusation. My mother flinches as if I'd struck her, her eyes welling up with tears. But not just tears of sadness; there's a deeper pain there, a sorrow that seems to transcend words.

"It was never my choice." She replies bluntly, causing the room to stand still.

The weight of her words settles over me, suffocating in their implication. I feel the rage flare up again, this time directed not at her, but at the man I called my dad. My mother's voice breaks through my tumultuous thoughts.

"I never wanted to give you up," she says, her voice cracking, "I fought *so* hard, sweet." As I stand there, absorbing her words, my mind churns. My entire life, I've operated under the assumption that my mother had given us up, that she had chosen to abandon us. But now, hearing her say it wasn't her choice, it shatters the narrative I had constructed to make sense of my past.

My thoughts, of course, drift to my father. He was the one who *'found'* me. I trusted him, believing he had rescued me from that home. But if my mother had been forced to give us up, it begs the question; what role did my father play in all this? Considering his actions in locking her up in a basement, it's obvious to me now that he's behind it all. Yet, it's still jarring to get confirmation of his deceit.

Despite our problematic relationship, I had always seen my father as a kind of saviour. Yet, this man I had trusted implicitly had actually orchestrated this entire nightmare. He didn't just take me from my mother; he condemned her to a life of darkness, hiding her from me all these years.

"You have to believe me, Marcus," she pleads, her eyes searching mine for any sign of understanding. "I never stopped fighting for you. Not for a single day." I swallow hard, the lump in my throat making it difficult to speak.

"I believe you," I whisper, the anger slowly giving way to a deep, aching sadness. "It's just a hard pill to swallow."

CHAPTER 2:
WHAT'S HIS IS YOURS

Sienna

Well, now those fucking eyes make sense. The revelation hits me like a freight train and everything is starting to come together. Each piece of the puzzle clicks into place with a sudden clarity that leaves me reeling. Noah, the tall guy from the basement, is Marcus' brother.

He was part of that nightmare, and though it's irrational, it's insane, Noah was different. The memory of him is a whirlwind of emotions; fear, confusion, and strangely, a kind of reluctant fondness. It's a messy, contradictory cocktail that defies logic, but it's undeniable; there was something about him that made me feel.. safe? Even if just for a moment.

This morning when he brought me breakfast. His demeanour had changed slightly; he was almost gentle in a way that felt genuine. We talked. It was bizarre, having this normal conversation in such an abnormal place. I never imagined I would find myself here, unravelling the revelation that he is Marcus' brother. Marcus' *brother*. The words echo in my mind, a surreal twist on the reality I thought I knew.

I had breakfast with Marcus' brother this morning.

Glancing at Marcus, I see his face awash with emotions. He's grappling with the truth of his past, the lies his father told him, and the reality of a brother he never knew existed. How could I possibly ever tell him that I've already met Noah? Knowing him, he would brutally murder Noah if he found out the truth, especially after what happened in the basement.

But Noah ended up being strangely humane with me. He even opened up about how his mother is dead, which now I know isn't true of course. In hindsight, it's evident that he, in his own tumultuous way, is just as much a victim of their father's insidious manipulation and cruelty as Marcus is.

The weight of my secret presses down on me like a leaden stone, but I know I must keep it to myself. This is Marcus' moment, a chance he's yearned for all his life. He has always longed for family, and I can't deprive him of this opportunity to connect with Noah.

Birdie interrupts the silence,

"how are we gonna find him then?" she asks. Marcus, visibly lost in thought, takes a moment to process the question. His brow furrows slightly as he considers the practicalities of locating Noah, whom I know is a lot closer than everyone likely suspects. A determined glint flashes in his eyes, a spark of resolve amidst the turmoil. He moves with purpose, striding toward his father's motionless form. The room seems to hold its breath as he kneels beside his father, his fingers deftly searching through the pockets of the lifeless body. With deliberate fingers, he begins to search through the pockets of that cold, unyielding flesh, a macabre scavenger in a place that once held the remnants of a father's authority.

As Marcus extracts his hand, a triumphant glare illuminates his eyes, and he holds up a phone and a set of jangling keys like trophies. The metal clinks softly as he swiftly unlocks the device, the screen casting an ethereal glow on his face. For a moment, his expression remains inscrutable as he scrolls through the applications in silence. Then, a smirk tugs at the corner of his mouth, a glimmer of amusement and triumph dancing in his eyes.

Without a word, he turns the phone towards us, revealing the screen that displays messages from a contact named 'Noah', confirming not only Noah's existence in their father's phonebook but also their recent communication.

"They were texting just last night." Marcus announces, his voice tinged with a mixture of disbelief and pride. "And, I can see his location."

Dean leans in, his brows scrunched as he processes the revelation.

"So, he's nearby?" he asks, his voice edged with anticipation. Marcus nods slowly, his gaze fixed on the phone screen.

"Yeah," he confirms, his voice steadier now and a sweet smile creeping onto his face. "He's not far at all." Marcus locks eyes with me and I grin back, a silent acknowledgment of the journey ahead and the unspoken support between us.

"Go. Go see him." I happily instruct. He takes a few steps closer to me and grasps my hands, pressing a firm kiss to my knuckles.

"There's no rush, sweet," he says. "I need to get you out of here first. You've been through so much. We need to get you cleaned up and-"

"No." I insist with a smile. "You have to go and find him. I'll be fine with everyone else." Skylar steps forward, her expression resolute.

"Don't worry, Marcus. I'll take care of her. Everyone can come back to my place." Marcus hesitates, staring intensely into my eyes. The determination in his gaze is palpable, but so is the worry.

"Sweet, are you sure?" he asks, his voice barely above a whisper.

"Yes. Go. This is important."

"Nothing is as important as you-"

"Go. I'll be fine, I promise." He searches my face for reassurance before finally nodding and releasing my hands.

As I raise my gaze, Delilah comes into focus. Our eyes lock in a silent understanding. Time seems to halt, the world holding its breath. Then, with an unspoken pact, the trio converges on me. Delilah, Skylar, and Birdie all rush over to me. They pull me into a warm, supportive embrace, their arms wrapping around me tightly. The comforting pressure of their bodies against mine is like a gentle rain shower on parched skin. The familiar scent of their hair, and the gentle murmur of their voices all blend together; grounding me. As I breathe in their scents, I feel my worries melt away.

We slowly pull away from each other, and I notice that Skylar's eyes are glistening with unshed tears.

"Hey, what's wrong?" I ask. Skylar's gaze drops, and she looks down at her feet before speaking in a shaky voice.

"I'm just.. I'm so sorry, Sienna. I should have been paying more attention. I was in my own world and I didn't hear a thing. I could've helped you." I reach out and gently take her hand, giving it a reassuring squeeze.

"Sky," I say softly. "There was no way you could have stopped this."

"I know," she whispers. "I just feel so useless." I shake my head, trying to convey the futility of her words. I take a deep breath and try to think of something to say that will ease her guilt.

"We were *both* in danger."

"But I should have been there for you."

"You were there for me, Sky. You always are," I say. "You're here right now." Skylar nods, still looking a bit tearful, but her expression softens.

I take a step forward and wrap my arms around her, pulling her into another tight embrace. Her body relaxes slightly as she leans into me, her tears finally beginning to subside.

"Okay," she whispers, her voice steady now. "Let's get going. We need to get you cleaned up." I nod, feeling a sense of relief wash over me.

As we begin to pull away, Skylar takes my hand preparing to leave and head to her house. Suddenly Marcus' voice cuts through the quiet.

"Wait." We all turn to look at him as he strides over to his mother. Reaching into his pocket, he pulls out the keys to his father's house; the metal glinting in the dim light. Holding them out to her, his voice is steady, but I can hear the mixture of resolve and tenderness in his words. "What's his is yours."

Charlotte stares at the keys, her eyes welling up with tears. She reaches out with a trembling hand, taking them from Marcus. The keys jingle softly as they change hands, a poignant transfer of power and responsibility. Her expression is a mix of sorrow, gratitude, and something else; perhaps a sense of bittersweet closure.

"Thank you," she breathes, her voice thick with emotion. Marcus nods, his jaw set with determination. He then turns back to me, his eyes softening. The unspoken promise in his gaze reassures me.

"I'll see you tonight, sweet." he says before turning his attention to the girls, "Keep her safe. Please."

CHAPTER 3:
BACK TO ORCHID'S
Dean

The room empties out, leaving just myself, Marcus and Marcus' dead dad. I've always known my life was pretty fucked, but the sheer number of corpses I've now witnessed has left me wondering if 'fucked' is too tame a term. If I were the type to go to therapy, I'd probably need to get my therapist their own therapist after explaining all of this shit.

I walk over to Marcus, who's staring down at the lifeless body with an expression I can't quite read. Maybe it's sorrow, maybe it's relief, maybe it's something in between. It's hard to tell with Marcus; his emotions have always been a mixed bag.

"Yo," I say, my voice softer than usual. "You sure you're ready to do this?" After a few moments, he tears his gaze away from his dad and looks at me. His eyes are bloodshot, and there's a vulnerability in them I'm not used to seeing. He's always been the strong one, the one who never lets anything get to him. But right now, he looks as lost as I feel.

"Yeah," he replies after a long pause. "Yeah, I'm ready. Let's go find our brother." I raise an eyebrow, confused.

"*Our* brother?" I respond. Marcus offers a small, proud smile.

"Yeah, *our* brother. You were here first."

For a moment, I'm taken aback. Marcus and I have been through hell together, but we've never put it into words like this. It's strange, hearing it out loud, but it's also.. kind of nice. Wholesome, even. And for two guys like us, moments like these are rare. I nod, feeling a lump in my throat.

"Alright. Let's go find our brother."

As we head out of the room, I can't help but glance back at Marcus' dad one last time. A part of me wonders if we'll end up like him; victims of a past we can't escape. But another part of me, the part that's still clinging to hope, believes we can break the cycle. We have to.

We step outside into the evening air, the cool breeze hitting us like a wake-up call. The city sounds in the background of music blaring, people shouting, the distant wail of a siren, remind us that we're back home. Back to the devil we know. It's a strange comfort, knowing that despite everything, the world keeps turning.

As we reach the road just outside the house where his dad now lies dead, Marcus slows his pace. He turns his head, casting a glance back, the shadows playing tricks on his expression.

"You okay?" I ask quietly, sensing the hesitation radiating from him. Marcus nods, his expression unreadable in the half-light.

"Yeah," he murmurs. "Just.. taking it in." I don't press further, respecting the silence that surrounds his grief. Instead, we cross the road to where our car is parked. I slip into the driver's seat, and Marcus settles into the passenger side, the door closing with a muted thud. The cool leather interior and the faint scent of rain-soaked asphalt bring a sense of grounding.

I adjust the rearview mirror with a determined flick, my other hand steady on the wheel. I glance at Marcus, catching the set of his jaw and the resolve in his eyes. I start the engine, its gentle hum filling the quiet evening air.

"What's the address?" I ask. Marcus shakes his head slightly.

"Not yet. Head to Orchid's first."

The gate, now hanging off its hinges from Skylar's reckless entrance, greets us with a crooked smile. Along with lines of crime scene tape fluttering in the breeze. I park the car nearby, the engine ticking as it cools down.

"What exactly are we doing here?" I ask, my voice low.

"Since dad mentioned the book before he.." He trails off, unable to finish the sentence. "I wanna make sure I have it. Clearly it's still important."

Of course, the book. Ever since that night we 'closed' it, an uneasy feeling has been gnawing at me, intensifying with every brush with death. The car crash that should have killed me, the tree that nearly crushed my skull, the combine that mercilessly claimed a couple of my fingers but somehow left the rest of me intact. It's as if some unseen force has been toying with my life, pulling me back from the brink time and again. And now, hearing Marcus mention the book, it all seems to connect in a way that makes my skin crawl. I can't share this with Marcus. Not yet. Not just because it would worry him, but because saying it out loud would make it all too real. And I'm not ready to face that reality just yet.

As we step out of the car, Marcus strides purposefully toward the tangled underbrush at the edge of the car park. I follow him, curiosity piqued, watching as he navigates the uneven ground with familiarity. The air is heavy with the damp scent of earth and foliage,the recent rain draping a shroud of moisture over the leaves and grass. He plunges his hand into the shadows of the bush where he'd tossed the book, his arm disappearing into the darkness. For a moment, he's still, as if considering whether he's in the right place. Then, with a slight tug, he pulls the book free from the muck.

What's interesting is that, although it had been raining and lying in mud, the book is entirely spotless. Not a speck of dirt mars its surface, the cover and pages seemingly unscathed by the elements. It's as if it had been shielded by an invisible barrier, untouched by the rain and the grime that surrounds it. The contrast is unnerving.

The mud clings to Marcus's fingers, darkening his jeans with stubborn smudges, yet the book remains pristine, its pages crisp and dry as if shielded by some invisible force. I suppose it's no surprise, considering the fact that we couldn't even put a fucking dent on this book before. But perhaps I assumed that closing the book would have broken the spell, diminishing its mystique.

"Alright, we got it. Let's get out of here," I say, assuming we'd be heading back to the car. But Marcus shakes his head.

"There's one more thing I wanna grab from inside."

As we approach the building, I spot the window we shattered last time, now hastily boarded up yet again. We come to a halt, both of us fixated on the crude patchwork; a jagged barrier held together by nails driven in at awkward angles, struggling to contain the splintered wood beneath.

"Round two, huh?" I nod towards the freshly boarded window.

"Seems like we're making a habit of this." Marcus replies with a wry smile. We step closer, our hands brushing against the weathered wood as we examine the handiwork. Without a word, we set to work, our fingers probing the gaps between the boards. The wood creaks and groans in protest as we apply pressure, our hands moving in tandem as if choreographed.

With practised ease, we pull and tug until the boards yield, exposing the shattered window beneath, shards of glass still stubbornly clinging to the frame. I toss the boards aside with a grunt, then follow Marcus as he climbs inside. As we navigate the debris and jagged glass strewn across the floor, the familiar crunch underfoot echoes through the silent building. Soft moonlight filters through the broken windows, casting long shadows that dance across the dusty surfaces.

We ascend the creaking staircase, the wooden treads complaining softly beneath our footsteps, the sound echoing through the silent hallway like a mournful sigh. Marcus bursts into the room, his gaze fixed on the floor behind the door, his attention razor-sharp and unyielding as he scans the space.

As Marcus crouches down to lift the floorboard where we originally found the book, I watch curiously, memories of our childhood flooding back.

"How did I never know about this?" I ask, incredulous. Marcus chuckles softly, his eyes crinkling at the corners, a spark of pride illuminating his expression.

"In the wise words of Dean Douglas," he replies, "we've been hiding forever." We lock eyes, and for a moment, everything just stops. There's a connection; strong and undeniable. I'm not sure what I'm feeling exactly, whether it's nostalgia, sadness, happiness or something else, but it's there.

Ironically, our childhoods weren't exactly storybook material. We became the 'bad kids' not because we enjoyed causing trouble, but because it was the only way we knew how to cope with the darkness that surrounded us. Breaking rules wasn't rebellion, it was survival. We turned to trouble and chaos as an escape, a way to bury the pain and trauma deep enough that it couldn't hurt us anymore. Or at least deep enough that we forgot about how badly it was hurting us.

Despite how close we are as a group, there are certain topics we just never touched. We never really talked about the shit that went down in our pasts. We were a family in that house. We'd kill and die for each other, no questions asked. But talk about the reasons we were in that home in the first place? No chance. It was like an unspoken rule; don't dredge up the past. Just hide and keep moving forward, no matter what.

And look at where that got us.
We've become complete monsters.

Marcus pulls out the small box from beneath the floorboards, opening it carelessly and immediately grabbing the ripped photograph of his mother from the back of the pile; its edges frayed and corners dog-eared. He shakes it in his hand a few times, as if confirming to himself that this is what he wanted, before stuffing it in his pocket.

I pause, taking a moment to absorb the desolate atmosphere of the room. Wandering towards the remains of my side of the bedroom; my focus lands on the endless array of scratches and slices in the wall. I remember every single one, somehow. The slits seem to ripple through my memory. When my parents sent me

23

here, I had managed to smuggle in a couple of knives in my pockets. I used to stay up all night just slicing the walls. It was my way of dealing with all the shit.

While everyone else tried to sleep, I'd be there, carving away like a madman. Sometimes I'd imagine the plaster was my old man's face or the endless parade of social workers who came in and out of the revolving door; not giving a single fuck about us. Other times, it was just about feeling something, anything, to drown out the numbness.

But those slashes in the wall didn't stay just slashes for long. The anger grew, and so did the violence. It wasn't just walls getting cut up anymore; it was knuckles, then faces. Fights became a regular thing. I'd brawl with anyone, everyone, as if beating the crap out of someone else would somehow beat the crap out of my own thoughts.

Then I spent some more time with Dot, the only social worker who ever seemed to genuinely care. She had this way about her, like she saw through all our bullshit. She'd sit with us, talk with us, actually listen. I don't know how she did it, but she got through. She got through to me. One morning, she brought in these cans of spray paint. She figured if I needed to leave my mark, it might as well be something worth looking at.

It wasn't long before I traded my knives for those cans. Instead of slicing walls, I started tagging them. Graffiti became my thing. It was a way to express all the shit I felt without tearing anything or anyone apart. It was colour and life in a place that felt grey and dead. Every tag was a piece of me, a burst of creativity where there used to be destruction. My aggression never left, but I learnt how to keep it controlled.

Which is of course why I shot somebody in the head this week.

Marcus snaps the floorboard back into place with a final, decisive thud. He stands up, dusting off his hands, and we look at each other.

"You ready?" he asks, trying to keep his voice steady.

"Am *I* ready?" I retort, raising an eyebrow. He chuckles softly and rubs his forehead.

"I'm not sure I'll ever be ready," he admits. "So let's get it done."

CHAPTER 4:

NICE TO MEET YOU

Marcus

As we pull up into Noah's estate, I can't help but stare in awe. In its centre stands a huge, old, classical-English mansion, the kind you see in movies or on postcards, but never in real life. Ivy crawls up the stone walls like nature's own wallpaper, and there's even a fountain in the driveway, water trickling down in a way that seems both elegant and incredibly unnecessary.

I glance at Dean, and his jaw is practically on the floor. He looks like he's just seen a UFO land in front of him, complete with little green men.

"You seein' this?" He mutters, more to himself than to me. I shake my head slowly.

"Oh, I'm seein' it."

"*Fuck*," he smiles. "You think he'll lend me a tenner?" I chuckle at his irreverent humour.

"Maybe if you ask nicely."

We step out of the car, and I feel like I'm in some kind of weird dream. The gravel crunches under our feet as we walk as slow as humanly possible toward the massive front door. I half-expect a butler to come out and shoo us away for lowering the property value by just being here.

"You sure this is the right place?" Dean asks.

"It's the only house here." I reply straightforwardly. Dean whistles low, shaking his head in disbelief.

The irony stings. My dad and I were scraping by in a rundown shithole, a place that barely held together. I always wondered why he was rarely home. Now, seeing this mansion, it all clicks. He'd been raising my brother too, but Noah got the mansion while I got the scraps.

We continue our slow approach, each step echoing in the dark silence, until we stand before the towering door. Just as we raise our hands to knock, the door swings open with a suddenness that startles us both. Standing there, framed by the opulent doorway, is a man who can only be Noah. His face is hard, eyes sharp and calculating, his presence exuding an air of quiet menace.

27

In his hand, steady as stone, he holds a gun; its barrel aimed squarely at Dean.

Good start.

"Unless you're begging for a bullet in your skull, I suggest you get the fuck off my property, Douglas." Noah's voice slices through the air like a blade, cold and firm. The threat in his tone is undeniable, sharp enough to make the hairs on my neck stand up. He looms in the doorway, his towering frame filling the space, exuding a dark authority that demands attention. His presence is intimidating, like the air itself is bending to his will.

Noah shares my dark hair and hazel eyes, but that's where the similarities end. He looms at least 6 foot 7. He's built like a fortress, not dramatically bulky but undeniably muscular, every line of his frame exuding strength and athleticism. His jaw is chiselled, his features hardened. There's no denying, he's a scary guy.

"Nice to meet you too." Dean mumbles as his eyes dart over to me; a silent plea for me to handle this. I swallow hard and consider the best way to navigate the conversation.

"Noah, wait." I interrupt. Noah's eyes narrow, his grip on the gun unwavering as he looks me up and down, sizing me up.

"Who the fuck are you?" He demands, suspicion and hostility clear in his tone. He looks me up and down another time.

"I'm your brother."

A smirk forms on his lips.

"You think you're funny?"

"No joke," I say, trying to keep my voice steady. "I know it sounds crazy, but it's the truth." Noah stares at me, a mocking smile spreading across his face before he turns to Dean, eyebrows raised.

"You gonna tell your little sidekick to shut the fuck up, or what?"

"I'm serious." I reply, standing my ground. Noah's eyes linger on Dean for a moment longer and then back to me, his smirk fading slightly but his grip on the gun still tight.

"Prove it. "

I nod cautiously, my hand inching toward the pocket of my tracksuit bottoms where I'd stashed the photograph. Just as my fingers brush the edge of it, Noah's gun snaps toward me like a coiled viper, his eyes locked on mine with a deadly intensity. I freeze, heart hammering in my chest, the weight of his gaze heavier than the cold steel aimed at my head.

"I'm just grabbing a photo, bro." I stammer, holding my hands up in a placating gesture. "It's proof."

Noah's eyes continue to bore into mine, and it's clear he's not easily convinced.

"Slowly," he growls. "And if you pull out anything other than a photo, you're both dead." I nod again, moving deliberately this time, my fingers finding the edges of the worn photograph.

As I cautiously retrieve the photograph from my pocket, Noah's eyes track my every move, his stare sharp and assessing. In that tense moment, it's clear that Noah is a force to be reckoned with, far beyond anything I've encountered before. I retrieve it from my pocket and hold it up; a faded photograph capturing my mother and I before I ended up in Orchid's. Along the left edge, the photo is torn, leaving me to assume my dad and Noah once filled the missing half.

Noah doesn't relax, but his gaze flickers briefly to the image. I can sense the gears turning in his mind, processing the implications of what he sees. He remains silent, his expression unreadable, weighing his options with the careful consideration of a seasoned strategist. Dean stands beside me, tense but alert. I feel him holding his breath, waiting to see how my brother will react. Noah squints his eyes slightly as he studies the photograph, then looks back at me, his stare piercing.

"Which one of you killed my dad?" Noah asks bluntly, his tone harsh. We pause, considering our approach. "I saw you both on the cameras so don't fucking lie to me."

"That would be my girlfriend." Dean replies, surprisingly chirpy, proud even. Noah's reaction is icy and detached, a chasm of emotional numbness

"Your *girlfriend,* huh?" he says, his tone dripping with disdain and a mocking inflection.

The laugh that follows is brief and chilling, betraying more embarrassment and annoyance than genuine sorrow. It's clear that in Noah's mind, such vulnerability, even in death, is a sign of weakness rather than tragedy. He steps back slightly, gesturing with the gun for us to enter. Dean and I hesitate, glancing at each other.

"Do you need a written invitation?" Noah snaps, his patience visibly thinning rapidly.

As we step inside, the opulent atmosphere envelops us; the place screams luxury. The marble floors, polished to a mirror-like sheen, stretch out like a rich tapestry, while the room's modern and antique accents blend seamlessly, evoking the grandeur of a bygone era. It's as if we've entered the lair of a cinematic mafia kingpin.

Dim lighting casts shadows across the room, making the rich wood panelling and ornate furniture look even more imposing. Chandelicrs suspended from the high ceiling cast intricate patterns of light, dancing across the walls like fireflies on a summer night. Every aspect of the decor exudes an aura of power and wealth.

The air is thick with the scent of cigars, leather, and burning fire, giving the place an old-world charm mixed with a dangerous edge. A grand staircase, swathed in a black runner, curves upward to the next floor like a crimson ribbon. To its right, a massive stone fireplace dominates the room, its mantle adorned with statues and a very fucking rich looking cigar box.

"Sit," Noah commands, gesturing toward a huge black leather sofa. We move to the sofa and sit, the leather cold and unbending beneath us. Noah's grip on the gun doesn't waver as he steps back, making his threat clear. "If either of you get up, I'll shoot." Noah strides over to a large, intricately carved chest in the corner of the room. He opens it, rummaging through the contents before pulling out a small wooden box. He opens the box, sifting through old papers and trinkets until he finds what he's looking for.

Holding what looks like the other half of the photograph, he saunters back toward us, but not before grabbing a cigar from the case on the mantel. With a flick of his lighter, he ignites the tip, drawing in a deep breath that fills the air with the rich, heady aroma of smoke. As Noah advances, the photograph clutched in one hand and his gun still aimed in the other, the cigar hangs casually from his mouth.

In this moment I can't help but think,
fuck, my brother's really cool.

Without a word, he holds out his hand to me, expecting the other half of the photo. I hand it over, and he fits the two pieces together.

As he studies the now-complete image, the room falls into an uncomfortable silence. The photograph confirms our shared history, but Noah's expression remains hard, unreadable. The seconds tick by like hours, until finally, he utters a low, contemplative 'Hm,' content that I've told the truth before tucking his gun away, a subtle release of tension.

He strides over to a plush armchair opposite the sofa where Dean and I sit. He sinks into the cushions, relaxing into a languid pose. His eyes remain fixed on mine, burning with an intensity that makes my skin prickle, as he savours another slow, considerate drag on his cigar.

"So," he says, his words dripping with quiet authority. "You're my little brother, huh?"

"Yeah." I nod, and for the first time, Noah smiles at me, a genuine smile.

"It's good to see you again, Marcus."

"You know my name?"

"I'm 4 years older than you, little man," he says, his eyes glinting with a knowing light. "I have memories that you don't." Noah's smile grows, and he leans back in his chair, the cigar still smouldering between his fingers. "I always knew you were out there somewhere. As I got old enough to start asking questions, Dad would tell me my memories of you were just fabricated, but I remembered you vividly."

I'm stunned, struggling to process the bombshell he's dropped. Noah's words are like a punch to the gut, shaking me to my core.

"He denied that I was your brother?" I confirm. Noah nods, his expression darkening.

"Yeah," he says gruffly.

"Why would he do that?" I ask, feeling a mix of anger and confusion. Noah shrugs, his shoulders rolling in a gesture of resignation.

"He's a confusing man." he says, his voice low and even. "Always was." I shake my head, trying to clear the haze of confusion from my mind.

"Where've you been?" he asks, interrupting my silence; curiosity and a hint of warmth in his tone. I take a deep breath and relax my body.

"Well, I didn't leave Orchid's until 2018." I reply, trying to sound casual despite the flutter in my chest.

"*Shit.* I almost forgot about that place." he says with a smirk, his eyes crinkling at the corners. "Where'd you go after that?"

"Dad came to collect me," I say. "I've been living with him ever since." Noah's brow furrows, confusion etched across his face.

"With Dad? How's that possible?" His words are laced with scepticism, and I can sense his mind racing to piece together the puzzle. I take another deep breath, trying to make sense of it all myself, but the more I think about it, the more tangled it becomes.

"He wasn't home much. I never understood why. He'd come back for a few days, then disappear for weeks. Now, of course, it makes sense. Apparently, he was living two *very* different lives." Noah exhales a slow, deliberate stream of smoke, his eyes clouding over

35

as he absorbs the revelation. He takes a moment to collect his thoughts before speaking again, his voice low and contemplative.

"As I said, he's a confusing man."

"Now," he starts again, leaning forward. "Let's address the elephant in the room. Why the fuck are you hanging around with this prick?" He jerks his chin toward Dean, who stiffens at the insult. I take a deep breath, bracing myself.

"Look, I don't know what issues you have with Dean, but he's been with me since Orchid's. He's got my back." Noah's gaze sharpens, an icy veneer sliding over his features as he zeroes in on Dean.

"I should put a bullet in your brain, right here right now," he says coldly. "But I'll spare you for my brother's sake, on one condition. You better stop taking our fucking business, Douglas." He points a finger at Dean, the threat clear.

Dean, instead of flinching, looks Noah dead in the eye, his posture relaxed and defiant.

"No need to worry, I'm not dealing anymore. I'm out of the game." Noah raises an eyebrow, his interest piqued.

"Huh. Why the sudden change of heart?" Dean shrugs nonchalantly.

"Things got ugly. Too many feds, too many enemies. I've decided it ain't worth the hassle." He admits. Noah's expression hardens.

"If you say so. But mark my words; if you ever think about crossing me or slipping back into the business, you won't get another warning."

"Understood." Dean nods with a sarcastic grin.

Noah leans back in his chair, finally relaxing a bit. He takes another drag from his cigar, the smoke swirling around his head like a halo of menace.

"Do you remember Mum?" He asks suddenly, his voice softer, almost hesitant.

"Not really," I admit. "All I've ever had was that photograph." I hesitate, then continue, "But I finally met her today." Noah's eyes widen, disbelief etched across his face.

"Met her?" he laughs, "Our mum's dead." I take a deep breath, the truth heavy on my tongue.

"She's not dead, Noah." I share. For a moment, I see a flicker of vulnerability beneath his hardened exterior.

"What do you mean she's not dead?"

"I met her earlier today." I admit, my voice trembling slightly. "She's been locked in Dad's basement all these years." Noah's expression shifts from confusion to a mix of shock and rage.

"The basement?" he echoes, his voice rising. I nod, swallowing hard.

"Yes. She's safe now. But she's been through hell down there."

Noah's face contorts with rage, a flash of anger that seems almost too intense to contain. His jaw clenches, and for a moment, I think he might explode. Then, just as suddenly as it appeared, his anger dissipates, replaced by a chilling calmness. He turns slowly to Dean, his eyes burning with intensity.

"Well," Noah says, his voice dangerously smooth, "tell your girlfriend I said thank you." Dean stiffens, clearly caught off guard.

"Thank you?" he repeats, confusion evident in his voice.

"Yeah. Thank you for taking him out. Saves me the trouble."

We sit in silence for a moment, the only sound being the soft echo of our breathing. His eyes, which had been locked intensely on mine for what felt like an eternity, finally drop to the marble floor, tracing the intricate patterns etched into the stone with a newfound introspection.

"I'd like to see her," Noah says suddenly, breaking the silence. His voice is steady, but there's an underlying urgency to his words. "Take me to her." I nod, feeling a strange mix of relief and apprehension.

"She's in dad's old house. The one we shared together." I tell him. Noah's expression shifts to one of disgust. He sneers, shaking his head in disdain.

"I'll get her a nice place. A *new* place." I nod again. That's exactly what she needs.

We stand up, ready to leave the house and Noah grabs a set of keys from an extremely impressive array of car keys on the back wall.

"Noah," I start. "I need to ask you one more thing."

"Make it quick," he replies, his tone still guarded but slightly more open.

"Do you have any idea why dad would have asked me about a book?"

For the first time since we arrived, Noah laughs; a genuine, hearty laugh that echoes through the grand room. He stands and walks back over to the chest, rummaging through its contents before pulling out a book very similar to mine. With a cocky grin dancing on his lips, he extends it toward me.

"Take it," he says, "I'm sick of hearing about that fucking thing."

CHAPTER 5:

PINK-HAIRED PRINCESS

Noah

I've just met her for the first time, my real mother, not the ghostly figure my father let me believe was dead and buried. Seeing her, broken and frail, was a punch to the gut. I hadn't felt that much anger in years, a rage so potent it made my blood boil. But I couldn't show it. Not in front of Marcus. Not in front of anyone.

I can't believe she was in that 'empty' room in the basement this whole time. They never gave me the keys to that room. They told me it was untouched. All the years I've spent torturing and murdering men down there, in the room next door, and my father managed to hide her from me. He and his loyal minion, Moth, who had always been like a shadow, always lingering around, always knowing more than he let on. More than he ever fucking should've. My old man and his henchman were more cunning than I ever gave them credit for. But now, they're both rotting, and good riddance.

When Marcus told me he had murdered Moth himself, I felt a sense of pride. Moth is no easy target. My little brother has shown his strength, and I'm impressed. It must run in the blood.

But then he hit me with the real kicker, the reasoning behind the kill. Apparently, Moth had confessed to the shit he did to Sienna, who I've now learnt is my brother's girlfriend.

Of course.

Little did Marcus know, I had joined Moth in doing so. I, obviously, kept my mouth shut about that. I never wanted to do that to Sienna. As stoic as I may seem, hearing her screams broke me in two. But Moth was high as a fucking kite, crazed, and pushing for us to take the job. Refusing would've been suicide, and worse, with me dead, Sienna would be left with no escape. Moth would drag her to his private warehouse, where he'd subject her to unspeakable horrors; rape, torture, and a slow, brutal, bloody murder. The thought of it was unbearable. I couldn't let that happen.

41

So I made the only choice I could; I agreed, knowing that I could use the situation to my advantage. I suggested taking Sienna to my father's house instead. It was a risk, but it gave me an opportunity to gain some kind of control of the situation. I had full access to that basement room. If I could persuade them to take her there, I'd eventually be able to get her out alive. It was survival, nothing more.

That basement is a place for grown men; enemies and cunts who deserved every second of pain and fear we inflicted on them. Never for sweet little girls. I tried to do something, anything, to make up for the horror she'd endured. I made and brought Sienna breakfast. Pathetic I know, but it was all I could do for right now. I had every intention of getting her out of there, one way or another. But luckily, Marcus showed up before I had to do anything more.

Thank fuck for that.

The drive over here had been a nightmare. Marcus wouldn't stop droning on about books the entire fucking time. Like father, like son. I'm sick of hearing about it. As if one cursed book wasn't enough, now there are two. Mine has been laying out events like clockwork since I opened it. And considering my father was just killed, the final event in the story, my book is finally complete. Done with.

I feel like I'm the only sane one left. While Marcus and our father have been fucking around with magical books, desperate to change the outcomes, I'm fully aware that they're only doing more harm. You can't mess with what's already set in motion. You can't fuck with fate.

And to top it off, I'm sick of Dean. I'm disgusted to find out that Marcus was his fucking Orchid's roommate and has been chilling with him ever since. I don't approve. The guy has been selling for years, constantly taking my dealers' business and giving them trouble. Not to mention the shit he used to cause for my mates back in the unit. He's a slimy cunt. A thorn in my side; always has been.
But it's okay, he won't be a problem much longer.
The book says so.

And now, here I am, standing outside yet-another house, this one belonging to somebody called 'Skylar', because Marcus wants me to meet his friends. This is the last place I want to be. I've got a business to run, enemies to watch, and a reputation to uphold. But family.. well, *my* family is complicated. So I'm here, against my better judgement, because my little brother asked.

Marcus raises his hand to knock on the door, and we wait. The seconds tick by before the door swings open, revealing a tiny figure standing in the doorway.

As soon as I see her, my entire world goes up in flames. I swear the world tilts on its axis.
I'm powerless to look away.

"This is Noah." Marcus says to her, a faint echo in my distracted mind.

She meets my gaze head-on, bold and unafraid, and something deep inside me stirs. It's possessive, almost primal. She's a goddess. She's a siren, looking up at me; beckoning me closer with those piercing blue eyes. She's got to be the sexiest little creature I've ever seen. It's immediately clear to me that I'd give anything to get my hands on her. Her delicate features, her petite frame; she's the perfect little package of fragility. And I know exactly what to do with that.

"Hey," she says, her tone teasingly melodic. "I'm Skylar." With intended grace, I step forward. Each movement is calculated, every stride laden with a magnetism I rarely unveil. My eyes feast on her face, lingering on the curve of her lips as they quirk into a subtle smile.

"Skylar..?" I ask, my voice low and commanding. She raises an eyebrow, a hint of amusement dancing in her eyes. I don't care. I know now that I'm not here to play games.

"A little formal don't you think?" she says, her voice husky and confident. I don't reply, instead I smirk, a slow, conscious movement. She's got no idea what she's gotten herself into. She thinks she's brave, standing there with her big girl talk and her flirty eyes. But I'll break her.

"Skylar Farmer." she continues, like she's giving me permission to know her name.

I close the distance between us, stepping into her space, watching the way her breath hitches as I invade her bubble. I lean in just enough to tower over her, my voice turning smooth and lethal.

"Well, Skylar Farmer," I say. "Pleasure."

I'm an ice-cold man, and this is what I've been missing; the rush of power that comes with possessing something that belongs to no one else. She belongs to me, and I know it immediately. She doesn't know what's coming for her yet, but I do. I'm about to do some bad things. Very bad things. My mind is a maelstrom of dark desires, and Miss Skylar Farmer is the spark setting them ablaze.

I've just found myself a pink-haired princess, and she'll soon know what it means to be owned by me.

She stares intensely into my eyes, almost challenging me. Her stare doesn't waver, and for a moment, we're locked in a silent battle of wills. Then, with a subtle shift of her weight, Skylar yields, her body angling to let us pass. The movement is almost imperceptible, but I know it's deliberate; a calculated surrender. As I pass her, I purposefully brush my shoulder against hers, the contact rough and possessive. It's a claim, a teaser of what's to come.

A warning that I'm no prince charming.

I feel her shiver slightly at the touch, and another satisfied smirk tugs at the corner of my lips. There's an immediate tension in the air. I can feel it. And I know she can too.

Inside, the others introduce themselves but I couldn't give a shit. I pretend I've never met Sienna, Delilah's the girl who shot my dad, the ginger one is a bird.

Blah blah blah.

I'm supposed to care about these introductions, supposed to engage, but they're all a distant hum. I'm a statue, frozen in place, my eyes fixed on Skylar and Skylar only; my mind already plotting. My pupils constrict, focusing all my attention on her. I don't blink.

I don't breathe. I'm like a man possessed; half-tempted to kidnap her on the fucking spot.

And then she catches me staring. Her eyes drilling into mine like a hot poker, and I give her a stern look; one that says I won't be deterred, I won't be swayed.

But instead of turning away..
she fucking smiles at me.

Not just any smile; a sly, naughty smile. Her lips curve upward in a subtle, knowing arc, as if she's sharing a private joke with me, one that only we understand. My cock hardens in response, but I don't react. I'm too far gone. Too locked in. I'm lost in the vortex of my own desire.

Birdie shouts over from across the room.

"Sky, can you get me a drink?" Skylar lets out a frustrated sigh and rolls her eyes, her irritation palpable as she begins to make her way towards the door behind me. As she approaches, her intensity doesn't waver. The room seems to shrink around us, every step she takes drawing her closer, until finally, she stops right beside me.

She stands close, her eyes locked onto mine with an inexorable stare. Leaning in just enough to invade my personal space, she whispers,

"Can I get you anything, Sir?" Her tone is dripping with mock politeness and formality. Brave girl. She's playing with fire, but what she doesn't realise is that I'm more than willing to get burned.

I narrow my eyes, a smirk curling my lips as I reply in a low, dangerous murmur,

"Just your cooperation, princess. Think you can manage that?" She lingers for a heartbeat longer, letting the tension build, then straightens and continues to the door; this time, her shoulder brushes mine as she passes.

It seems she's keeping score.

Marcus calls me over, his voice cutting through the haze of my thoughts.

"Noah, come join," he says, gesturing towards the group. Reluctantly, I make my way over to where they're gathered. I try to focus on the general chit-chat, nodding at the right moments, but my mind keeps drifting back to Skylar. The conversations around me blur into a background hum until I catch something that piques my interest.

"So, where are you planning on going now?" Delilah asks, her voice tinged with worry. "The police are still on your backs." She says. Marcus sighs, rubbing the back of his neck.

"I'm not sure, but it's getting late. We'll figure something out in the morning."

I see an opening, sliding in with casual ease.

"You could all stay at my place for a couple weeks. It's secure, not too far but it's out of the way, and you wouldn't have to worry about the feds. They wouldn't step foot on my property." I suggest, my tone casual. Delilah looks sceptical.

"I don't think we're all gonna fit in one house." she says. I chuckle, low and sure of myself. Dean joins in, shaking his head with a grin.

"Except it's not a house, darling. It's a fucking estate." He says. Marcus laughs and nods in agreement. I give a nonchalant shrug, pretending like it's no big deal.

"Consider it an open invitation. You'll be safe there, and it'll give you all some time to figure out your next move."

The truth, of course, is that I have an ulterior motive. With Skylar under my roof, I can keep her precisely where I want her; at my mercy, under my watchful eye, and within my grasp. As I observe her, study her, and unravel the secrets of her psyche, I'll gain the upper hand. And once I know exactly what makes her tick, I'll use that knowledge to prey on her. Manipulate her. Bend her to my will.

And the best part? She won't even realise it until it's too late.

"Well, I'm down." Marcus says, looking around, waiting for the others to follow. The nods come quickly, murmured agreements, everyone falling into line. Except Dean. "Dean?" Marcus asks. He doesn't respond right away, too busy rolling a joint, his hands moving faster than they should. I can see the tension in his shoulders, the way his jaw clenches. He hates this idea. Not because of the house, but because of me. I can't resist the urge to poke at him, to remind him of the shift in dynamics.

"Ah, come on, Douglas." I taunt with faux-genuinity "It'll be nice for Marcus to spend some time with his big brother." Dean's jaw tightens slightly, his eyes screwing as he glances briefly at Marcus, then back down at his joint. He doesn't dignify my jab with a response, but I can see I've struck a nerve.

Dean grunts noncommittally, lighting and taking a drag from his joint. The smoke swirls around his face as he exhales slowly, his gaze fixed somewhere in the distance.

"Yeah," Dean finally mutters with a nod. "Sounds good."

As Dean begrudgingly agrees, I smirk inwardly, relishing the subtle power play. He knows who holds the reins here, and it's not him. Marcus values me and I have qualities that Dean simply can't match. I see through his attempts at composure. He knows better than to challenge me openly. He sees me as untouchable, and he's not wrong.

Dean's bravado doesn't impress me. He likes to think he's dangerous, dealing his shitty weed and throwing fists around like it means something. But now, I'm here. He's used to being the big fish in a small pond, but in my ocean, he's just another minnow. His life has been a parade of petty crimes and adolescent bravado. I knew a few guys he had beaten up back in the young offenders' unit. Always picking fights he knew he'd win, thinking it made him hard.

But he's stepping into my world now, a world where I've carved out my place. A world where every single decision is life or death.

I exude arrogance because I've fucking earned it.

The group starts to disperse, everyone moving towards the door. I hang back with Sienna, making sure we're out of earshot from the others. She's been through hell, and I need to make sure she's okay. Considering I'm largely to blame.

"Sienna," I say softly, catching her attention. "How you doing?" She looks up, her eyes a mix of vulnerability and strength.

"I'm surprisingly okay, Noah." she replies, her voice barely above a whisper. I take a deep breath, the weight of my actions heavy on my chest.

"I'm so sorry, Sienna. I'm a fucking monster. I played a role I never wanted to play, but if I had refused, I would've been killed." I explain, "and with me dead, you'd be in a hell you'd have no chance of escaping from." She nods, understanding but still wounded.

"I forgive you."

"I want you to know," I continue, my voice earnest, "I wasn't going to rest until I got you out of there." Her eyes search mine, as if trying to decipher my soul.

"I believe you, Noah. And weirdly, you made me feel safer there." Her words bring a strange sense of relief. I've done unspeakable things, but her forgiveness feels like a lifeline.

She glances around, making sure no one is listening.

"Please, can you keep this between us?"

"If that's what you want." I promise, my tone firm and sincere. "I swear." She extends her little finger towards me, a gesture so innocent it almost breaks my heart. I hook my pinky with hers, sealing the promise, and meaning it.

CHAPTER 6:

SUSPICIOUS

Dean

I linger by the door, my hand on the knob, ready to leave. But something makes me turn. My eyes lock onto the scene unfolding behind me; Noah and Sienna, huddled close, making a pinky promise and smiling at each other like they've known each other forever. The sight makes my stomach churn. They've supposedly just met, yet there's an ease between them that doesn't sit right with me.

I grind my teeth, trying to keep my composure, but I can't shake the suspicion that Noah had something to do with Sienna's capture. He just appears out of nowhere, in full contact with Grizzly and his gang, but for some reason the group is all for him. I know better than to challenge Noah openly. He's got this aura of untouchability, and I can see why Marcus is drawn to him. But it doesn't make it any easier to stomach. Marcus might be eager to get to know his real brother, but I'm not convinced. There's something off about Noah, something that doesn't add up. And until I figure out what it is, I'll be watching him like a fucking hawk.

He finally notices me standing there. As he glances over, our eyes lock for a brief, tense moment. He gives me that infuriating smirk, the one that makes me want to reach up and punch his cocky face in. He knows exactly what he's doing, jabbing at me, pushing my buttons. And I hate to admit it, but it's working.

Noah strides towards the door, his towering frame casting a shadow over the room. As he approaches, he stops right in front of me.

"Something wrong, Douglas?" he asks, his voice dripping with condescension, his tone implying that he knows better. I don't flinch.

"All good. Just keeping an eye out," I reply evenly as I take a drag of my joint, my tone suggesting more than casual concern.

"Keeping an eye out for what, exactly?" he presses.

"I just wanna make sure you know where you stand," I say, my voice low and measured, each word laced with underlying threat. He smiles, his face dripping with arrogance.

"Oh, I think I've got a pretty good idea," he says. I lean in closer, my voice low and serious.

"Don't mistake Marcus' trust for an open invitation. I don't trust you as far as I could fucking throw you." I warn. Noah laughs, a cold, mocking sound that sets my teeth on edge. He glances down at my hand, a sneer forming on his lips.

"How'd you lose your fingers?" he asks, not out of genuine concern, but as if hinting that I'm an easy fight.

I hesitate for a split second, the truth flashing through my mind of Skylar turning on that fucking combine harvester, but I decide on a different narrative.

"It's a long story," I say, keeping my voice steady, hinting at something darker and more dangerous. I smirk slightly, letting him fill in the blanks with whatever badass scenario he can conjure up. Noah smiles arrogantly and pats me on the shoulder in a patronising gesture.

"See you at the house, yeah?" he says as he swerves around me and heads out the door.

Prick.

I trudge over to where Sienna stands, her demeanour fragile yet resilient, a stark contrast to the tension that just transpired with Noah. I approach her cautiously,

"You good?" I ask. She looks up at me with tired eyes, offering a faint smile.

"Yeah I'm good. A little tired, but good." I pause for a moment, choosing my words carefully.

"I saw you guys making a little pinky promise. What was that all about?" Sienna's shoulders tense slightly, but she manages a small, sheepish smile.

"Oh, we were just joking around." She lies. I nod, trying to keep the conversation light.

"Got it. So, what do you think of him?" I ask, hoping to squeeze something out of her.

"He seems nice," she shrugs. I raise an eyebrow slightly, taking another drag of my joint. Sienna's answer is too neat, too practised.

"Nice, huh?" I repeat, letting the smoke curl from my lips. "You know, I get the feeling there's more to him than meets the eye."

She looks away towards the door where Noah exited.

"Yeah, well, it's hard to get a read on someone in just a couple hours," she replies, her tone dismissive. But I'm not buying it. I step closer, lowering my voice.

"Look, Sienna. He's part of the gang that orchestrated this whole thing. You don't think he has secrets?" I hesitate, watching her closely for any reaction, but her expression remains guarded. Her eyes widen slightly, and she shakes her head, though her reaction is more instinctual than convincing.

"I'm not sure what you're suggesting."

"I'm just throwing things out there," I say quickly, attempting to ease the tension. "Just.. trying to make sense of everything, you know?" I watch her carefully, waiting for her response, but her expression is diplomatic.

"Yeah, I understand," she replies softly, her voice tinged with apprehension. I nod slowly, accepting her answer for now.

"Good," I say, my tone thoughtful. "Well, give me a heads up if anything seems off, okay?"

"I will," she assures me, her voice quieter now.

I watch her for a moment longer, then glance towards the door where Noah disappeared moments ago. The unease settles in my gut like a heavy stone.

"Just don't do anything stupid, okay?" She says with a smile. I smirk, but there's no humour in it.

"Don't worry. Stupid's not really my style."

10:43p.m. I pull up in front of Noah's sprawling estate, Delilah sitting beside me in the passenger seat and Skylar lying leisurely in the back. The mansion rises before us, grand and dramatic, surrounded by well-manicured gardens and imposing gates.

"Holy shit." Skylar gasps. "I might just have to suck him off for some spending money."

"Skylar, what the actual fuck?" I say, head in hand.

"What? It's called a strategy."

Delilah's eyes widen as she takes in the sight.

"Woah, this place is huge," she breathes out, her voice tinged with a mix of awe and uncertainty.

"Yeah I know," I mutter, more to myself than to her. Something about this whole setup feels off, like we're walking right into the lion's den without realising it. But for Marcus' sake, I'll play nice.

As we tread through the gates, into the driveway, I trail my fingers through the fountain, the cool water soothing against my skin. The sound of trickling water blends with the soft rustle of leaves in the breeze, creating an atmosphere that should be serene but instead feels strangely tense.

I'm drawn to the row of expensive cars parked along the driveway, their sleek bodies angled in an intended, intimidating line. Of course he'd have his collection of supercars parked as if they're poised to spring into action at any moment.

We get it, you're big and scary.
And really fucking rich.

Noah pushes open the double doors in a slow, easy motion.

"Welcome home." He says casually. He guides us to the left, bypassing the gigantic staircase, and into a spacious living room adorned with modern art pieces and dark, comfortable furniture arranged around a sleek fireplace. It's all so.. moody. "Feel free to hang out here if you want," he mentions, gesturing towards the large sofa before leading us further into the expansive kitchen.

The kitchen is a chef's dream, with state-of-the-art appliances, and a large island that doubles as a breakfast bar.

"Help yourselves to anything in here," Noah says, opening the cabinets and double-door fridge to reveal a variety of snacks and beverages neatly arranged. "And there are four bathrooms scattered around the house, so no need to worry about waiting."

As he continues the tour, Noah moves swiftly, almost as if he's done this countless times. He leads us down a hallway branching off from the kitchen, stopping at various doors to point out the layout. When we circle back to the foyer, he gestures towards a sleek, vintage black phone mounted on the wall.

"If you need anything ordered in, just use this phone," he explains. "My driver will pick it up and bring it over."

I roll my eyes.

Of course he has a constantly-available driver.

As we ascend the grand staircase, Noah leads us down a sleek corridor that reeks of old money and the pungent scent of cigars. The second floor opens up to another staircase and a wide hallway. Floor-to-ceiling windows allow the moonlight to filter in, bathing the hallway in a soft glow. The walls are adorned with modern wood panelling, adding a touch of sophistication. Polished brown-stain concrete floors beneath our feet give a subtle echo as we follow his lead.

He points us towards the row of closed doors lining each side.

"This floor has enough bedrooms, so just take your pick. They're all pretty comfortable." he says with a careless wave.

"Yes, I'm sure they are." I mutter under my breath. But no one seems to notice my sarcasm. Instead, they're all oohing and ahhing over the opulence like a bunch of groupies at a rockstar's tour bus.

"I gotta finish up some stuff in my office. Just give me a shout if you need anything," Noah adds, his tone relaxed. He starts to turn away, his steps leisurely as he moves back towards the staircase leading down. Just as everyone starts to disperse, he pauses and looks back towards Skylar.

"Oh, and Farmer," he says with a slight grin, his eyes twinkling with mischief, "your room is up on the third floor. First door on the left."

Skylar blushes slightly as Noah proceeds to wink at her; her cheeks turning a faint shade of pink. Birdie and Sienna exchange knowing glances, their smiles widening as they giggle and squeal softly to Skylar about the flirtatious gesture. I stand a few steps away, watching the interaction with a furrowed brow and tight jaw. Sky's excitement over Noah's advances is hard to ignore; she's too gullible, too fucking naive.

I keep a close eye on his retreating figure, my scepticism about him only growing stronger as I watch him disappear into the opulence of the mansion. The lavish decor and sparkling chandeliers may try to dazzle me, but my instincts remain firmly rooted in the conviction that Noah is trouble; and nothing about this gilded cage can change my mind.

I'm pulled back into reality by Delilah calling me over to the room she's picked.

"Dean! Check this out!" Even *she's* all happy and excited; in awe about the room and the mansion in general. I feel like an outlier, aware of the storm brewing while everyone else remains oblivious. With a sigh, I mutter under my breath.

"Coming."

61

CHAPTER 7:
TOGETHER AT LAST
Marcus

I follow Sienna into her chosen room, closing the door softly behind us. The moment we're alone, I turn to her, my heart pounding with relief and overwhelming emotion.

"Sweet," I whisper, my voice thick with unshed tears. She looks up at me, her eyes shining with a mixture of exhaustion and trust. I can't hold back any longer. I yank her into a fierce hug, wrapping my arms around her like a shield against the pain and fear she's endured. She melts into my embrace, her body trembling as she clings to me, burying her face in my chest.

"I was so scared," she whispers.

"I know. I snap, my eyes locked on hers with fierce intensity. "But I'll always find you. It doesn't matter what trail of blood I have to leave behind."

We stand there for a long time, just holding each other, the room's silence filled with the steady beat of our hearts. Gradually, her trembling subsides, and she pulls back slightly, looking up at me with a soft smile.

"Is Butter okay?" She asks. I smile, my thumb brushing a stray strand of hair away from her face as I answer.

"Yes, Butter's fine, sweet." I reassure her, "I have to go back tomorrow to get my bike. I'll bring her back for you." Her eyes light up at the mention of her beloved little butterfly.

"Can I come with you?" she asks, her voice hopeful.

I hesitate, the protective part of me wanting to keep her locked in the house forever and as far away from any potential danger as humanly possible. But then I look into her eyes and I'm done. How could I deny that face? She's been through so much, and if this will bring her a bit of comfort, then I'll make it happen.

"Of course," I say, smiling down at her.
She beams up at me, the shadow of fear lifting from her face for the first time since I found her. I pull her into another hug, kissing the top of her head. The scent of her freshly washed hair fills my senses, clean and

familiar. I breathe deeply, letting the fragrance wash over me like a soothing balm. After being in that basement, her hair had been tangled and smelled unlike it ever had before. Now, it feels like I've truly got my angel back, the way she's meant to be.

"You must be exhausted." I state.

"I've never been so tired, Marcus." she shares. I nod sympathetically, trying to hide my own emotions.

"Did Sky lend you anything to sleep in?" I ask, trying to sound normal, as I gently sit her down on the edge of the bed. She nods, pointing to a small bag on the floor. I grab the bag and pull out a pair of soft pyjamas, then kneel slowly on the floor in front of her, just like I've done so many times before.

But this time, as I carefully remove her borrowed clothes, I'm met with the bruises and cuts marring her thighs and behind; my heart clenching painfully at the sight. The moonlight casts an eerie glow over the room, making everything feel like a bad dream. I carefully slide off her underwear, my fingers tracing the lines of her bruised skin like a map of pain. Each touch is like a tiny betrayal, like I'm complicit in her suffering. My breath catches in my throat as I realise the true extent of the damage; her thighs have actually been sliced, the dark bruises interspersed with deep, angry gashes.

I always put her pyjamas on for her, tuck her in and whisper sweet nothings in her ear. It's a ritual that's supposed to be about care and protection. But now, it just feels like a cruel fucking joke. Because underneath these innocent little pyjamas, she's been savaged in the most intimate way.

I gently tug on the fabric of her new, borrowed garments, as if the fabric could somehow scrub away the brutal reality. The soft cotton whispers against her skin like a mournful sigh, and I feel like I'm trying to erase the evidence of what I allowed to happen to her. But it's too late for that.

I'm putting a plaster on a broken bone.

As I pull up the bottoms, I try to be as gentle as possible, my touch feather-light against her damaged skin. I have to fight to keep my expression neutral for her sake.

I kiss her body gently, starting from her toes and moving upwards, savouring the warmth and softness of her skin. Each kiss is a tender gesture, reassuring and loving. Her curls spill across her face like a curtain of innocence, adding to her deservedly-peaceful appearance. I take my time, making sure to cover every inch of her skin, lingering on the gentle curves of her neck and the soft slope of her shoulders. Once I've kissed her body to my satisfaction, I slide the pyjama top over her head, trying not to jostle her too much.

I burrow her into the bed snugly, making sure the duvet wraps around her comfortably. Leaning over, I stroke her forehead and run my fingers through her curls, gently smoothing them out. My tired angel closes her eyes immediately.

"Sleep tight, sweet," I whisper, before I withdraw and turn off the light.

Walking towards the window, I light a blunt, seeking a moment of respite from the endless emotional turmoil from today's unfathomable events.

I started the day in a shitty B&B without Sienna.
Now I'm ending it in a mansion with Sienna back, a dead dad and a new brother and mother thrown into the mix.

Pretty fucking normal.

The sweet, pungent aroma of marijuana fills the air, and I take a deep drag, feeling the smoke curl around my tongue and down my throat. The instant rush of relaxation washes over me, easing the tension in my shoulders and calming the racing thoughts in my mind. As I exhale, my eyes droop slightly, and I let out a slow sigh, feeling my muscles relax and my breathing slow.

The smoke has a way of quieting the noise in my head; like a twisted rubber band snapping back into shape.

I take another hit, feeling the effects intensify. My vision blurs a little as the cannabis takes hold. I lean against the window, feeling the cool breeze on my skin as I watch the smoke curl out into the night air; hearing Sienna's tiny breaths in the background. It's not perfect, but it's a small moment of peace in a day that's been one giant clusterfuck.

"Marcus?" Sienna's soft voice interrupts my thoughts, drawing me back to her side.
God I missed that beautiful little voice.

I turn to see her gazing at me with those big, innocent doe-eyes.

"Yes, sweet?" I respond, my voice gentle.

"Will I ever be your girlfriend?" she asks, quiet and hesitant. The question catches me off guard and I chuckle lightly, taking another long drag.

"No, sweet," I say. "I don't think so." Her expression falls slightly, but she nods.

"I love you, Marcus."

"I love you too, sweet. More than anything."

With a small sigh, Sienna's eyelids flutter closed, exhaustion finally claiming her. I watch over her for a while longer, feeling a swell of protectiveness and gratitude that she's safe with me now.

CHAPTER 8:
HARD TO GET

Noah

2:35a.m. I finish up downstairs, making sure everything is in order. I've been on the phone non-stop, dealing with the fallout from Moth and, more importantly, my father's death. Calls to trusted dealers, whispered conversations about retaliation and alliances shifting in the underworld. I have a more important role now that my dad is gone. A role I've been primed for since I could crawl.

The house is quiet again, thank *God*. Having to keep everyone here just to ensure Skylar will be close by is a fucking hassle. I prefer my peace and quiet, and a full house grates on my nerves. I'm not exactly the most social person to begin with, and the fact that I have to force chatter and smiles with an entire group, just to get to know my brother and keep Skylar under my watch, is already driving me fucking nuts.

Then on top of that, you toss Dean Douglas into the equation, and I'm seriously considering offing myself.

Every time a door slams or someone laughs, my muscles tense. But I remind myself that this is temporary. The noise, the small talk, the tension with Dean; it's all part of the game. A game I intend to win. Keeping Skylar here, keeping her off-balance, is worth every bit of discomfort.

Heading upstairs, I catch movement behind one of the doors; the one I gave to Skylar. There's banging, movement, the sound of drawers being yanked open and slammed shut. My curiosity spikes, and I stop in front of the door, listening. She's up to something.

I knock on the door, waiting for a response. Silence. I rap again, more firmly this time, but there's still no reply. A bit concerned, I decide to open the door. Skylar is there of course, rummaging through the drawers, her back to me. She spins around, her eyes narrowing when she sees me.

"I didn't say come in," she snaps, her voice icy and her posture defensive.

69

"I knocked," I reply smoothly, stepping into the room. "You didn't answer."

"That usually means fuck off, genius."

Her unnecessary verbal abuse should piss me off, but instead, I bite down on a chuckle. My eyes rake over her, taking in the way her body moves; the way she seethes. God.

She's sexy when she's mad.

"What are you looking for?" I ask, my voice calm and collected. In actuality, I'd like to teach her a lesson for that sharp tongue of hers; show her what happens when she talks back. She huffs and turns back to the drawers, clearly unwilling to share. I lean against the doorframe, watching her every move.

"You know, Farmer," I say, letting the condescension drip off my words. "If you need something, you could just ask. This is my house, after all." Skylar freezes, her hands paused mid-reach, before continuing her search.

"I don't need anything from you," she spits out, her tone dripping with venom. I step closer.

"I think you're going to need me more than you realise."

She stops rummaging and looks at me, her eyes challenging mine.

"Is that so?" She questions. I nod, holding her gaze with an intensity that I know unsettles her.

"Yes. And the sooner you accept that, the easier things will be for you, princess." For a moment, we stand there, locked in a silent battle of wills.

"Well, since you decided to put me in your weird little sex dungeon, I have no room for my clothes!" She snaps. I stop, raising an eyebrow.

"Sex dungeon?" I repeat with a grin. Skylar glares at me, her cheeks flushing slightly.

"Yes! The hooks, the.. other stuff. What is all this shit?"

I chuckle, the sound low and amused.

"I see you've been exploring."

"Listen, fuckface-"

"*Fuckface?*"

"I don't know what you think you're going to accomplish by putting me in this room," she spits out, her tone acidulous, "but I'm not interested, and I *really* don't appreciate the lack of drawer space."

Did she seriously just call me fuckface?

I raise an eyebrow, a slow, predatory smile spreading.

"Don't worry, I'll make sure you have room for your things." I step closer, my voice dropping to a whisper, "but don't pretend you're not curious."

Her breath catches, just for a second. Gotcha.

She doesn't reply, her defiance faltering for a split second. I press on, enjoying her discomfort.

"What's with the attitude, princess? I have to say I preferred it when you were calling me sir."

"Well don't hold your breath," she laughs. "I can assure you that'll never happen again."

"I wouldn't be so sure."

"You're beyond delusional," she says with a scowl, but the aggression in her voice is tinged with something else; something that excites me. I step closer again, enjoying the way she stiffens as I invade her space.

"Oh yeah?" I murmur, my voice dripping with confidence. She doesn't reply.

I chuckle softly, taking a few more steps closer until there's barely any space left between us.

"You're in my house now, princess." I warn, lifting a hand to brush a stray lock of pastel pink hair away from her face. "And if you keep pushing, I might have to put this room to use." Her skin prickles under my touch, but she doesn't pull away. Her cheeks flush deeper with anger and frustration as she looks me up and down like a high school bully.

"Good luck with that." She shoots back, clearly unimpressed. I take one last lingering look at her, my smirk widening.

The pretty-pink hair gets more ironic the more she opens her mouth. It's like I'm looking at this adorable little candyfloss dream and thinking she's all sweetness; but then she hits me with these witty, spiteful comebacks out of nowhere. She's a tough nut to crack. Unpredictable. I wouldn't be surprised to learn that she's plotting world domination in her spare time. And I'm all for it.

"I think it's about time someone taught you how to behave." I suggest, my voice low, as I turn to leave. I can feel her eyes burning into my back as I take a step away from her, leaving a silent challenge hanging between us like a thread. "Goodnight, Farmer." I say over my shoulder.

I close the door behind me with a soft click, the sound echoing through the silent hallway. A sly smile spreads across my face, a thrill of satisfaction coursing through my veins. Her discovery means she's fully aware of my intentions towards her. The realization is sinking in, and fuck, it's delicious.

She's just uncovered a tiny piece of my world, and now she'll be on edge, wondering what I'm going to do about it. She thinks she's got me figured out, but she's only seen the tip of the iceberg. It's like a game of cat and mouse, and what she doesn't know yet is that this game only ends one way. I take a deep breath, feeling my pulse race with excitement. This is what it means to be alive; to be a predator, to be a hunter. I smile to myself, savouring the thrill of the chase.

But fuck, she's a firecracker. This is going to be a much bigger challenge than I thought. Her insufferable, sassy little attitude was certainly unexpected. Every snarky comment, every raised eyebrow made me harder than a rock. She's feisty, rude, and unyielding, and I fucking love it. The thrill of breaking through that tough exterior, of showing her who's boss, is more exhilarating than I could have imagined.

She has no idea what I'm capable of, what depths of depravity I'm willing to sink to in order to get what I want.

And what I want is her.

CHAPTER 9:
WAKEY WAKEY

Marcus

The morning light seeps through the curtains, casting a soft glow over the room. I wake slowly, aware of Sienna nestled against me, her warmth a comforting weight. Her eyes flutter open, still heavy with sleep, and she smiles drowsily at me.

"Good morning," she mumbles, her voice still thick with sleep.

"Morning, sleepy," I reply softly. The relief of having her safe and sound washes over me anew.

"How are you feeling?"

"Happy," she says simply, her smile widening as she snuggles closer. I raise an eyebrow. 'Happy' is probably the best, and least expected, reply she could've given to that question.

We lay there for a while, savouring the quiet intimacy. Her steady breathing, the way her body moulds to mine. After a few moments, I shift slightly.

"I'm gonna get up and make us some breakfast." I say, my voice low and husky. Sienna pouts, her eyes barely open, her face scrunched up like a child who's been told it's time to leave the playground.

"It's only 8a.m. You're never up this early. Can't we stay here a tiny little while longer?" she whimpers with a faux-sad expression. I chuckle and then, without warning, tickle her sides. She squeals, squirming in my arms. I follow it with a light smack on her behind, and she swats at me playfully.

I grin, standing up and pulling on classic my tracksuit bottoms and white t-shirt.

"You get up whenever you feel like it, sweet," I say. Sienna splays herself out on the bed dramatically, stretching her limbs like a cat and sighing theatrically.

"Never," she declares with mock defiance, "this bed is *so* cosy." I laugh softly, watching her indulge in the comfort of the bed. For a moment, I just stand there, admiring her. Her natural beauty, the way her hair fans out on the pillow, the serene expression on her face; she looks like pure perfection. It's a sight I could get used to waking up to every single morning.

"Alright, sweet," I say, leaning against the doorframe. "But don't blame me if you miss out on your favourite breakfast." She cracks one eye open and looks at me sceptically.

"What are you making?" she asks, curiosity piqued despite her dramatics. I grin, turning to leave the room.

"A full English of course," I say through the crack in the door, my voice teasing. "But if you don't want any, that's fine, I'm sure Dean would be delighted to take yours off your hands," I add with a wink.

I can hear her groan of protest just as I close the door, a smile tugging at my lips. As I head downstairs to the mansion kitchen, I still can't believe this is my brother's house. The sheer size and opulence of it is overwhelming. This could've been me too.
Man, my dad is a prick.

Reaching the kitchen, I open the massive fridge, its coolness washing over me as I grab all the ingredients. The sizzle of bacon hitting the hot pan fills the room. I move efficiently, cracking eggs into another pan, their edges crisp and turning golden. The tomatoes and mushrooms release a mouthwatering scent as they cook, mingling with the savoury smell of the sausages.

I'm just starting on the baked beans, stirring them gently in a saucepan, when I hear footsteps behind me.

Turning, I see my brother Noah entering the room, his hair is tousled under a cap and he's still shaking off sleep. He's wearing a compression top that highlights just how ripped he is. The guy looks like he could bench press a small car.

"Morning," he says, yawning. "What's all this?"

"Just making breakfast," I reply. Noah raises an eyebrow, glancing at the spread.

"Nice." He smirks, grabbing a mug and pouring himself some coffee. "It smells good."

"Thanks, man." I smile.

The kitchen is filled with the sounds and smells of cooking, the beautiful aroma of breakfast foods blending together. I plate the bacon and sausages, setting them on the counter next to the fried eggs. The beans are simmering nicely, and I give them one last stir before turning off the heat.

Noah leans against the counter, sipping his coffee. Despite the early hour and his sleepy demeanour, he's got this constant alert look. It's honestly quite unnatural how someone can look that menacing before 9a.m.

"So, how's Sienna?" he asks.

"She's good," I say, smiling to myself as I think about her upstairs, likely still sprawled out on the bed. "She's happy. Which is all that matters." He nods, watching me work.

"You're doing pretty well with this. Got the timing down and everything."

"Yeah, I've always liked cooking." I admit. Noah's face softens a bit, a rare expression for him.

"Mum does too." he shares. I pause, turning to look at him fully. He nods, looking over at my bacon.

"You know, she had this trick for getting the crispy edges on the bacon while keeping it tender in the middle."

He steps up, taking the tongs from my hand and showing me how to arrange the bacon in the pan just so, and then lowering the heat slightly.

"You let it cook slower, give it time. Keeps it from getting too tough." he shares. I watch him, absorbing the information. He hands the tongs back to me. "See how that goes," he says. "She taught me that as a kid. I used to help her in the kitchen all the time."

There's a moment of silence between us, filled only with the sounds of cooking. It's a comfortable silence, a new thing for us.

"I wish I had some memories with her." I acknowledge. Noah looks at me, his expression unreadable.

"Yeah I know, I wish you did too. But at least you can make some new ones now, right?" He says. I smile, feeling a strange warmth in my chest.

"True that."

Just as I'm flipping the last of the sausages, I hear soft footsteps padding down the stairs. I turn to see Sienna, still sleepy-eyed and in her borrowed-pyjamas, looking adorably rumpled. She stifles a yawn as she enters the kitchen, her eyes lighting up at the sight of the food.

"There she is." I greet her with a grin.

"Yum," she smiles, rubbing her eyes. "This smells amazing, guys."

"I knew the promise of food would get you out of bed." I tease, grabbing a plate and arranging the food with a flourish. I shape some of the food into a heart; the sausages forming the outline, and the eggs and tomatoes filling the centre. "Just in time to get the first plate while it's hot," I say. She giggles, taking the plate from me and giving me a grateful smile.

"Thank you."

As she makes her way to the huge dining table, Birdie, Dean and Delilah follow behind her, all looking a bit more awake.

"Mmm," Birdie sings, skipping across the kitchen. She grabs a plate and holds it out for me to dish up. Dean gives a nod of approval as he sees the spread laid out before them.

"Mornin', all," He says, grabbing a plate and starting to serve himself.

"Wow, you guys really went all out," Delilah adds, her eyes wide with appreciation. Noah shakes his head.

"Credit goes to Marcus here," He says, clapping a hand on my shoulder. "He's the one running the show this morning."

"Hey, we worked as a team."

"Jeez, could you guys get any further up each other's arses?" Dean says, screwing up his face dramatically. The room goes quiet for a beat, the tension palpable. Noah's jaw tightens slightly, but he keeps his cool.

"Feeling left out, mate?" He says, raising an eyebrow.

"Nah, just making an observation." Dean shrugs grumpily. Noah smiles and replies,

"You always this charming in the morning?"

"Yeah, what's up with you today?" I chime in. Dean shrugs and takes a rough bite of a piece of bacon.

"Just hungry." He says nonchalantly, before heading over to the dining table with his plate.

As I plate up mine and Noah's breakfast, carefully arranging the food with a bit of flair, I notice Noah's gaze darting towards the entrance of the kitchen. He seems to be waiting for someone, his attention divided between his coffee and the doorway.

"There you go, man." I say, sliding his plate over to him. He doesn't hear me; his mind occupied.

"Hellooo," I say as I wave my hand in front of his face to get his attention. He snaps quickly out of his daydream, giving me a brief smile. "Your food," I remind him, gesturing down to his plate.

"Yes, sorry. Thanks, bro." Noah finally acknowledges. He takes the plate with a distracted nod, clearly still waiting for someone.

"Shouldn't we wait for Skylar?" He asks, glancing over his shoulder again. I laugh softly, shaking my head as I grab a knife and fork for myself.

"If you wait for Skylar, you'll starve."

I take a seat at the table, grabbing a piece of toast and starting to spread some butter on it. As I glance back towards the kitchen, I see Noah still hanging around, seemingly lost in thought. He's leaning against the counter, his eyes fixed on the doorway once again.

Curious, I watch him as he carefully begins plating up an extra serving of breakfast. He dishes up a generous amount of food, more bacon, sausages, eggs, and beans; taking his time to make sure it's all perfectly arranged. He then wraps the plate meticulously in kitchen foil. He takes extra care to ensure it's well-wrapped and secure, pressing down to keep everything insulated and hot. His attention to detail is clear.

Once he's satisfied with his work, Noah leaves the foil-wrapped plate on the kitchen island before heading over to join the rest of us at the table. As he takes his seat, I catch his eye and give him a teasing, knowing smile. Noah catches my eye and immediately knows what I'm smiling about. He tries to suppress a smirk but fails.

Hm, I think my brother has a little crush.

CHAPTER 10:

SHADOWS OF DOUBT

Dean

Breakfast is over, *thank God.*

The whole meal had been like a boxing match, Noah and I exchanging verbal jabs beneath the surface of the casual conversation. Every comment had felt like a strategic shot, each of us trying to come out on top without outright throwing a punch. Round one might be over, but I know this fight is far from finished.

As the group slowly disperses, I follow Delilah back upstairs. The mansion's grand staircase seems to echo each step, a rhythmic reminder of the irritation simmering inside of me. The sun streams through the tall windows, casting long, golden shadows that flicker as we ascend.

When we reach our room, Delilah closes the door softly behind us. She turns to me, her expression a mix of concern and curiosity, eyes searching mine for answers.

"What on earth has gotten into you today?" She asks. "You were snappy all through breakfast." I let out a heavy sigh, running a hand through my hair in frustration. The plush carpet beneath my feet does little to ground my scattered thoughts.

"It's Noah." I say immediately, not bothering to soften the edges of my frustration. "I've got a real bad feeling about him."

She raises an eyebrow, her curiosity piqued but still tinged with scepticism.

"Noah? Really? He seems chill." she questions. I shake my head, pacing up and down.

"No, baby. There's something off about him, and it's driving me fucking crazy that nobody else seems to see it." Delilah sits down on the edge of the bed, patting the spot next to her, a concerned look in her eyes. I join her, my mind racing as I try to articulate my thoughts.

"It's everything, Delilah. The way he talks, the way he looks at people. The constant, arrogant fucking smirk on his face. He's hiding something, I know it." I continue. She tilts her head, considering my words.

"Okay, I hear you." She responds softly. "But.. hiding what exactly?"

I hesitate for a moment, then decide to voice the suspicion that's been lurking at the back of my mind. To share my little sprinkle of information.

"I saw him with Sienna last night, they were making a pinky promise with each other. And neither of them would tell me what it was about"

"Dean, *really*? A pinky promise? That's not exactly a crime." She states, with a confused smile.

"My point is, there's no way they only met yesterday." I let out a deep breath, "You don't think it's possible he had any involvement in Sienna's abduction? He was talking to Moth and Grizzly on a regular basis. He must have an important role in their operations. I mean, just look at his fucking house!"

Delilah's expression turns serious, her eyes narrowing.

"So, you're suggesting that he kidnapped Sienna?" she clarifies. I shake my head, feeling the need for some quick damage control. My Delilah is a blabber-mouth after all.

"I don't know that for sure, Delilah. I'm just throwing it out there." I mumble, backing down slightly. "But I *know* something's up with this guy."

She looks at me with a mix of concern, confusion, and warmth for a few moments, her eyes searching mine.

Her brow furrows as she wraps her arm around me, drawing me in for a gentle hug. I lean into her touch, rubbing my temples in frustration.

"I'll keep an eye on Noah," she whispers, her voice soothing. "We'll work it out together." Her words wash over me like a soothing tide, and I nod, feeling a profound sense of relief. Delilah has always had a way of knowing exactly how to calm me down. She's not trying to offer grand solutions or promise that everything will be perfect, nor is she dismissing my concerns as absolute fucking paranoia. Instead, she's simply being present.

We sit in silence for a long while, our eyes locked on each other's, the connection between us like a gentle thrumming in my chest. Her features are soft and relaxed. Time seems to stretch out as we sit there, lost in each other's eyes. The world outside recedes, leaving only the two of us, suspended in this moment of quiet intimacy. As I place my hand on her thigh, I can feel my heart rate slowing, my breathing evening out.

And then, something shifts. It's as if a switch has been flipped, and her eyes darken, growing more intense. Her pupils dilate, and her lips part slightly, inviting me in. I feel my own eyes responding hungrily, my heart rate quickening as I drink in the sight of her. I know that look on her face all too well. I raise an eyebrow, a silent question of, 'what happens now?' And then she sucks in her bottom lip, her eyes never leaving mine.

Her breathing grows shallow, and before I can fully process what's happening, she pounces on me. Her lips crash into mine with an eager, desperate fervour. She grabs my face with both hands, her fingers digging in gently as she pulls me closer. The kiss is fierce and consuming, a mix of relief and passion that erupts between us. I'm caught off guard by the sudden surge of intensity but quickly respond, sliding my hands around her waist and pulling her onto my lap.

Delilah's weight settles onto my lap as she straddles me, her body pressing firmly against mine. The kiss grows even more desperate, her lips moving with an urgency that mirrors the pounding of my heart. My hands instinctively grip her waist, pulling her closer, feeling the heat and intensity of her touch.

Her hands slowly shift down, guiding my fingers to her lower back and then further, until they rest firmly on her ass. She lets out a soft, approving moan, her body arching into my touch as if savouring every second. I let out a breathy laugh.

"You know exactly what you want, don't you?" I murmur between kisses, my voice rough with desire.

She grinds against me, her hips circling in a slow, sensual motion. My fingers dig into her ass, controlling her movements. Delilah's breath hitches as I guide her rhythm, my fingers pressing deeper into her flesh. Her eyes flutter shut, lost in the sensation. My hands roam up her back, feeling the smoothness of her skin beneath her shirt. I tug it upwards, exposing more of her, and she raises her arms to let me pull it off completely. I toss it aside, and she's already working on my belt, her fingers nimble and insistent.

"Fuck," I mutter as she grinds harder, the friction driving me wild. Her hands are everywhere, exploring my chest, tracing the lines of my abs. I capture her mouth again, kissing her fiercely, our tongues tangling as the heat between us intensifies. She whimpers, her hands sliding down to my crotch. She teases me through my tracksuit bottoms, her touch light and maddening. I can't take it anymore. I flip us over, pinning her beneath me on the bed, my mouth trailing hot kisses down her neck.

She moans, arching into me, her hands clawing at my back. I hook my fingers into the waistband of her shorts, pulling them down slowly, savouring the sight of her. She's breathtaking, her skin flushed, her eyes dark with need. I position myself between her legs, my body thrumming with need. She pulls me closer with her legs wrapped around me, her eyes begging me to take her hard.

Just as I'm about to lose myself in her, a sharp knock on the door shatters the moment. We both freeze, our eyes snapping open in unison. Delilah sighs deeply, rolling her head back against the bed in frustration.

"Seriously?" She pants, her voice dripping with exasperation. "Right now?" Still leaning over her, I can't help but smirk as I let out a resigned breath through my nose. The smirk lingers on my lips as I slowly push myself off her, both of us trying to reorient ourselves after the abrupt interruption. Just then, the door knocks again, followed by Birdie's loud shout from the other side.

"Hey, stop fucking for a minute! I have to tell you something!"

Delilah grabs her top, pulling it back on as she shakes her head; clearly frustrated but also unable to suppress a small, rueful smile.

"We'll continue this later." I say, winking at her as I saunter towards the door. Opening it, I'm met with a disapproving Birdie; her pink, sparkly phone glued firmly to her hand. Her gaze moves from me, looking a bit dishevelled, to Delilah, who's now hastily adjusting her shorts. Birdie's eyebrows raise in a knowing look, her expression a blend of teasing and judgement.

"Knew it," she declares matter-of-factly, her tone equally playful and serious. Without a response, she struts past me like a sassy cat and heads straight for Delilah.

Birdie shows Delilah her phone screen, and Delilah's eyes light up with excitement as she reads the message. She lets out a delighted squeal, jumping up and down and throwing her arms around Birdie.

"No way! You got it?" Delilah exclaims, her voice bubbling with happiness. Birdie beams, nodding enthusiastically.

"Yup."

"That's amazing, Bird!"

I walk over, curious.

"Got what?" I ask. Birdie, grinning from ear to ear, turns the phone towards me.

"I've been accepted as a lifeguard at the best surf beach in the country!" She shares. Delilah hugs her again, practically bouncing with joy. I blink, then break into a wide grin.

"Wow. The bar must be pretty low if they're letting you in," I tease, nudging her playfully. "You know that means you'll have to get your precious hair wet, right?" Birdie rolls her eyes but can't suppress her smile. It's quite sweet really.

"Yes, Dean. I'm aware."

"For real though, congrats. That's actually pretty sick. Just make sure you don't drown." Birdie gives me a mock-serious look.

"Thanks, Dean. It means a lot coming from someone who probably thinks 'Baywatch' is a documentary."

"Hey, I know my way around a pool," I retort, unable to hide my genuine happiness for her. "I just prefer to leave the life-saving to the pros like you." Birdie laughs, her eyes sparkling with pride.

"I start next month!" she squeals.

"How long will you be down there?" Delilah asks.

"Until the spring," Birdie replies. Delilah's face falls, and she pouts, sad and dramatic.

"Oh Bird, I'm gonna miss you."

"I'm gonna to miss you too," Birdie says, giving her a reassuring squeeze. "But my parents rented me this incredible beach-front apartment so you can all come and visit, whenever you want." Delilah's eyes brighten at this.

"Absolutely! We'll make it work."

CHAPTER 11:
BOOK TALK

Marcus

I stand in the kitchen, the lingering scent of breakfast still in the air. I start clearing the plates from the table, my movements deliberate as I stack them in the sink. Noah is washing up, and I take a moment to watch him, noticing how out of place he seems. I don't picture Noah as the type of guy to do much housework. I'm sure he has a maid who does this for him.

But it doesn't take long to realise why he's doing it. His gaze keeps flicking towards Skylar, who's sitting at the table, eating the breakfast he kept warm for her. Every time she looks up, he straightens, ensuring he's in her eyeline.

"You've got a good chance with her, you know," I say with a casual smirk. Noah glances at me, a hint of confusion in his eyes.

"Why's that?" He asks. I let a grin slide across my face.

"Oh, she's really into drug dealers."

Yes, I'm aware that my brother isn't exactly a 'drug dealer'. But I figure being the leader of a criminal empire as big as his, there's enough overlap to make the comparison. Also, I'm yet to have any banter with my long-lost big brother, and this seems like a good place to start. Noah's eyebrows shoot up.

"What you on about?" he snaps. I chuckle, nodding towards Skylar.

"It's a running joke with us. She fucked a couple of her dealers. She has a thing for '*bad boys*'. So, I figure you kinda fit the bill."

Noah's expression shifts subtly. There's a flicker of irritation in his eyes as he processes what I said.

"Really?" he says, his voice low and edged with something I can't quite place. Noah's gaze returns to Skylar, and I can see the change in his demeanour. The playful glint is gone, replaced by a harder edge. Despite my attempt at humour, it's clear that Noah isn't happy.

Change the subject, Marcus.

"So," I begin, my voice steady but curious, "do you have any idea why Dad asked me about the book before he died?" I ask. Noah sighs deeply, setting a plate in the drying rack with more force than necessary, seemingly annoyed that I'm interfering with his Skylar fantasies.

"Because he was desperate to change the outcome."

"The outcome?" I echo.

"Yeah," Noah says. "Dad gets murdered at the end of my book."

I'm suddenly struck by two realisations at once, the chilling thought that the events of Noah's book have unfolded in reality, and the unsettling fact that he has already read and finished it. I had assumed that, since the book was sealed, he hadn't opened it yet.

"Wait, yours is completed?" I ask, my voice barely above a whisper.

"Yeah, Dad died. It is what it is." Noah replies nonchalantly, his focus still more on Skylar than on our conversation. His tone is detached, almost cold, which strikes me as strange. He seems surprisingly unfazed, considering our dad has just been murdered, and that he knew it was coming.

"Mine is closed too, but Dean.. he's still having near-death experiences." I share. Noah glances at me briefly, a flicker of possible interest crossing his face before he turns back to Skylar.

"That's weird, man." He says, clearly distracted once more.

"What was the story you wrote?" I press, trying to keep him engaged.

"It wasn't really a story," he replies, scrunching his eyebrows in thought. "It was more like a wishlist."

"A wishlist?" I ask, intrigued despite his evident distraction.

"Yeah," he says, finally looking at me. "I just wrote stuff like 'Mum is still alive', 'I'm going to be fucking rich', 'Dad needs to die'. You know? Cringy shit like that."

I stare at him, processing his words. It dawns on me that the magic must not have come from the story but from the book itself. Noah and I had the exact same book, yet what we had written inside was entirely different.

The book's power lies in the pages, not the content. Noted.

"So it's the book itself," I murmur, more to myself than to him. Noah nods absently, his attention drifting back to Skylar.

"What was yours about?" He asks. I launch into a brief summary, explaining the plot without going into too much detail. Noah definitely listens, but whether he's actually absorbing the information is another question entirely.

"So, how did you seal it if it's not completed?" He asks with a puzzled look.

"I went and found Millie and we were able to close it together. The book was glowing like crazy." I explain.

"It glowed?"

"Yours didn't?" I ask, intrigued.

"No. There was a '*boom*' noise but that's about it." Noah shares as he turns to face me fully now, his focus finally breaking away from Skylar. "What happened after you closed it?" He asks.

I take a deep breath, trying to gather my thoughts.

"Dean looked better," I say, my voice steady. "He wasn't sick anymore. But then an argument started. It got pretty heated. I could hear police sirens approaching and, long story short, the night ended with Skylar running Millie over." Noah raises an eyebrow, a mix of intrigue and an odd sort of admiration crossing his face.

"What do you mean she ran her over?"

"Sky stole a car and got into a chase," I explain.

"Stole a car? Wow." Noah lets out a low whistle, smirking in Skylar's direction. "So the queen is dead, huh?" He continues with a jokey tone.

"Yeah," I reply, letting out an awkward laugh at his cold response, but it quickly dies in my throat. I sit with it for a second, the weight of his words settling over me. I think more. And more. And then it hits me like a ton of bricks.

"Holy fuck," I mumble, my eyes widening in disbelief. "The queen is dead." Noah looks at me confused, a frown creasing his brow.

"Yeah, I just said that."

"No," I say, my voice trembling with realisation. "The queen is dead. That's why the story is still playing out."

Noah stares at me like I've lost my mind, the smirk slipping from his lips, replaced by a look of quiet disbelief. The coldness in his eyes unsettles meso sharp and detached, it's as if nothing can touch him. Not our father's death. Not Millie's. Not even the looming danger of the book's unresolved magic. He's an island, standing apart from it all, indifferent. Unbothered. The implications of Millie's death and what it means for the book's narrative weigh heavily on my mind, a burden that becomes increasingly harder to bear alone.

He stops washing up and turns off the tap, his movements intentional. He picks up a tea towel and dries his hands roughly, the fabric making a harsh sound against his skin. Each movement seems precise. He strides toward me, halting just inches away, his gaze locked onto mine.

"Stop stressing about the book," he says, his tone low. "What will be, will be." Before I can respond, he presses the tea towel to my chest with an intentional push. The gesture is forceful but not aggressive, like he's giving me an order. He then swerves past me, his shoulder brushing mine as he walks away, his posture relaxed and confident.

Noah's footsteps echo as he strides away, leaving me standing in the kitchen, clutching the tea towel to my chest. The cloth is now a physical token of the power play that just unfolded. As I stand there, I can't shake the sense that his words were more than just a casual remark. It felt like a definitive statement, a final word on a subject that I refuse to accept as settled. The implication was clear; the outcome of the book, the events that are unfolding, are beyond our control. That sense of inevitability, of resignation to fate, is something I can't afford to entertain.

The more I think about it, the angrier I become. The idea that we should simply accept Dean's hinted death as an unavoidable part of our fate is unacceptable to me. Noah's dismissive attitude towards the gravity of our situation stings. It's almost as if he's suggesting we should all just roll over and accept the hand fate dealt us. As if the best we can do is turn Dean's possible demise into a dramatic, tragic finale. I, for one, plan to rewrite that ending with every ounce of determination I've got.

I start drying up, the rhythmic motions of scrubbing and rinsing grounding me as I try to process the implications. The kitchen, now quiet except for the gentle hum of the refrigerator, feels almost serene. Just then, Skylar strolls up, her breakfast plate in hand, clearly in no rush. Without so much as a glance, she flicks her wrist and drops the plate into the sink. It clatters against the metal, but she's already tossing me a lazy grin and sauntering off. I look at the plate, now the lone occupant of the sink, and let out a dry, resigned laugh. Because of course, just as I think I'm done, there's always one more thing to handle.

CHAPTER 12:

GIRLFRIEND?

Sienna

I'm standing in Skylar's room, wearing a pair of flared low-rise jeans with an obnoxious heart-shaped buckle; along with a pink tank top that shows way more skin than I'm used to. I'm suddenly very aware of my bruises and cuts. The clothes feel like they're mocking me, highlighting the marks that I'm struggling to come to terms with.

As I tug at the hem, trying to make it cover just a bit more, I'm caught in a tug-of-war between two conflicting emotions. On one hand, I feel like I should hide the bruises. They're a reminder of something painful, something I'd rather not have others see. Hiding them feels like a protective barrier, a way to maintain some semblance of control over my own vulnerability. But on the other hand, there's this nagging feeling that hiding them is a form of surrender; like admitting that they have power over me, that I'm afraid of how others might perceive them. I glance in the mirror, realising quickly that it's not just as simple as 'this outfit shows off the bruises'; it's that it makes me feel like I'm being forced to confront them in a way that's uncomfortable.

I feel a surge of sadness. Each mark tells a story I'm not ready to share, a story that's still unfolding within me. The choice to cover them or not feels like a choice between vulnerability and strength, between acceptance and denial. The more I think about it, the more I realise that the conflict isn't just about what others might see; it's about how I see myself. How I reconcile the person I am now with the person I was before, and how to navigate a world that seems cruelly determined to remind me of both.

"I don't think this is quite my style," I admit, glancing at Skylar, who has made herself right at home on the bed, legs swinging back and forth as she's absorbed in her DS game. She glances up for exactly two seconds, takes in my outfit, and then dives back into her game as though it's a matter of life and death.

"You look cute." She chirps helpfully.

I roll my eyes and start rummaging through her bags and drawers again, looking for something that feels more like me. Her clothes look like they belong to a Bratz doll; crop tops, miniskirts, and low rise everything as far as the eye can see. I pull out a tiny leopard-print cami, trimmed with pink lace along the top, and hold it up, giving her a look.

"Seriously, Sky? How do you even breathe in this?" I ask, holding the top up for her inspection, feeling both amused and slightly horrified.

"It's called fashion, Sienna." She declares with such confidence that I almost want to salute her.

"Fashion or torture device, I can't tell." I mutter under my breath. Sensing my struggle, Skylar puts her game down and sits up, determined to save me from my fashion crisis.

"Here, let me help you find something." She says as she starts digging through a drawer, tossing aside crop tops and miniskirts with a flourish. "There's got to be something in here that works."

After a bit of digging, she finally pulls out a simple pair of cream trousers and a soft blue top. "What about these?" She asks, holding them up like a prize; hoping for my approval. I take a deep breath, feeling a wave of relief wash over me at the sight of the clothes; nothing outrageous, nothing that seems designed to squeeze my body and spirit into submission.

103

"Much better. Thanks," I reply, a genuine smile breaking through.

Just as I'm adjusting the waistband and smoothing out any wrinkles, the door creaks open. Marcus strides into the room with the kind of casual confidence that makes you feel like he's always been here. Skylar looks up from her spot on the bed, her DS game momentarily forgotten.

"Seriously Marcus? No knock?" She scoffs. Marcus raises an eyebrow, giving a mock bow.

"So sorry, your majesty." He says with a sarcastic grin. Skylar rolls her eyes dramatically and goes back to her game, clearly unperturbed.

Marcus' gaze shifts to me, and his expression softens.

"You look beautiful, sweet," he says with a sincere smile. I feel a small blush creep up my cheeks.

"Thank you."

Marcus then glances around the room, taking in the piles of discarded clothes scattered across the floor. He raises an eyebrow in mock concern.

"You ready to go?" he asks, his tone a mix of amusement and worry.

"Please," I reply, eager to leave the chaos of the room behind. As we turn to head out the door, his eyes land on a particularly suspicious ring-hook on the wall. His brow furrows in genuine concern this time.

"What's with the hooks?" He asks Skylar, his voice low and serious. Before Skylar can retort, I quickly grab Marcus's arm, tugging him along.

"Don't ask," I say firmly, trying to stifle my own discomfort.

As we step out into the warm summer afternoon, the sun bathes everything in a golden glow, casting long shadows across the driveway. Marcus and I are heading towards Dean's stolen ride when I notice Noah standing by one of his many cars, the boot wide open. Curiosity gets the better of me, and as I pass by, I peer inside. My eyes widen at the sight of an array of guns neatly lined up inside.

"Nice collection, Noah," I joke. "Looks like you're preparing for the apocalypse." Noah turns around, a wry smile tugging at the corner of his mouth.

"Something like that," he says. "With the two biggest players gone, I'm in charge now. That alone puts a target on my back. And believe me, their deaths? It's blood in the water. Our enemies are already circling, thinking we're vulnerable." I nod, pretending to understand the gravity of pressure on his shoulders.

"Well, good luck with that," I say, trying to inject some levity. "Just don't count on us for backup." Noah chuckles, though the sound is devoid of real humour.

"I'll try not to," he replies, closing the boot with a decisive thud.

We continue toward Dean's stolen car, but before we reach it, Noah calls out.

"Why don't you take one of my cars instead?" He asks. Marcus shakes his head.

"Thanks bro, but we can't bring it back. We're gonna go get my bike," he says. Noah smirks and tosses Marcus a set of keys.

"No worries. Take the Range Rover, I've never been a big fan of it. Makes me feel like some rich yoga-mum. Call it a loan." He says. I raise an eyebrow at Noah's nonchalant attitude. It's almost impressive how literally throwing away a car is just a casual thing for him; must be nice to be that rich. Marcus catches the keys, gives them a quick once-over, then looks back at Noah as if trying to decide if he's joking.

"Thanks, man." Marcus says, slightly hesitant but grateful.

We climb into the Range Rover, the interior exuding an aura of expensive luxury. As we drive away from Noah's place, the car's smooth, quiet ride feels almost surreal compared to the chaos we've been through. The leather seats are buttery soft, and the dashboard gleams with high-end tech. I sink back, letting the comfort momentarily wash away my lingering anxiety.

The drive to the B&B is peaceful, the sun casting elongated shadows across the road as the afternoon wears on. For a while, we don't speak, content to let the quiet hum of the engine fill the space between us. Marcus keeps one hand on the wheel, the other resting comfortably on my knee.

As we pull up outside the cottage, the familiar sight stirs a whirlwind of emotions within me. The quaint façade feels tainted by what I endured during my time there. As the engine purrs to a stop, the silence looms heavy between us, and I can feel the tension coiling in my stomach.

Marcus turns to me, concern etched into his features.

"You wanna wait outside?" He asks, low and gentle. I shake my head, a shaky breath escaping my lips. The idea of him doing it for me is tempting, a protective gesture that feels warm and safe. But there's a part of me that knows I need to face this. I take a moment, gathering my thoughts, and despite the anxiety gnawing at me, I respond,

"No, I want to go in."

Marcus studies me for a moment, his hazel eyes searching mine for any hint of doubt. I can almost see the battle between wanting to protect me and believing in my strength.

"Okay," he concedes, his tone reluctant but supportive. We step out of the car under the warm embrace of a summer afternoon, the sunbathing everything in a golden hue that feels almost idyllic. However, despite the beauty of the day, a sense of dread tinges the air around me. With each step towards the front door, my heart races, thudding relentlessly in my chest.

As we get closer, my stomach drops at the sight of the door hanging ominously off its hinges; a gentle breeze whispering through the entryway. A wave of anxiety crashes over me, flooding my senses with the memories of that horrific moment; the thunderous sound of the door being kicked open, the chaos that ensued as I was ripped from everything I held dear. I can still hear the echoes of panic and fear that reverberated through that moment.

Could Butter have left?

Gritting my teeth, I take a hesitant step forward, each footfall heavy with the weight of dread and uncertainty. My mind races as I cross the threshold, instinctively scanning the dim interior for any sign of movement. As I venture deeper into the room, the wooden floor feels cool beneath my feet, grounding me in a reality I desperately want to escape. That's when I see them; patches of dried blood smeared across the floor, stark and grotesque against the sunlit wood. A chill snakes through me, my breath hitching in my throat as a wave of confusion washes over.

It's unsettling, but rather than evoking the panic I expected, it leaves me feeling strangely numb. How can something so visceral and horrifying feel so removed from my own existence? I blink, trying to process what I'm seeing. The blood shouldn't belong to me; it couldn't be mine. But even as I tell myself that, a part of me wants to recoil, to walk away from this gruesome evidence of violence. But I'm not sad.

Instead, I'm left with an unsettling yet promising sense of detachment, as though I'm watching someone else's nightmare unfold. The images in my mind refuse to align with the horror at my feet; I can't connect the dots between the bloodstains and my own reality. Yet, amidst the chaos of my racing thoughts, something catches my eye. There, perched calmly on a shelf, is Butter, her silhouette bathed in golden sunlight.

She is here.
She stayed.

"Butter," I whisper, tears welling in my eyes as I marvel at her fragility and beauty. She flutters her wings gently, her presence a small, comforting constant in a world that feels so unstable. Butter, my steadfast little companion, flits gracefully from the shelf to my finger. "I missed you." I murmur, my voice quivering with emotion. She responds with a gentle flutter of her wings, almost as if she's saying she missed me too. I cradle her gently in my palm, captivated by the way her wings glimmer like stained glass. I can't help but smile through my tears, the connection between us feeling more precious than ever.

A giggle escapes my lips as I extend my finger, inviting her to take flight. With a graceful leap, Butter flutters into the air, and I spin around in delight, laughter bubbling up from somewhere deep inside me. As I turn, I catch Marcus' presence in the corner of my eye. He's leaning against the doorframe. Time seems to freeze as I meet his gaze. He isn't smiling, at least not fully, but oh, the way he looks at me makes my heart skip.

His hazel eyes are locked onto mine, filled with something so deep it nearly takes my breath away. In that moment, it feels like I am the only thing that matters in the entire universe. Everything else dissolves into a shadowy haze, as if the rest of existence could burn to ash, crumble into dust, leaving no trace behind, and he would remain unfazed; enthralled only by the essence of me.

Marcus' expression is intense, his eyes filled with a beautiful kind of admiration. I can see it in the way he watches me, as if he's witnessing something precious and rare. It's the way he sees me, completely and without reservation, that makes me feel like I'm alive, rather than surviving.

He ambles past me without a word, his focus shifting to the task at hand. He places his duffel bag on the bed, the soft thud breaking the quiet. Without hesitation, he begins to methodically gather our clothes and belongings, his hands moving with practised ease. Each item is carefully folded and placed inside the bag. I watch him, momentarily mesmerised by the quiet strength in his actions. There's something comforting about the way he takes charge; his calm demeanour contrasting with the chaos that's surrounded us.

His broad shoulders move with confidence, muscles flexing subtly beneath his shirt as he works. In his quiet steadiness, I find an anchor for my own tumultuous thoughts; a deep sense of calm washes over me, reassuring me that no matter the storm, he is here, and he knows what to do.

After a few minutes, Marcus finishes packing and turns to face me. He reaches for Butter's enclosure, which is resting on the bedside table, and hands it to me with a gentle touch; his fingers lingering against mine for a brief second. Just as I take hold of the enclosure, Marcus' hands slip around my legs, his strong arms lifting me effortlessly. I see Butter fluttering nearby and, with my free hand, I reach out, catching her gently in mid-air.

A soft gasp escapes my lips as I'm hoisted higher into the air, my world tilting as I'm slung over his shoulder like I weigh nothing at all. Marcus chuckles, the sound rich and low, vibrating through me as he holds me securely against him. My laughter mingles with the soft flutter of Butter's wings. Everything feels surreal, like we're in a world of our own.

His hand rests on the back of my thigh, steadying me as he strides toward the door. As he carries us out of the room and toward his beloved bike, I find myself feeling lighter. I look back at the cottage and small smile tugs at the corners of my lips. It's a quiet smile, one that holds no bitterness, just a gentle acknowledgment that the worst is over. The cottage no longer feels like a place of torment, but rather a setting in a book of my own.

A book finally closed.

As we ride back to Noah's, I can feel the exhilarating zip of wind against my face. I never thought I'd admit it, but I missed the bike. Marcus leans into the curves with effortless precision, the bike slicing through the air at a hundred miles an hour as though it's a part of him. Each acceleration sends a jolt through me, the speed blurring everything around us into streaks of green and grey.

It's funny, really. I'm gripping him so firmly, literally hanging on for dear life, and yet instead of feeling terrified, I'm completely enchanted. The wind rushes around us like a wild melody, and I can't help but marvel at how his reckless abandon feels oddly.. sexy. Sure, we may be one small jolt away from certain death. But you know what? If I die in a fiery explosion, I might as well go out swooning, right?

As we continue down the winding road, I notice that Marcus isn't heading back the way we came. My curiosity piques as we veer off onto a path I recognize. The landscape starts to look familiar, and my heart skips a beat when I realise where we're headed.

"This isn't the way home," I shout over the roar of the engine, my voice barely audible. Marcus doesn't respond immediately, his focus clearly on the road.

"I know."

The anticipation builds as we approach a spot that has become etched in my memory. I can barely make out the glint of sunlight reflecting off the river's surface as we draw nearer. Memories flood back; the river where I'd found a tiny bunny and then, quite dramatically, ended up taking an unintended dip. It feels like a lifetime ago.

Marcus pulls the bike over to the side of the road, bringing us to a smooth stop beside the familiar riverbank. As the engine quiets, I feel the exhilarating rush of speed give way to the calmness of this peaceful spot.

He removes my helmet with a tender touch, his fingers brushing against my skin. I look up at him, my heart still racing from the ride, and see a soft, knowing smile on his face.

"Remember this place?" he asks, his voice low and warm. I nod, a smile spreading across my face.

"How could I forget?"

The riverbank where everything had felt so perfect yet so complicated.

I stare at the water, my thoughts drifting back to that day. It was here that everything changed for us. Marcus had confessed his love for me; raw and honest. And unexpected. I can still picture the moment we leaned in for that kiss; his eyes sparkled with hope and sincerity, reflecting a vulnerability that took my breath away.

But instead of leaning in, I panicked. A wave of fear crashed over me, and in my haste, I pulled away; not just physically, but emotionally as well. I remember the harsh words that tumbled from my mouth, unkind and unfiltered. I was unable to embrace the gift he was offering so freely, and that decision weighed heavily on my heart. Even now, as I watch the river flow, I can't help but wonder how different things might have been if I hadn't let fear take control.

We walk hand in hand to the riverbank, the only sound around us the soft rush of the water over the rocks. The sun is lower now, bathing the world in a warm, golden glow that softens the edges of reality, almost like a memory. We reach the edge of the river, and without a word, we sit down on the grass. The ground is slightly damp, but I don't mind. It feels good to be here, away from everything, just the two of us. I watch the water flow by, its surface catching the last of the sunlight, sparkling in the quiet.

There's a peace in this moment that I haven't felt in a long time. It's like all the chaos and fear that's been swirling around us has finally settled, if only for a little while. I glance over at Marcus, who's staring out at the river with a thoughtful expression, and I feel a wave of warmth towards him. Being here with him, in this familiar place, feels right.

The stillness of the river is comforting, but I begin to notice that something is off. Marcus is quiet. His usual confident demeanour replaced by something I can't quite put my finger on. His eyes are fixed on the water, but I can see his mind is somewhere else entirely.

"So.." I start, my voice breaking the silence, "what are we doing here?"

He glances at me, the corner of his mouth twitching into a half-smile, but there's a seriousness in his eyes that makes me nervous; like whatever he's about to say matters, a lot. He finally breaks the silence, his voice steady.

"Last night, when I told you that you'll never be my girlfriend," he pauses, his eyes locked on the flowing river as if searching for the right words. "Well, I meant it."

My heart drops like a stone, the weight of his words sinking in before I can fully process them. A sudden tightness grips my chest, a wave of sadness swelling that I wasn't prepared for. I try to mask the hurt welling inside, forcing a laugh that falls flat, barely masking the tremor in my voice.

"Because you don't do labels, right?" I joke, but even I can hear how hollow my attempt sounds. Marcus' expression doesn't change, his brow furrowing like he's grappling with something crucial. My attempt to brush off his words doesn't seem to ease the tension hanging between us.

"You're right, I don't do labels," His voice sends a cold shiver down my spine, the pit in my stomach growing heavier. My mind races with confusion.

"It's not because I'm afraid of commitment or because I don't care about you. It's because.." he begins, his voice measured, almost too calm. "It's because that label doesn't feel right for us." The words hit me like a cold splash of water, and my heart sinks. I can't comprehend why he wouldn't want to be my boyfriend, to make this official. "I've never been one for doing things the typical way. *We've* never been typical, have we?" He asks.

I shake my head, more out of reflex than anything else. I'm still trying to wrap my head around what he's saying. His words cut deeper than he probably realises. It's true, we've never been typical. My whole life has never been conventional, never followed the normal paths that everyone else seems to navigate so effortlessly. I've always craved something solid, something secure, and I want that with Marcus. Calling him my boyfriend would be something normal, something to hold onto in a life that has never felt particularly stable. And now, it feels like even that is slipping through my fingers. My thoughts are a whirlwind of confusion and hurt, spinning faster with every word he says.

"So, when I said you'll never be my girlfriend," his voice drops, colder now, sharper, "I meant it." He states flatly, and in that instant, I feel as if my heart is fracturing into a thousand pieces.

He really doesn't want to be with me.

But then, Marcus shifts, his hand reaching into his pocket. My breath catches as I watch, time slowing as he pulls out a small box. For a second, my mind goes blank, unable to comprehend what's unfolding before me.

He opens it to reveal a delicate gold ring, shimmering softly under the fading light. The sight is breathtaking and surreal, but it does little to calm the storm brewing inside me.

"I don't ever want you to be my girlfriend, sweet," he says, his voice firm yet tender. "I want to skip that part. I want to go straight to the part where you're my wife."

I freeze, heart racing in a frenzy that feels both exhilarating and terrifying. His hazel eyes hold an unwavering depth as he gazes at me, and all at once, I'm overwhelmed.

"Sienna Saunders, will you marry me?"

My heart races, every beat echoing louder than the last. The shock is too great, the emotions too raw, and for a moment, everything inside me seems to freeze.

Tears well up in my eyes, blurring my vision. I'm overcome with a tidal wave of relief and joy; a deep, undeniable love that makes my chest ache. I try to speak, but the words catch in my throat, too choked by the overwhelming emotion. All I can do is nod, a silent, tearful confirmation of what I can't find the words to express.

As soon as the first tear spills down my cheek, I can't hold back the flood. I'm sobbing, the tears streaming freely as I look up at Marcus. My vision is clouded, but I can see the tears brimming in his eyes too. They reflect the same raw, intense emotion that's surging through me. Without thinking, I crash into him, flinging my arms around his neck, clinging to him as if I can't bear to be apart. Marcus' one hand settles on the small of my back, his hold is both strong and gentle, comforting me as I bury my face in his shoulder, letting the tears flow uncontrollably.

"So, is that a yes, sweet?" He whispers teasingly. I nod vigorously, my smile breaking through the tears.

"Yes, Marcus. Yes, a million times."

CHAPTER 13:

ART OF SEDUCTION

Noah

11:49p.m. I push through the door, the weight of the day dragging on me like a chain. The soft click of my keys echoes through the silence as I hang them up, the tension still coiled tight in my muscles. Today was hell; hiring new people, managing the internal power struggles of my organisation, and taking care of a few dealers who clearly didn't know their place. The weight of it all is pressing heavily on my shoulders, and I long for the rare calm of my space. I grab myself a bottle of water and drag myself through the expansive hallways, the echo of my footsteps amplifying the solitude of the night.

I push open the door to my bedroom ready to collapse, but as the door swings open, all thoughts come to a screeching halt.

My little pink-haired menace, sitting on my bed like she owns it.

Yes, I never explicitly said nobody was allowed in my room, but I gathered it wasn't something I'd need to spell out. It's the kind of thing that goes without saying. It's strictly off-limits by default. But little Miss Skylar? She's breaking every unspoken rule without even flinching. It pisses me off, but at the same time, it's.. hot. Real fucking hot.

My first impulse is to slam the door, pin her down on the mattress and fuck her as a punishment. But as I take in her provocative, effortless allure, I find myself oddly impressed. She's not just invading my space; she's owning it with an air of audacious confidence that's undeniably sexy. *How long has she been here?* The question pulses in my mind as I take in her strong, almost smug demeanour. It's such a daring move, so unlike anyone else I've encountered.

I smirk as I close the door behind me, the soft click of the latch echoing in the quiet room. My gaze locks onto her with a predatory intensity. I stand there for a moment, just watching her, letting the silence stretch.

"Skylar Farmer." I say, my voice low and charged with an edge of amusement.

"Noah Bear."

"No, not personally." I reply. Skylar's expression shifts to one of puzzled disapproval, her eyebrows knitting together as she looks at me. "Get it? Noah Bear. Know-a-bear?" I explain, attempting to make the pun land. She blinks at me, clearly unimpressed.

She stares at me, unimpressed, and I exhale, dropping the joke like the waste of breath it is. My voice turns serious, my eyes narrowing as I take a step closer.

"Why are you in my room, Farmer?" I ask. Skylar's eyes narrow, and she shoots back almost immediately.

"Why do you like me?" She snaps.

"What's not to like?" I say simply. She doesn't skip a beat, her frustration mounting as she gets up from the bed and begins to pace like a caged animal.

"I'm serious! What do you want from me?"

"Sorry?"

"Do you want sex? Is that it? Or are you just bored? Because I'm not some trophy to be won, Noah! I'm not-" She continues to pace, her steps growing more erratic before she catches me smiling and stops right in front of me.

Yeah that definitely didn't help.

"Is this some kind of game to you? Do you have a checklist of women you need to fuck to make yourself feel better? Huh? Because let me tell you, *sir*, I'm not interested in being another mark on your list! I'm not here for you to prove a point or for you to get some sort of thrill. I have my own life, my own goals! Okay?" Her voice trails off, and she stops abruptly. She looks at me, her eyebrows scrunched together in a mixture of defiance and confusion.

Meanwhile, I'm standing there, utterly bemused. I hadn't expected this kind of reaction.

"Sit down." I order with a single chuckle. Skylar's eyes flare with irritation.

"No." she snaps, her voice sharp. I clench my jaw, my expression turning more serious.

"I'm not gonna ask you again."

Her defiant stance begins to falter under my intense gaze, and she sighs heavily; frustration evident in every line of her face. After a moment, she relents, dropping onto the edge of the bed. She crosses her arms tightly, her posture rigid, trying to look as mad as she can manage. But even in her attempt at anger, she's far more adorable than intimidating. Tempting.

I lean against the doorframe, watching her silently. I give her the space to process, letting the room settle into a quiet that feels almost tangible. Gradually, her defiant stance softens. Her eyes drop to the floor, and I can see the tension in her shoulders ease, even if just a little. The irritation in her expression fades, replaced by something deeper. As I observe her, it's already crystal clear to me what's going on in that pretty little mind.

I think back to what I learned earlier, to the dealers I dealt with today. It's obvious to me that they were the kind who use and discard without a second thought. If she's let herself get close to men like that, men who don't give a damn beyond their own gain, then I know exactly why she's standing here so guarded now, her defences sharp, ready for the next hit.

She expects me to be no different. She's bracing for the same treatment; waiting for me to take what I want and leave her hollow like the rest. Her attitude is just a mask, a way to protect herself from more disappointment. I can see the fear she's trying to hide, the vulnerability she doesn't want me to touch. But she has no idea what she's dealing with. I'm not like them. Her fear, her insecurities, they don't stand a chance against the weight of what I intend to take; and I won't be leaving her in pieces.

I let out a heavy sigh, pushing off from the doorframe.

"I'm not here to use you, Farmer." I say sternly. I take a step closer, voice low and firm. "Let me make something real fucking clear." I continue, "This isn't some fling. You don't get to walk away. I'm going to fucking own you, every part of you. You can hate me, scream, fight, it doesn't matter." I look deeper into her pretty blue eyes, "I'll be under your skin, in your fucking bones, haunting your every thought. You think you can run? I'll hunt you down, drag you back, and remind you exactly who the fuck you belong to."

There's a finality in my tone, something that leaves no room for argument. There's nothing soft about it, nothing sweet. Just the hard truth. I'm not letting her go, and she better get used to the idea. When she doesn't respond, I let out a slow breath, steadying myself. I'm not frustrated, just feeling the weight of her uncertainty. I cross the room, the silence thick. Reaching the large cabinet against the wall, I yank it open, rummaging through until I find what I'm looking for, a fucking huge box. I stroll back to her, noticing how her eyes follow my every move, cautious but curious. I set the box down in front of her with a solid thud.

"Now that we've got that out of the way," I say, my tone firm but softer, "let's paint."

She stares at the box, her confusion plain as day.

"Excuse me?" she asks, her voice laced with bewilderment. I don't respond. Instead, I crouch down and open the box, revealing its contents; paints, brushes, canvases, everything. I start taking them out, one by

125

one, spreading them across the floor in front of her. She watches me, still trying to figure out what the fuck I'm doing, but I stay focused on the task, letting the action speak for itself.

Once everything is laid out, I pick up a canvas and a brush, holding them out to her. She's still staring at me like I've lost my mind, but I don't waver.

"C'mon," I say, my voice steady. She hesitates, eyes flicking between the canvas and my face, trying to make sense of this sudden shift. When she finally takes the canvas and brush, I nod, satisfied. "Paint." I tell her, as if it's the most natural thing in the world.

I shift from a crouch to sitting on the floor, getting comfortable as I squeeze out the colours onto a palette. Skylar watches me intently, her eyes narrowing slightly as she glances between the paintbrush in her hand and me. I can sense her hesitation, the internal struggle playing out behind her guarded expression. Finally, she exhales deeply; her shoulders relax just enough for me to notice before she shifts to sit down beside me on the floor.

"Atta girl." I murmur.

Dipping the brush into the colour of her choice, she starts to paint, her strokes hesitant at first. It's clear she's not thrilled about this, but she's doing it. Begrudgingly. Skylar continues painting, her brush moving more fluidly with each stroke. The tension in her face starts to fade, the lines of stress and anger slowly melting away. I sit there in silence, just watching her. Every flick of her wrist, every dip into the paint, it's like I'm seeing her unravel bit by bit.

Her focus shifts entirely to the painting in her hand. The raw, chaotic energy she came in with is being transferred onto the canvas, leaving her features calmer, softer. She's letting go, even if she doesn't realise it. And all I do is watch, taking in every subtle change.

After a little longer, Skylar stops painting and turns the canvas around to face me, her expression dead serious. I glance at the painting, and for a split second, I'm unsure how to react. The artwork is.. Definitely something.

She's painted us.
In a way.

As I study the painting, I realise it's not just poorly done, it's also disturbingly graphic. The scenes she's conjured are twisted, depicting her figure torturing mine in various brutal and unsettling ways.

We both stare at the painting, trying to keep straight faces, holding onto whatever sternness we can muster. But it doesn't take long before I see the corners of her mouth twitch, and I feel my own restraint slipping. Skylar's the first to break, a small giggle escaping her lips, and I can't help but follow. The laughter builds until we're both genuinely laughing, the sound filling the room, and for a moment, all the tension and unspoken words dissolve.

As our laughter fades, we lock eyes, and I notice something different in her gaze; hope, maybe, and a certain calm that wasn't there before. The tension that had gripped her earlier seems to have unravelled, leaving her looking more relaxed, almost at ease. I reach out and take the canvas from her hands, examining it with a thoughtful expression. With my other hand, I surreptitiously dip my finger into some light blue paint, making sure she doesn't notice.

"You know," I say, keeping my voice casual, "I think it's missing something." Her brow furrows slightly as she leans in.

"What?" she asks, looking like she's ready to dive into a deep art critique.

That's my moment. Without missing a beat, I swipe my paint-covered finger across her cheek, leaving a streak of blue. Her eyes widen in shock, and then her expression hardens so fast I barely have time to react.

Oh yeah, she wants to kill me.

I watch, amused, as she processes the violation, her expression growing darker by the second. She's quiet, too quiet, and I notice her hand tightening around the paintbrush in her hand like it's a weapon. That little face of hers scrunches up in fury, but all I can think is how damn cute she looks.

It's like I'm battling with a very abusive Strawberry Shortcake.

I try to keep my amusement under control, but I can't resist. The corner of my mouth tugs up into a smirk. That's all it takes.

She lunges at me with the paintbrush, violent and fast, but I'm faster. I easily knock it out of her hand, my leer growing wider. But then I see the determination in her eyes, and before I know it, she's going for the palette. I yank it out of her reach with a smug grin, enjoying this a little too much.

"You've gotta do better than that, baby." I chuckle. She huffs, clearly annoyed, but the fire in her eyes hasn't dimmed one bit. She's relentless. Her eyes dart to the open tubes of paint, and I catch on to what she's planning a split second before she moves.

As she makes a move for the paint, I catch her wrist midair and, without a second thought, twist it around, using just enough force to guide her down to the floor.

In one swift motion, I grab the other wrist and pin her there, her back against the hardwood. I hover over her, my grip on her wrists firm as I hold them above her head. My other hand presses down on the floor beside her, keeping her in place. My jaw clenches as I look down at her, my gaze stern and threatening; her piercing, ice-blue eyes staring back at me.

"You really think you've got a chance?" I say, my voice low and controlled. There's a weight to my words that goes beyond the paintbrush and palette.

She meets my eyes, and we both know exactly what I mean. It's not just about the little fight we're having over art supplies. I'm telling her, without needing to say it outright, that she's not going to win against me in any sense. She can't fight it. Whatever it is that I want from her, I'll have it. She glares up at me, her frustration blatant.

"You think you can just pull out some paints and now everything's cool? That's not how this fucking works."

I smirk, unfazed by her attitude.

"Princess, if you wanna play with paints, we can play with paints." I use my free hand and dip it into a blob of black paint, before pressing my paint-covered palm firmly against her throat. The paint leaves a dark handprint around her neck, and I tighten my grip just that little bit more than necessary, my fingers pressing into her skin in a way that's both possessive and intense.

"This stuff doesn't wash off easily," I murmur, my voice dropping to a dangerous purr. "So why don't we make sure everyone knows exactly what we've been up to?" As she struggles to gulp, her throat constricted by my hand, I can feel her pulse thrumming beneath my fingers. Hot and alive. Her efforts to break free heighten my awareness of the control I wield over her. My breath quickens, an animalistic growl rumbling deep in my chest. When I finally release her, it's slow, with a controlled exhale, like I'm granting her a gift she doesn't deserve.

I sit down on the edge of the bed, my eyes never leaving her as she stands up in front of me. The black handprint around her throat is stark and sharp against her skin. A slow, satisfied smile creeps across my face as I take in the sight. I pull off my shirt, tossing it aside. She crinkles her nose, a mix of distaste and intrigue, but I catch her eyes wandering down to my abs, lingering just a heartbeat longer than she probably intends. Then, her eyes crawl up again, landing on my chest, and her face drops.

"That's a lot of scars." She says bluntly, both eyebrows raising. I smirk.

"Proof I'm hard to kill, sweetheart."

"Go crazy," I say, my tone suggestive, as I stretch out on the bed with a casual, dominant ease. I gesture to the array of paints and brushes on the floor, a smirk playing at the corners of my lips as I watch her reaction. She gives me a disdainful look and replies bluntly,

"I despise you." I don't respond at first; instead, a genuine smile blooms on my face. With a defiant huff and an exaggerated roll of her eyes, she snatches the palette from the floor, her movements brimming with resolve. As she strides over to me, she plants her hands on my chest and delivers a firm shove. Although it doesn't budge me an inch, I can feel the anger coursing through her touch. I'm momentarily caught off guard, not used to being manhandled like this, but *fuck* is it turning me on.

I let myself fall back onto the bed, arms crossing behind my head as I settle in comfortably, the smirk on my lips never wavering. She straddles me, and I look up at her, savouring the unexpected thrill of being under her control. Her eyes are fierce, but I can see the flicker of excitement in them, matching my own. She works on my chest with the palette in hand, painting in silence. Every stroke of the brush, every flick of her wrist, is mesmerising. I stay completely still, just watching her. Her focused expression, the way her brows furrow in concentration, and the subtle sway of her hips as she moves. The silence stretches between us, but it's not uncomfortable.

As Skylar finishes painting my chest, tilting back to admire her work, I pull my phone from my pocket. I hold it out to her with confidence.

"Take a picture," I say, offering the phone with a casual flick of my wrist. "The password's 221515." She glances at the phone and then back at me, a look of genuine incredulity crossing her face.

"Why the fuck would you give me your password? Have you ever met me?" She asks. I chuckle softly, meeting her gaze with a mixture of arrogance and genuine interest.

"I don't have a thing to hide from you, my princess."

Her expression shifts, and I catch the faintest hint of a smile tugging at the corners of her mouth. She tries to suppress it, but she can't hide from me. Skylar snaps a picture with my phone and then turns it around to show me. As the screen lights up, I see the painting she's done; a stunning galaxy spread across my chest and up my neck. The colours swirl together in vibrant hues of blue, purple, and pink, capturing the essence of the cosmos with an impressive depth.

I tilt my head, examining her work. The intricate patterns and the way the colours blend together are surprisingly impressive. It's clear she's put a lot of effort into it, and the result is striking. I let out a low whistle, genuinely impressed.

Then, I pause, my eyes locking onto the middle of my chest. Right where my sword tattoo should be. My brow furrows. The sword's still there, but it's been transformed; the blade now serves as the body of a butterfly, its wings spreading outward, delicate and vivid, blending seamlessly into the stars around it. She hasn't just covered up the tattoo; she's used it, turning something hard and sharp into something graceful and alive. Beautiful.

"A butterfly?" I murmur, half-amused, half-bemused. She shrugs, still fighting that smile.

"It suits you." She says. I can't help but chuckle. Somehow, she's turned my darkness into something light, and against all odds, it doesn't feel wrong; it feels strangely right.

"Not bad at all, Farmer." I admit. She raises an eyebrow, a mix of pride and defiance in her expression.

"You doubted me?"

"Never." I say, flashing her a grin. She snorts, rolling her eyes with an obviously fake disgust.

"If it's so good, maybe I should charge you for it."

With that, I stand up, brushing off some of the dried paint and giving her a once-over.

"Alright, missy, I think you need to get some rest," I say, my tone firm but with a hint of a smirk. "You know, cool off a bit before you try to kill me again." She scrunches her eyebrows, but there's a flicker of a smile. I lean in slightly, adding with a casual tone, "and if you're feeling brave, you're welcome to stay in my bed tonight." Skylar raises an eyebrow judgmentally.

"Rest? It's not even 2 a.m."

I'm about to respond when she suddenly grabs the hem of her top and yanks it over her head, tossing it aside without a second thought. It drops to the floor, and without warning, she's standing there, half-naked, like it's no big deal. My brain short-circuits for a second. Women don't do this around me. They don't have the balls to pull a stunt like this. But Skylar? She's got no fucking fear.

I'm rooted to the spot, caught completely off guard. My eyes rake over her body, taking in every curve, every inch of exposed skin, and it's driving me insane. My pulse kicks up, thoughts spiralling.

135

What the fuck is she doing?

"What, you've never seen a pair of tits before?" She says. My jaw clenches so hard I can feel the tension in every muscle. I'm fighting the urge to lose control, to just take her right here. But there's something about that attitude of hers that gets under my skin in a way I can't ignore. Normally, I wouldn't tolerate this kind of disrespect from anyone, but with her, it's different. I hate it, and I love it at the same time. Skylar casually flops onto the bed, sprawling out on her stomach as if she's completely at ease. Her bare back exposed and inviting.

"Your turn," she says bluntly. My mind races as I take in the sight of her, and I'm struck by how she's completely shifting the dynamic between us. This isn't how things usually go. Women I deal with are usually more compliant, less daring. But here she is, making me question myself. Despite the shock, a grin creeps onto my face. I can't deny that I'm impressed. Her audacity is disarming, and it's got me intrigued.

I move to the box of paints, my steps steady but my mind racing. How the hell am I letting this happen? I'm supposed to be the one in control, but here I am, eagerly complying with her demands. There's a part of me that wonders why I'm allowing this shift without enforcing some kind of punishment. But nonetheless, I lean over her, the mix of colours spread out on the palette in my hand.

"Alright, princess," I say, my tone both mocking and indulgent. "What you want, you shall receive." I start painting her back, and it quickly becomes apparent that I'm not just applying colour; I'm deliberately making this as intimate as it gets. I use both the brush and my fingers, letting the paint blend and smear in ways that are both intentional and teasing. My fingers glide along her skin, sometimes tracing light, almost ticklish strokes, and at other times pressing firmly enough to make her squirm. I make sure to take my time, savouring each touch, each shift of her body under my hands. Every time I move my hand, I'm acutely aware of the way she reacts.

As I paint, my mind drifts to darker, more primal thoughts. I'm painfully aware of how easily I could have her right now. How effortlessly I could hold her still. I focus momentarily on her flimsy little shorts and knickers that cling to her hips. The sight of them, so easily removable, is driving me wild. All it would take is one firm grip, a quick tear, and I'd be having my way. My body responds to the fantasy, a hard, urgent pressure that I'm struggling to control. I try to stay focused on the task at hand, but it's almost impossible not to let the images of what I could do seep into my mind.

I finish painting, the final strokes of colour blending seamlessly across her skin. I step back, admiring my work with a smirk.

"Job done." I murmur, my voice tinged with satisfaction. Reaching into my pocket, I pull out my phone and snap a picture of the masterpiece. I throw the phone down onto the bed beside her, my grin widening as she glances at the screen. Her eyes go wide, taking in the intricate sunset I've painted. The colours are vivid and mesmerising, capturing the last light of day in a breathtaking way. She's genuinely stunned, her usual tough exterior softening as she looks at the painting. I watch as she sits up, her eyes still glued to the phone screen.

"Woah, what the fuck," she says, her tone a mix of surprise and genuine admiration. "That's actually sick."

"Thank you, princess," I reply smoothly, leaning back and letting the compliment roll off me. She continues to examine the photo, zooming in and scrutinising every detail, clearly impressed. Meanwhile, my gaze drifts over her half-naked body, unable to ignore the way her bare skin looks in the dim light. It's a battle not to let my eyes linger too long, and the sight is becoming harder to ignore.

Finally, I reach my breaking point. I grab her shirt from the bed and toss it at her in a firm gesture.

"Alright, now be a good girl and get to bed." I command, trying to sound stern but probably just sounding grumpy. She catches the shirt and shoots me a begrudging look, her attitude still firmly intact. As she puts her top back on, she drops my phone onto the bed and stands up. She heads for the door, glancing back with a smirk.

"*Yeah*, sorry to break it to you," she starts, "but I'm not a good girl." She says with a laugh, the sound echoing in the room as she walks out. I watch her glide out, a mix of frustration and fascination simmering inside me like a pot that's slightly too full. This girl is anything but predictable, and it's becoming increasingly clear that she's not going to make things easy for me.

CHAPTER 14:
HE'S NEW HERE
Marcus

The sun is high, and I step out into the garden just as lunchtime is in full swing. Before me lies the sprawling estate; a mafia-king style mansion garden. It's an absurdly huge expanse of green that's probably visible from space. Seriously, this place is so big, I'm half expecting to find a lost civilization hiding in one of the hedges. But, hey, I guess that's what you get when your rich brother's idea of a home is a royal fucking palace.

I make my way across the stone path, the sound of my footsteps echoing in the open space. The stones are immaculate, almost offensively so, like even the earth itself bends to Noah's will, too afraid to leave a single mark on his kingdom. Everything here screams control, order. Power. Their voices float over, and I catch the tail end of a conversation that makes me smirk.

"I just think it's too much hassle," Birdie's saying, her tone dripping with that rich-girl apathy. "Being chased by a snail for the rest of your entire life? No thanks." She continues. Skylar snorts, clearly not impressed.

"Of course *you* wouldn't take the money, Birdie. You're already fucking swimming in it." Birdie shrugs, not even denying it. Skylar grins, mischief written all over her face. "Personally, I'd trap the little bastard in a safe, chuck it in the ocean, and call it a day." Noah, lounging next to her, raises an eyebrow, clearly ready to pick apart her plan.

"Yeah okay, and what happens when the safe rusts and the snail breaks out? Or better yet, what if someone finds it, opens it up, and accidentally sets the snail free?"

"You got a better solution?" Skylar asks.
"Just shoot it," Noah says, deadpan, as if that's the end of the discussion. Skylar whips her head toward him, eyes blazing.

"The snail is invincible, you moron. You can't just shoot everything that pisses you off." She replies. Noah leans back, giving her a lazy, amused look.

"Clearly. If that was the case, I'd have shot you days ago." He snaps back. Sienna, sitting off to the side with Butter on her hand, sighs and jumps in with a more practical approach.

"Or you could just move to a different country every couple of years. The snail's slow. It'd take forever to catch up."

My sweet, always the voice of reason.

Birdie rolls her eyes, crossing her arms. "Honestly, this whole thing is just ridiculous." She mumbles. Skylar's eyes light up with a new idea.

"Oo, okay, what if I just keep it in a glass tank as a pet? That way, I can watch over it all the time." She suggests. Noah raises an eyebrow.

"What if someone smashes the glass?" He questions. Skylar scowls at him.

"Why the fuck are you so obsessed with violence?" She shrieks.

"Did you seriously just ask that?" Birdie interjects, "the guy kills people for a living." Noah

shrugs,   a   smirk   playing   on   his   lips.
"I'm just thinking practically. Not everyone has the patience to be a fucking snail babysitter."

I finally sigh and sit down next to Sienna, grabbing a handful of crisps from the table. Their back-and-forth is entertaining, but I've heard enough. As Noah and Skylar continue their relentless bickering about the stupid snail scenario, Dean strolls over with a scowl on his face, clearly unimpressed. His mood is anything but cheerful, and the ongoing argument only seems to irritate him further.

I'm desperately trying to think of a way to move the conversation along when I notice that both of them have tiny smudges of black paint on their necks. Noah has dark remnants that look almost deliberate, and Skylar has a couple of telltale black lines across her throat. It's a curious detail, considering their current tension, and it immediately grabs my attention.

I smirk, unable to resist the urge to dig a little deeper.
"What's with the paint?" I blurt out before I can stop myself. The effect is instant and almost comical. Noah and Skylar both turn their heads sharply in my direction, Sky's face going pale as if she's seen a ghost. It's clear they weren't expecting anyone to notice, let alone call them out on it.

I guess they've had a busy night.

Skylar's face flushes with embarrassment and she becomes instantly defensive. Her eyes dart around, clearly uncomfortable. It's as if I've unearthed a secret she wasn't prepared to expose. Her shoulders stiffen, and she's suddenly very intent on avoiding eye contact. Noah, on the other hand, remains calm, his expression shifting to a smug, knowing grin. It's clear he's fully aware of what's going on and doesn't mind flaunting it. He leans back with a self-satisfied smirk.

"Just a little late-night art," he says smoothly. "You know how it goes."

I see Noah's enjoyment. His calm demeanour and the arrogant glint in his eyes show that he's not only aware of the situation but is relishing the attention. Across from him, I see Dean's expression darken, tension rolling off him in waves. He's clearly irritated and wants to change the topic fast.

"Wow, isn't that interesting." He snaps, sarcastically. Immediately, the conversation comes to a halt. Everyone goes quiet, leaving a thick, uncomfortable silence. The tension between Dean and Noah is electric; it's clear this isn't just a casual disagreement. They're staring each other down; their eyes locked in a silent, deadly standoff. The hostility radiates off them like heat from a fire, each man's gaze sharp enough to cut through steel.

Delilah, sensing the hostility and desperate to break the uncomfortable silence, suddenly pipes up, her voice just a little too obnoxiously bright,

"So, Marcus, what's the deal with the books?" The question comes out rushed, almost like she's grabbing at the first thing that comes to mind. I clear my throat, grateful for the distraction.
"I don't know," I say, leaning forward, resting my elbows on my knees. "I've got a lot to think about. I'm trying to put the puzzle together, but I just need some time."

Before I can say anything else, Dean chops in, his voice sharp and clearly teetering on the edge.
"What if we don't have time?" He snaps, his frustration palpable. "The universe is fucking me at every single turn. I've lost two fingers, for fuck's sake. When is the next time gonna be the time that this book actually finishes me off?"

His words strike with a daunting weight, bringing the harsh reality of the situation home to everyone present. The tension is thick, and no one seems to know what to say. Dean's eyes blaze with a fierce mix of anger and fear, and for a fleeting moment, the only sound cutting through the stillness is the soft whisper of the wind rustling through the towering trees.

An uneasy silence blankets the garden, the weight of Dean's words lingering like a spectre. My brother, seated directly across from him, can't fully suppress the faint smirk that tugs at the corner of his mouth, though he quickly attempts to mask it. Dean catches the gesture, his glare intensifying, but instead of responding with words, he grabs a drink from the table and downs it in a swift gulp. Without uttering another word, he pushes back his chair, the legs scraping sharply against the stone as he rises and storms inside, the tension discernible in his wake.

Delilah shoots up from her seat, quickly trailing after Dean as he storms off. I let out a heavy sigh, rubbing my forehead as if that could somehow ease the stress that's been building in my mind. My thoughts are a tangled mess, and every time I try to piece them together, it feels like I'm only making it worse. I glance around at the others, noticing how everyone is avoiding eye contact. The pressure's getting to us all. I'm supposed to have this figured out, supposed to be the one keeping everything together. But right now, it feels like everything's slipping through my fingers. I lean back in my chair, staring up at the sky, wishing for some kind of clarity. The sun's bright, almost mocking in how cheerful it is compared to the storm that feels like it's inevitably brewing.

Skylar pipes up, her voice cutting through the heavy silence.

"Why don't we all go and hang out at the tunnel? It might make everyone feel better." I glance over at her, trying to gauge if she's serious. The idea of heading down to the tunnel doesn't exactly scream 'stress-free' to me, especially considering the fact that Skinny Jeans body was just found down there. But I mean, Skylar's trying, and I can see she's desperate to lift the mood.

"The tunnel?" Noah questions, raising an eyebrow. Skylar rolls her eyes, exasperated. "Ugh, noob." She mutters.

Sienna giggles softly, stepping in to explain. "It's just our spot. We've been hanging out there since we were kids. It's where we go to chill." Noah looks between them, clearly intrigued. I'm not thrilled about the idea, but I'm also not ready to shoot it down just yet. I glance at Skylar, giving her a look that says, *'Are you sure about this?'*; to which, she smiles, doubling down on her suggestion. The tunnel has too much baggage for my liking, but honestly, it could be exactly what we need to clear the air.

CHAPTER 15:
UNCOVERED SECRETS

Dean

Some genius had the bright idea of dragging us down to the tunnel, and somehow, I got roped into it. Now here I am, trudging through the woods, getting closer to that shitty little spot we've claimed as our hideout for years. There's an old, ratty sofa abandoned there, like it's some kind of living room for ghosts. We've been coming here forever to chill, smoke, paint and pretend we're not *completely* fucked up.

But now, this place feels different. Heavy. And surprisingly, it's not just because there's a massive gap in the floor where some dead guy was buried. It's because Noah's here. I can't even put my finger on why

I fucking hate him so much. Sure, we've got some history; old street dealer bullshit involving his crew, but it's nothing personal. He's a smug bastard, sure, always hanging around like he thinks he's the king of the world. But there's something deeper gnawing at me. Maybe it's that cocky way he carries himself, all calm and collected, like nothing rattles him. Or maybe it's *because* I can't quite figure him out, and that's what pisses me off the most.

Then there's the whole Sienna situation. I've got a gut feeling he's tied up in her abduction, but with no proof, it's all just speculation. And the worst part? Sienna seems perfectly fine around him. Happy even. Which just makes me feel even more off-balance.

Ah fuck, I don't know.

I'm the first to make a beeline for the old sofa, throwing myself down into its worn-out cushions like it's the only thing that makes sense anymore. The others are still milling around outside, but I'm not about to waste time pretending I'm thrilled to be here. I pull out my rolling papers and start working on a joint, trying to drown out the nagging thoughts about Noah and everything else that's been getting under my skin lately.

Delilah wanders over and plops down next to me, her presence as familiar as it is comforting. She watches me roll the joint for a moment before nudging me with her elbow.

"You okay?" she asks, her voice soft, but there's a hint of concern there too. I give her a genuine smile, one that actually reaches my eyes.

"Yeah, I'm fine," She smiles back, and it's one of those rare, unguarded moments that remind me why I keep her close.

"Well, you better be. We're not doing the whole brooding thing again tonight, okay?" She jokes playfully. I let out a small laugh, appreciating her attempt to lighten the mood.

"Yes, ma'am." I laugh, my smile lingering as I light up the joint.

The rest of the group starts to settle in, each finding their spot. I watch as Noah strides past, all tough-guy swagger, as if he owns the place. His eyes scan the walls of the tunnel, and he points at the graffiti.

"Has this always been here?" He asks. I don't even bother looking up from my blunt.

"No," I mutter, keeping my tone flat, "I did all the graffiti." He glances at me, one eyebrow raised, and I can feel him waiting for some kind of reaction. I just keep rolling, ignoring the weight of his stare. I'm not giving him anything. Let him wonder if I'm pissed off or if I even care. The truth is, I don't know which it is myself.

"Looks nice, man." He says.

I glance up, just for a second, catching the genuine tone in his voice. It's almost unsettling. I don't know if he's messing with me or what, but I'm not interested in figuring it out. I go back to rolling my joint, keeping my expression blank. I don't give two fucks if he thinks it's nice. I didn't do it for him, and I'm not about to start caring what Noah thinks.

As I finish rolling the joint, I hear Noah mutter, "You're welcome," dripping with sarcasm. I don't bother looking up. The flick of the lighter follows. As I take a drag, letting the smoke fill my lungs, I finally glance up and catch sight of Noah settling onto one of the logs. He's got a cigar in hand, the tip glowing as he lights it. Of course, he'd pick a cigar; gotta one-up me, even with something as simple as what he's smoking.

He meets my gaze, puffing out a cloud of smoke, his eyes locked on mine like he's daring me to say something. I won't lie, despite all my talk, the guy is fucking intimidating. There's something in his eyes, a coldness that sends a chill down your spine. It's not just that he's tough; he looks like a killer.

Probably because he *is* a killer.

That sadistic stare of his is a reminder of exactly who I'm dealing with. I'm a fighter, sure, but *fuck*. Noah's on a whole different level. The kind of guy who looks like he could end you without breaking a sweat. It's enough to make me think twice, just for a second. I exhale, the blunt's smoke swirling up around me, and look away. Not giving him the satisfaction.

We've been sitting around for hours now, the sun beginning to set, everyone trying to act like we're here to unwind. Birdie, always the one to lighten the mood, suggests,

"How about a game of 'Never Have I Ever'?" I don't have the energy to protest, so I go along with the idea. Skylar's all in, of course.

"Fuck yeah! I'll start." She squeals.

"Never have I ever been arrested?" Skylar, Birdie and I all put a finger down without hesitation. I watch as Noah's hand stays perfectly still, not a finger budging. Skylar narrows her eyes at him, disbelief written all over her face.

"Hold on, you're telling me you've never been arrested? You, of all people?" she asks, incredulous. "You're literally an open criminal." Noah leans back, giving her that arrogant smirk he's perfected.

"I don't get caught, princess." He replies nonchalantly. Skylar scoffs, but I catch a hint of amusement in her expression.

It's my turn next, and I decide to raise the stakes.

"Never have I ever killed someone." There's a pause, a noticeable shift in the air. Slowly, Skylar, Marcus, Noah, and Delilah each put a finger down. An awkward pause follows, before the group bursts into giggles. Then it's Noah's turn, and he seems ready to dive right in.

"Never have I ever betrayed someone." He says it casually, like it's just another question, but his eyes are locked on mine. For a fleeting moment, I wonder if he's hinting at something specific or if it's just my overactive imagination. I maintain a neutral expression, even as my mind races with paranoia.

Sienna, Butter in hand, takes her turn next.

"Never have I ever done drugs." She says. Everyone except her drops a finger, and Delilah wastes no time calling her out, a playful grin on her face.

"Sienna, don't lie, you've smoked weed before." Sienna rolls her eyes, looking a bit defensive.

"Yeah, against my will. And it was awful!" There's some laughter, and it's lightened the mood a bit, but I'm still on edge. I can feel Noah's gaze, like a knife digging into my back.

"Never have I ever dyed my hair." Delilah says. Skylar immediately drops a finger, groaning.

"Woah, that's not fair." Skylar protests. We all

chuckle, but I can't help but notice how Noah's still watching me.

"Never have I ever been caught trying to steal from someone," he says, and this time his gaze isn't just calculating, it's predatory. My stomach twists. I know exactly what he's alluding to. There was a situation back in the young offenders unit. I tried to lift some cash off a guy who looked like an easy target. Got the absolute shit beaten out of me instead.

How the fuck does Noah know about that?

I shift in my seat, trying to play it off, but my mind is spinning. He's got dirt on me, and he's making sure I know it. Delilah takes her turn, but her words drift over me like background noise. All I can think about is Noah, about how much he knows. How he's peeling back my layers in front of everyone, one question at a time.

Before I can steady my nerves it's Noah's turn again, and I brace myself.

"Never have I ever," he starts, his eyes stabbing into me, "kept a secret that could've changed everything." As soon as the words leave his mouth, it's like the world stops spinning. The ground drops from under me. My mind goes blank for a second, and all I can think is; he knows.

Oh my God, he fucking knows.

I feel the blood drain from my face, a sudden coldness washing over me, followed by a wave of heat that makes me break out in a sweat. My heart pounds so loudly in my chest, I can barely hear anything else. My vision narrows, the edges of my vision blurring as I focus on Noah, on the way he's looking at me.

The joint I'm holding wobbles between my fingers, and I barely notice as ash falls to the dirt. I try to stay still, but I can't. My hands are trembling, and I shift on the spot, desperate to draw air into my lungs. It's futile. The woods around us seem to close in, the trees pressing down like they're suffocating me. The world narrows down to the space between us, and all I can feel is panic, pure and raw. My stomach twists, a sick feeling crawling up my throat.

I can't stem the tide of memories rushing back, my long-buried secret clawing its way to the surface.

Marcus can't find out. He can't find out that I knew. He *can't*.

I remember the day I found the file, like it was yesterday. We were just kids, stuck in that shitty children's home, with peeling wallpaper and a stench that never went away. I was in our bedroom, trying to kill time by moving the furniture around; anything to distract from how miserable that place was. That's when I spotted it, dusty and yellowing, wedged behind the wardrobe, waiting to be unearthed.

I pulled it out, flipping it open. And there it was, plain as day; Marcus had a brother. A real, biological brother, out there somewhere. The kind of family connection I'd never have. My first instinct was to tell him. I should've told him. But then, the selfish part of me kicked in. What if he found his family and left? I'd be stuck in that hellhole alone, without my best friend, without the only person who made that place bearable. I couldn't let that happen. So, I burned the file. I never spoke a word.

But I knew.

I kept that secret buried deep, convincing myself it was for Marcus' sake. But deep down, I knew the reality; I was terrified of being left behind. Terrified of losing the only family I'd ever known. Noah's stare is cutting into me, and there's a twisted satisfaction in his eyes. He's got me cornered, and he knows it. The smug bastard knows exactly what he's doing. I'm struggling to keep my breathing steady, trying not to let the others see just how fucked I am right now. But I can feel it, everything I've tried so hard to protect is slipping through my fingers like sand.

I can't take it. The pressure in my chest is too much, my vision blurring as everything starts to spin. I stand up, needing to escape before I completely lose it. Marcus glances up, concern etched on his face.

"You alright, mate?" he asks. I can't even look at him. The guilt is clawing at my insides, but I force myself to nod.

"You look a little pale." Noah adds, his voice dripping with mock concern as he takes a puff on his cigar.

"I'm fine, bro." I manage to get out, my voice tight. "I just.. need a minute."

I turn to leave, but suddenly Sienna's butterfly starts flapping in my face, wings fluttering wildly as if it senses the chaos inside me. The tiny thing buzzes around, adding to the disorienting swirl in my head. I swat at it, not hard, just enough to get it out of my way, but my movements are rougher than I intend.

"Dean!" Sienna's voice is sharp, a mix of surprise and anger. I can feel everyone's eyes on me, but I can't control my body. I can barely think straight, my mind is a mess of panic and regret, and this fucking butterfly won't leave me alone! I push at it again, stumbling forward, my hands trembling as I try to get away from the group, away from Noah's smirk and the memories that are ripping me apart inside. But the butterfly just keeps coming, its tiny wings beating around my head.

"Dean, what's going on with you?" Delilah asks. I can't reply. I see Marcus reach up and snatch the butterfly from the air. The tiny creature flutters in his hand, finally stilling as he cups it gently. Sadly, I don't have the luxury to appreciate the gesture. As I stagger away from the group, I feel a jarring snag on my foot. I look down to see my shoe wedged tight in the metal of the old train track, the iron teeth catching with an unforgiving grip.

I try to yank my foot free, but the track's metal seems to hold on with an almost mocking tenacity. Panic rises in my chest, my breaths coming out in short, frantic bursts. Every pull only makes the situation worse, my foot feeling more and more trapped. My vision starts to blur, not just from the dizziness but from the growing realisation that I'm stuck.

"No fucking way." I mutter under my breath, tugging desperately. I can't believe this is happening, not now. The metal track seems to laugh at my struggle, remaining obstinately fixed.

The butterfly launches itself from Marcus' grasp, immediately diving back toward my foot, its wings beating frantically around the spot where I'm ensnared. I swat at it, struggling to concentrate, but it seems determined to pester me.

Then, from somewhere in the distance, a low, ominous rumble begins to swell, gradually growing louder and reverberating through the air. Everyone freezes, the sound pulling us all into a sharp, tense silence. It takes a moment for the realisation to sink in, but when it does, it hits like a punch to the gut.

A train.

The distant roll sharpens into something more defined, transforming into the unmistakable clamour of metal grinding against metal. The train's whistle pierces the air, a haunting sound that starts as a faint echo, but grows, blaring progressively louder with each passing second. My heart races, each frantic beat mirroring the threat that looms closer. I pull at my foot with renewed desperation, panic flooding every nerve in my body.

"Dean!" Delilah's scream slashes through the air, raw and filled with terror. The sound jolts me, but my foot stays stuck, the track holding on tight, refusing to let go.

The group around me bursts into frantic motion, but I'm only vaguely aware of their urgent shouts and scrambling bodies; my whole world narrowing down to the sight of my foot caught in the track and the menacing roar of that train barreling toward us. I pull harder, the metal digging into my shoe, but nothing gives.

The train's growl gets louder, closer, and I can almost feel the vibrations through the ground. Panic surges, cold and sharp, as I begin to understand just how little time I have. Frantic hands claw at me, tugging desperately at my leg, my foot; anything they can grasp in a desperate bid to liberate me from the unyielding embrace of the track. The light from the approaching train becomes visible now. A blinding beacon, a searing beam that intensifies with each pounding heartbeat. The ground beneath us shudders, the vibrations building into a deafening, earth-shaking roar that rattles my very bones.

"God, this is it," I whisper, my words lost in the atmosphere. I close my eyes, bracing myself for the onslaught of inevitability. The thunderous clatter of the train envelops me, a monstrous force that seems to consume the world whole.

And then, just when the end feels unavoidable, Marcus delivers one final, desperate tug. Pain shoots through my ankle as it twists free, a sharp, burning sensation that ignites my nerves. In an instant, I'm yanked through the air, flung backward with a force that knocks the wind from my chest. The train surges past, a colossal blur of metal and noise, the wind from its speed whipping violently across my face. It's so close that it warps my mind.

For a moment, the world falls into stillness. Sprawled on the ground, I gaze up at the canopy of trees, my chest heaving as I struggle to reclaim my breath. My heart pounds a relentless tattoo in my ears, the echo of survival ringing in my head.

The others are on the opposite side, likely staring towards me through the blur of the passing train. It feels as if a colossal wall of steel has risen between us, the engine so loud it drowns out everything else. I can't hear a thing, except the train and the knelling in my ears.

The moment unfurls like an eternity, a surreal freeze-frame where time itself seems to stretch thin. At last, the train roars past, its cacophony gradually dissipating into the distance, leaving in its wake an eerie stillness. Straining against the ground, I push myself up onto my elbows, the gritty earth rough beneath my palms, and gaze across the tracks.

The group stands frozen in place, their faces a tumultuous mix of shock, fear, and something more sinister; a flicker of darkness that betrays their thoughts. No one says a word. They fix their stares on me, and I can see it in their eyes, a shared recognition.

This shit just got very real.

CHAPTER 16:

YES, ANOTHER FUCKING CHASE

Marcus

What the actual *fuck* is going on?

First Dean freaks out over Noah's question in a stupid game of 'Never Have I Ever,' and then nearly gets himself flattened by a fucking train. I can't wrap my head around it. I look at Dean across the tracks. He's pale and shaken, and the rest of us aren't far behind. We're all rooted to the spot, not really sure what to do next. One minute, it's a game; the next, we're staring death in the face.

Delilah bolts across the tracks, throwing her arms around Dean as soon as she reaches him. He's still catching his breath, but he holds onto her like she's the only thing keeping him grounded. She probably is. The rest of us just stand there, looking at each other, and it's clear we're all thinking the same thing. No one says it, but the looks passing between us say everything.

Dean's not safe. Not even close.
The book isn't done with him yet.

If I were a normal person at this moment, I'd probably be thinking, 'Well, at least that's over.' But I've learned the hard way not to be too quick to assume everything's wrapped up nicely. Optimism and I don't mix well these days. And apparently, my instinct is right. As if on cue, I hear a shout from down the track. My head snaps around, and I'm met with three police officers marching toward us.

Shit.

The group shifts uneasily, the weight of the moment sinking in. Everyone's eyes dart around, clearly unsure of the next move. Noah takes a step forward, positioning himself between the group and the approaching police officers; his cigar still clamped between his fingers. His demeanour is unyielding, and he remains cool and collected as he faces them. The officers, recognizing him immediately, address him with a mix of respect and wariness.

"Noah Bear," one of them says, clearly familiar with his reputation. Noah meets their gaze, his expression hard and unphased.

"Is there an issue?" he asks, his voice low and assertive, cutting through the tense air. His confidence is palpable, and he doesn't flinch under their scrutiny.

One of the officers begins to reach for his walkie-talkie, presumably to call for backup. Noah reacts in a split second. He unexpectedly pulls out a gun and, without hesitation, fires at the walkie-talkie. The device explodes into pieces, clattering to the ground.

"You *really* don't wanna do that." he warns, a sinister grin spreading across his face. I'm struck dumb. My eyes widen, and my mouth probably falls open as I watch the whole thing unfold. It's like watching a scene from an action movie, except this is real life, and it's happening right in front of me. I glance at the others, their faces reflecting the same stunned amazement I'm feeling. Noah isn't just playing the game, he's redefining it. I can't lie, my brother is pretty fucking sick.

The officers look completely thrown off, their confusion and surprise evident. His casual handling of the situation flips the script entirely. He just stands there, gun in one hand, smoking his cigar with the other like he rules the world. Noah doesn't take his eyes off the police as he speaks, his voice steady and low.

"Marcus, take everyone to the cars," he says. "I'll be there in a minute."

I hesitate, my eyes flicking between Noah and the officers. There's a part of me that wants to stay, to see how this all plays out, but I know better. When somebody like Noah gives an order, you don't question it. I start backing away, leading the group toward the cars. The coppers aren't just standing there, though, they're getting antsy.

"Don't fucking move!" one of the officers shouts, his voice cutting through the air like a whip. But I don't stop. None of us do. We're getting the fuck out of here.

The moment we're out of the police's line of sight, we all break into a run, feet pounding against the dirt and gravel as we race toward the cars. We reach the cars, breathless but moving fast. Sienna and Skylar bundle into the backseat and I slide into the driver's seat, hands gripping the wheel. I watch the others speed off, the car kicking up dust in its wake.

As we huddle in the car, the silence is deafening. Skylar's staring out the window, chewing her lip, while Sienna fidgets in the backseat, her knee bouncing anxiously. I glance around, but there's no sign of Noah yet. The seconds tick by, stretching out unbearably. Then, faintly at first, I hear sirens in the distance. My chest tightens.

I tap my fingers on the steering wheel, trying to keep calm, but my patience is wearing thin. I grip the wheel harder, urgency pounding in my veins.
  "Come on, Noah," I mutter, the words escaping through gritted teeth. Every second that passes cranks up the pressure.

The flash of blue lights appears in the distance and I can't wait any longer. I reach for the keys, jamming them into the ignition with trembling hands, ready to floor it. But just as I'm about to start the engine, Noah strolls out of the woods, still puffing on his cigar like he's got all the time in the world. He's completely unfazed, the picture of calm, and it's actually really pissing me off how cool he looks right now.

He saunters over to the car and slides into the passenger seat, the rich scent of the smoke trailing behind him. For a moment, I just stare at him, caught between relief and disbelief. He looks over at me, raising an eyebrow.
  "Drive, then." He says, calm and confused. I blink at him, my astonishment momentarily overriding my panic. I can barely contain a chuckle.
  "You're fucked, you know that?" I admit. Without waiting for a response, I slam the car into gear

and peel out, making an immediate U-turn; the tires screeching against the asphalt.

The police sirens are deafening, slicing through the night with a relentless wail. Every inch of the road ahead is a battlefield of flashing lights, screeching tires, and the throbbing pulse of adrenaline. I whip the wheel, taking a sharp turn onto a narrow side street. The car skids, tires screeching in protest as we narrowly avoid a row of parked cars. The atmosphere is thick with the scent of burnt rubber and the tang of diesel from the police car closing in behind us.

"Left." Noah barks unexpectedly. I barely have time to think before, just as Noah's command leaves his lips, another police car screeches around a corner up ahead. It's charging straight for us, trying to cut off our escape.

"Do you have x-ray fucking vision or something?" I snap. I wrench the wheel sharply to the left, the tires screaming in protest as they grip the ground, whipping us around the narrow bend in a wild skid.

Each turn feels like a desperate gamble, and the relentless glare of the pursuing police car looms in my mirrors like a dark omen. Suddenly, I hear the distinct click of a window being rolled down. I glance over, only to see Noah calmly puffing on his cigar, the night air whipping into the car. And I thought *I* was relaxed in chases.

"What are you on the run for anyway?" he asks, his voice maddeningly calm, like we're just out for a casual drive. I blink, momentarily thrown off by the absurdity of his question.

"Really? Right now?" I snap, dodging another police car as it veers into our path. The side mirror just misses clipping it, and I slam on the gas, pulling ahead. But Noah just looks at me, waiting for an answer, smoke curling   lazily   from   his   cigar.

"I uh," I grit out, swerving to avoid a pedestrian sign. "I killed some guy." Noah doesn't even flinch, understandably, just raises an eyebrow. "I buried him back at the tunnel. I guess they're watching over the area now." I continue as I slam the brakes to avoid yet another police car that suddenly appears in front of us. The car jerks, and I throw it into reverse, speeding backward down the narrow street. Noah just nods, blowing another puff of smoke out the window.

"Got it," he says. "Who'd you kill?"

For a split second, my thoughts spiral back to that night; my first kill. I can still see his face, twisted, the way his eyes widened in shock when he realised he wasn't getting out alive. I remember the cold, detached fury that had washed over me, a part of me I didn't even know existed until that moment. It was like flipping a switch, and once it was done, there was no going back. That night changed everything. It changed me. I'm not the same person I was before that moment, and I never will be.

"A cunt who had it coming," I finally say, my voice cold, as I gun the engine, pulling us much further ahead now.

Noah just nods, like that's all he needed to know. He doesn't press for details, doesn't pry into the twisted mess that led me to that point. I'm sure he gets it, I know he's been there too. Or maybe he just doesn't care.

As we tear through the streets, I notice the police cars are trailing a little further behind. Their lights still flash in the rearview mirror, but they're not as close as they were. There's a chance, a small one, but a chance nonetheless. I know of a tight alleyway up ahead, barely wide enough for the car. It's risky as fuck, but If we can just squeeze through, we'll be out of sight before they even realise where we've gone.

I jerk the wheel with all my strength, causing the car to slide sideways and skid into the cramped alleyway. The car scrapes against the alley walls, the screech of metal against brick is loud; painful, even. The car bucks as it scrapes through, sparks flying from the sides, and for a split second, it feels like we're going to get wedged in tight. But then we're through, bursting out of the other side of the alley. I barely have time to straighten the wheel before I ramp up the speed.

The speedometer climbs past 100mph as I rocket towards Noah's house. My grip on the wheel loosens just a little, and I start to feel that familiar rush.

Marcus Bear has done it again.

The police sirens are distant now, barely a whisper behind us, and the roads ahead are wide open. I hear the girls in the back let out simultaneous sighs of relief, the tension in the car slowly melting. A smile spreads across my face, pride swelling in my chest. It's almost becoming routine at this point, but *fuck* it never gets old.

As we step out and get a good look at the car, it's clear the thing is wrecked on both sides. Scratches, dents, and who knows what else; it's a miracle we even made it here. I glance at Noah, expecting him to be at least a little pissed, but he just looks at the damage and smirks.

"Just a scratch," he says, completely deadpan.

"Hopefully you've got the cash to cover it," I shoot back, glancing mockingly up at the mansion looming behind us. Noah chuckles richly, completely unfazed.

He glances back at the house, then at me.

"Don't worry about the feds. They won't be sniffing around the tunnel anymore. I've taken care of it." He assures. I stare at him, still trying to wrap my head around this level of control. It's the kind of power I thought only existed in movies.

"How do you do it?" I ask, genuinely curious. Noah looks at me, a small smile playing on his lips.

"You're a Bear, Marcus," he says, his voice steady. "You can do it too."

CHAPTER 17:

THREATS, THREATS, THREATS

Noah

I'm thoroughly impressed by what I just heard; yet another kill under Marcus' belt. My little brother is a force, no doubt about it. He's proving himself in ways I didn't expect, showing the kind of grit and ruthlessness that could make him a great partner in the organisation.

I finish off my cigar and step into the house, the door clicking shut behind me. I'm ready to call it a night. My feet carry me up the first flight of stairs, each step echoing in the quiet hallway. Just as I'm about to reach the top of the stairs, I spot none other than Dean-fucking-Douglas; standing at the top of the stairs, blocking my path.

For fuck's sake.

I stop in my tracks, eyeing him with a mix of annoyance and resignation. He's pissed off, and the feeling is mutual.

"What do you want?" I ask, my voice flat. I'm not in the mood for this right now. He doesn't move, just stares down at me like he's got something to prove.

"We need to talk," he says, his tone dripping with the kind of forced intensity he probably thinks is intimidating. It's not. I let out a slow breath, rolling my neck like I'm loosening up before a fight.

"Yeah? Well, I need to sleep. So unless this is life or death, it can wait." I reply. Dean doesn't budge, his expression like stone, but I can tell he's determined to drag this out.

Dean doesn't say anything, just stands there, eyes locked on mine, like he's daring me to take this seriously. I don't. I continue up the last few stairs, intent on walking right around him, but he steps further to the side, purposely blocking my path. The move is subtle, but it's enough to make my blood simmer. We're in my house. He might think he's a big man, but this is my domain, and I won't tolerate being challenged under my own roof.

I stop in front of him, letting the silence hang for a moment. Then I lean in just enough to make sure he gets the message.

"You're in my fucking castle, Douglas. Don't push your luck." I threaten. Dean's face tightens.

"I want answers."

"Yeah, I bet you do." I grin, enjoying the way his frustration bubbles up. "Unfortunately, it doesn't work that way."

"What's your game?" He asks. I chuckle, the sound low and dangerous.

"My game? You brought this on yourself." I say, my voice calm but laced with menace.

He clenches his jaw, staying silent, but I can see the rage burning in his eyes. He wants to say something, to lash out, but he's holding it back.

"If you wanna show me disrespect," I continue, stepping closer, "then I'll be your worst fucking nightmare." I smirk, leaning in slightly. "Don't underestimate what I know, or what I can find out." As I move myself closer to him, Dean tilts his head up, meeting my gaze with that tough look he's always fronting. But it's almost funny, seeing him have to look up at me like that.

Being this tall, towering over people, it makes everything I do more fitting. I love how it adds to the intimidation factor, and makes my job that much easier. There's something about looking down at someone, especially someone like Dean, that just reaffirms my place at the top. It's an ego boost, really.

"How did you know?" He asks, surprisingly quiet.

"Somebody had to find the file, Douglas. And clearly it wasn't my brother," I smile.

"I'm not fucking scared of you," he spits out, his voice low but firm.

"That's your problem, Douglas." I say, savouring the absurdity of it. "You should be."

"I'm not the only one with secrets." He retorts.

When Dean says it, I can tell he's hoping to get under my skin. But instead of annoyance, I feel a flicker of respect. Decent response for once. I let a slow smile spread across my face.

"The difference is, you're guessing. Putting two and two together and hoping you'll get four. You've got no proof, no context," I laugh, "you're way out of your depth."

Dean's lips curl into a smug smile, and I arch a brow. The fuck is he grinning at? He looks like a Cheshire fucking cat, undeservedly full of himself. I'm not intimidated, never by him, but something about the way he's looking at me stirs my curiosity.

"What if I don't need proof?" he finally says, that shit-eating grin still plastered on his face. I stare at him for a second, barely holding back a laugh. Alright, Douglas. Let's see what you've got.

A low chuckle escapes me, and I rub my jaw, letting the tension roll off as I look down at him.

"Humour me," I say, my voice calm but with that edge I know gets under his skin.

"Do you think Skylar would be happy to know that you and Sienna have been spending time together? Making pinky promises?" He says. The laugh dies in my throat, but my smirk stays. Ah, there it is. He's swinging, and I'll give him credit; it's a decent hit. But not enough. Never enough.

"Though she'd never admit it, Skylar's wrapped around my little finger." I share, "But it's a decent threat, Douglas. You're getting better at this."

I know how to twist people, how to make them loyal without even realising it. Dean's trying to hit me where it hurts, but he doesn't know just how tight my grip is. Dean's smugness falters for a second. Just a flicker, but I catch it.

I start up the stairs again, shoulder brushing past him with force. Dean doesn't move to stop me this time. For a second, I think he's finally getting the hint, but then his voice cuts through the air again.

"What would Skylar think," he says slowly, dragging the words out, "if I told her you've been eyeing Sienna a little too closely?"

I pause, my back still to him, my jaw tightening. That little fucker. He knows that's a lie, but it's just slimy enough to plant doubt. And Skylar.. well, she's clearly got her triggers. I take a breath, letting it slide off my back, keeping the poker face locked in tight. I turn slightly, just enough to glance over my shoulder.

"So you'd lie?" My voice is low, controlled, but there's an edge to it, like a warning beneath the calm exterior.

Dean just shrugs, that smug grin still plastered on his face, like he's enjoying this little game.

"If it gets the job done."

Alright, time to shut this fucking show down.

I turn back fully, stepping into Dean's space so fast his cocky smile falters. I can feel his breath hitch as I get up close, towering over him, looking down with nothing but cold intent.

"You like to lie, don't you, Douglas?" I say, voice barely above a growl, but it lacerates through the atmosphere between us. My eyes lock onto his, unblinking. I lower my voice, letting each word dig under his skin. "You lied to your best friend," I say, slow

177

and intentional. "You knew he had a brother and you kept it quiet. How the fuck do you sleep at night, huh?"

His jaw tightens, but he doesn't say a word. I can tell I'm getting to him, though. He can't hide the guilt flashing across his face.

"You were supposed to *be* like his brother, right? His ride-or-die? But nah, you kept it all to yourself. And for what? So you could stay top dog in his life?" Dean's breathing gets heavier. I'm right there, chipping away at whatever bravado he has left. "You're the one with the big bad secret, Douglas. You went and fucked over the only person who actually trusts you." I let out a low chuckle, shaking my head.

I see his eyes darting away briefly, trying to escape the weight of what I'm saying. But there's no fucking way I'm letting him off that easy; not when he's throwing around threats like that. I've gotta make sure he's too rattled to even think about going through with any of it.

"Why you looking away now, huh?" I growl, stepping even closer, invading his space. "You might be able to lie to Marcus, but you can't lie to me. I know what I'm fucking doing."

Dean's gaze snaps back to mine, more intense now. His jaw clenches so hard I can almost hear it.

"You're not as untouchable as you think." he says, his voice steady but sharp. It's not a full-blown threat, but it's clear he's not about to roll over either. I can see it in his posture, the way his chest rises and falls like he's keeping his nerves in check. He knows I've got him cornered, and we both know I mean business.

I smirk as I glance at him again, noticing the sheen on his forehead.

"I'm not the one sweating, Douglas," I say, my tone mocking as I let out a low, sinister laugh. He doesn't reply, though. He's holding back, and I can tell. I turn slowly and make my way up the stairs. "Remember where you stand in my fucking house." With that, I start climbing the stairs again, every step deliberate and slow. As I reach the top, I can feel his eyes burning into my back, but I don't look back. I don't need to. He knows exactly who runs this shit.

CHAPTER 18:
GUNPLAY

Noah

As I ascend the stairs, I start heading toward my room, planning to unwind from the day. But then, a thought crosses my mind, and I veer off course, deciding to pay Skylar a visit instead.

I reach her door and swing it open without knocking. Skylar's sitting on her bed, scrolling through her phone, her expression focused until she notices me. The second she sees me, her face tightens into an annoyed scowl.

"Why don't men ever fucking knock?" she snaps, her tone sharp and irritated. It's clear she's not in the mood for any interruptions, but I just smirk.

"My mistake, princess." I say calmly, backing out and closing the door. I give it a firm knock and then wait for her to respond. From inside, she shouts,

"Fuck off!" Her voice laced with frustration, but I just chuckle. Ignoring her protest, I open the door once more, stepping back inside with a nonchalant shrug.

As I mosey back in, I head straight for the bed where she's sitting, still absorbed in her phone. I watch her for a moment before I speak up,

"I'm just coming in to check on you." She doesn't look up or acknowledge me, her attention still locked on her screen. I can't help but let my lips curl into a smirk as I watch her. That little attitude is just *so* sexy. I lean in slightly, tilting my head. "Is there a problem, Farmer?" I ask, drawing out the nickname with a touch of dirty amusement.

She looks up at me in slow motion, like something straight out of a horror film. Every inch of her glare seems to crawl up my body with painstaking slowness, as if she's trying to project her fury through sheer willpower. It's both terrifying and hilarious; here I am, a 6 foot 7 criminal kingpin, and she's a tiny ball of sass with baby-pink hair, staring daggers at me like she's about to summon some kind of dark force.

"Yes," she says, her voice dripping with venom. "There is a problem."

She just keeps staring at me, her gaze piercing through the room like a hot knife through butter. It's that kind of stare that makes you think of the old saying, *'If looks could kill.'* But right now, I'm thinking, if her stare could actually manifest into something, she'd probably have me six feet under and buried in the back garden.

"Would you like to elaborate on the problem?" I ask, the edge in my voice more teasing than anything.

"My drug dealer died," she snaps. I raise an eyebrow, unfazed.

"So?" I say, shrugging. "Dealers get killed all the time." Skylar finally breaks her stare, rolling her eyes as if I'm the dumbest person she's ever encountered.

"Yeah," she huffs, "but then I went to go ask my other dealer, and guess what?" I raise my brow again, playing along.

"What?"

"He's dead too!" she shouts, throwing her hands up, clearly pissed. I bite back a smirk, keeping my face as neutral as possible.

"I'm sorry for your loss," I say, layering the words with as much sarcasm as I can manage.

Skylar's face twists with irritation, and before I can even blink, she's shoving past me, her tiny frame packing a surprising force. She starts pacing the room, her steps sharp and furious, like she's trying to incinerate the floor beneath her. I just watch, arms crossed, enjoying the show. Skylar stops dead in her tracks, turns on her heel, and just stares at me. Her eyes narrow, and for a second, I think she might throw something.

"Why did you kill both of my dealers?" She asks, voice sharp as glass.

"Why did you let both of your dealers fuck you?" I shoot back, unflinching.

Skylar's eyes flare wide, and I can tell I've struck a nerve immediately. Her eyes flicker with insecurity, embarrassment even, but she swallows it down fast, quicker than I expected.

"Because I was horny," she fires back, her chin lifted like she's daring me to say something else. I can't help but laugh under my breath. That's Skylar for you.

"You're better than that." Her face darkens with annoyance, and she strides right up into my personal space. This is the second time today I've had someone square up to me in my own house.

A new record.

She rolls her neck and plants her hands on her hips.

"I don't need a lecture from *you* about my sex life." She spits.

"I'm not lecturing you, I'm setting boundaries." I step closer, and the move forces her to take a step back, her defiance momentarily faltering. I can see her fighting to regain her composure as she eyes me. "From

183

now on, nobody touches you, but me." The firmness in my voice leaves no room for argument, my authority clear and uncompromising.

"Sorry?" She laughs, her voice dripping with defiance as she tries to regain her space.

"You heard me, Farmer," I say, my eyes locked on hers.

I take another calculated step forward, forcing her to retreat. She tries to stand her ground, but every inch of space I close down on her makes her push back. It's instinct. It's power. She's getting cornered, and she knows it.

"You're insane if you think you can tell me who I can and can't-"

"I don't *think*, baby. I'm telling you. This isn't up for discussion. It's a command. And trust me, you'll want to obey." I cut her off.

"You don't control me, Noah. Nobody does." She says. I let out a low chuckle. My God, it's so hot when she says my name.

"Wanna bet?"

Her back hits the wall, and I take the last step, boxing her in. She's trapped between the wall and me now. She swallows hard, looking up at me, but I can tell her mind's racing, searching. Then, out of nowhere, her lips curl into a smirk, eyes flicking around the room before landing back on me.

"Y'know," she starts, her voice still full of sass. "I think the reason you're so insistent on telling me who I can and can't fuck, is because you're insecure." She says, still giving me that little smirk. "Overcompensating with all of this maybe..?" She tilts her head, mocking me, and her gaze flicks to the ropes and hooks on the walls.

I arch a brow, my expression unchanging, though inside, I can't help but be amused at her pathetic attempt to hit a nerve. A slow smile spreads across my face as I watch her.

"Careful, princess," I growl, my voice low and teasing. "You wouldn't want me to have to punish you for that mouth."

"Oh my God. I'm right, aren't I?" She laughs, "you're boring in bed."

I don't respond immediately, keeping my cool, but she's pushing it. Every word out of her mouth feels like a challenge, like she's begging me to prove her wrong. My grip on my self-control is slipping fast, and my thoughts, well, they're not just dark. They're graphic. Filthy. Her little comment about me being 'boring' in bed? She has no idea. I want to fucking tear her apart, make her regret every word she just said; make her beg for the things she's mocking me for. The ropes in this room? They're not for show, and the thought of her tied up, helpless under me, only makes me more desperate to prove her wrong. I can feel it all playing out in my mind: her eyes wide, attitude gone. *Fuck.*

Skylar keeps pushing, her attitude as fierce as ever.

"I bet even *Sienna's* having more interesting sex than you," she taunts, her eyes dancing with defiance. I watch her, unimpressed but intrigued.

"Keep talking, Farmer." I say, my voice deliberately low and threatening.

"It's true," she says, her voice remaining confident. "She told me he held a knife to her throat while they *did it*." I smirk, feeling a dark satisfaction.

"Well, it's cute that my little brother's been playing with knives.." I take another small step closer, pressing her even more firmly against the wall. My voice drops to a cold whisper, "but big brother plays with guns."

I slowly pull my gun out of my waistband, watching as Skylar's eyes flash with confusion and a hint of fear.

"What's that supposed to mean-" Before she can finish, I yank her wrists up, jerking them hard above her head. She gasps, her protest cutting off into a squeal as I move quickly, grabbing the rope hanging from the hook on the wall. I wrap it around her wrists, pulling it tight, forcing her arms to stretch painfully above her. The rough rope digs into her skin, pinning her against the wall with a brutal finality.

Skylar's breath quickens as she starts to show real fear. I slide the barrel of my gun under her chin, tilting her head up so she has no choice but to look at me. Her eyes widen as she meets my gaze, a mix of resilient defiance and dread swirling in them.

"Noah, what are you doing?"

"Feeling a bit nervous now, are we?" I taunt, the gun's cold metal pressing against her skin, making her shiver. Her lips part, but no words come out. I let the gun hover just beneath her chin, the pressure firm but not enough to hurt.. Yet.

"Tell me, princess," I continue, my voice low and dangerously calm. "Did you really think I'd just stand here and let you run your mouth without consequences?" Her eyes dart around, searching for an escape that isn't there. I keep the gun steady, enjoying the way she's forced to focus entirely on me, her bravado crumbling. "Because, *I* think you know exactly what you're doing," I say as I let the gun press a bit harder, making her flinch slightly.

She tries to squirm,

"I don't know what you're talking about. Fucking untie me, you weirdo!" Her demand hangs in the air, but I ignore her plea, my gaze locked onto hers.

"You want me to prove you wrong, don't you?" I taunt, relishing the way her jaw tightens, the fire in her eyes dimming to a wary flicker. The realisation dawns on her; she wanted to push me, to test the limits, and now she's learning just how perilous that choice was.

"That's not-"

"Well here you go, princess. You've got my attention." She struggles against the ropes, but it's futile. The more I talk, the more I see the panic set in. It's clear she didn't expect me to take her taunts seriously, let alone react like this.

"Now, shut that pretty fucking mouth," I growl, the command rough and final.

With one hand still gripping the gun under her chin, I use my other hand to hook a finger into the waistband of her little shorts. She tries to look down, probably trying to gauge what's happening, but I make it impossible for her by tightening the gun under her chin, forcing her to meet my stern, unyielding stare.

"Noah," she whimpers, her voice suddenly small and pleading. The shift from her usual defiance to this quiet, almost mousy desperation is jarring. It's a tone I've never heard from her before, and it's extremely satisfying.

"I thought I told you to be fucking quiet," I remind her, my voice cold and unfeeling. She swallows hard, her breath coming in shallow, uneven gasps. I can see the tension in her body, the way her muscles tighten with apprehension. This is where I want her; nervous, on edge, completely aware of how little control she has.

It's turning me on to see her struggle against the ropes, knowing that the more she fights, the tighter they pull.

I lock eyes with her, the heat in my stare making it clear this isn't some innocent game. My scowl's fierce; I'm not truly angry, but I want her to feel the weight of my intent. With a predatory growl, I hook a finger into the waistband of her shorts again. My grip is ironclad, and in one brutal yank, I rip the fabric away from her, watching it tumble to the ground like a shredded trophy. As that fabric flutters down, my thoughts turn feral.

I let my gaze devour her; the sight of her bare skin, so close and so available. The curves of her thighs and ass now fully revealed. Her knickers, a delicate baby-pink lace with a sweet little bow on the front, remain, now the only barrier. I feel like a fucking animal. I take a deep breath through my nose, my jaw clenched tight. The tightness in my chest and the raw, urgent need surging through me are almost unbearable.

I hook my finger into the lower part of her knickers. Slowly, provokingly, I run the back of my finger over her sensitive skin, teasingly trailing along her clit before descending lower. The second I feel how soaked she is, a low, guttural sound escapes me, and I have to swallow hard to keep myself in check.

"*Oh*," I murmur, my voice dripping with contempt. "Is someone enjoying herself?" I tilt my head, leaning in closer, watching her carefully. "All that attitude, and here you are, soaking right through your knickers." I look down as I trace her again, savouring the way her body betrays her.

I press my finger in slowly, just enough for her to feel the tip slip past her entrance. Her body responds instantly, a subtle shudder running through her as she clenches around that small intrusion. I can feel the wetness coating my fingertip, and I push in just a little deeper, not enough to give her any real satisfaction but enough to torment her. She's fighting it, trying to squeeze her thighs together, but I keep her pinned, my finger still barely inside her, feeling her body tense with every tiny movement I make. Each slow, intentional push stretches her slightly more, her pussy clinging to my skin as I press in just a fraction deeper before pulling back again.

To my surprise, she lashes out, trying to kick me. I have to give it to her, she's fucking brave. Most people would be begging by now, but not Skylar. She fights. Unfortunately, it's not going to work. I catch her ankle mid-kick and shove her harder against the wall with a force that makes her gasp.

Her entire body is now pressed between the wall and my hand, which is gripping her throat tightly, holding her in place. Her back is arched so severely that only her ass and shoulders touch the wall, leaving her torso suspended, tense and exposed.

"Think you're brave?" I growl, pressing down hard enough to make her panic.

"Okay, I get it! Let me go." She manages to choke out. I smirk, rubbing my thumb back and forth slightly.

"You're not going anywhere until I've made my point, baby." I promise.

With that, I press the gun to her lips, it's cold steel making contact with her warm skin. I tap it lightly twice, each gentle knock a clear, unmalleable order.

"Open your mouth for me, princess." I command softly, though the underlying menace in my voice is unmistakable. Her eyes widen, a tempest of fear and disbelief swirling within their depths. As she thinks, her breaths come in sharp, erratic gasps. She hesitates, her eyes locked on the gun, knowing exactly what this means.

Her voice trembles as she whispers,

"Is the gun loaded?" I let out a soft, mocking chuckle.

"Why would I tell you that? I thought you wanted some excitement?" I taunt. Her pale blue eyes plead with mine. The colour is almost unnaturally vivid, like shards of frozen crystal reflecting the dim light of the room. The hue is almost otherworldly, reminiscent of the clearest winter sky just before dusk; deepening into an iridescent sheen that seems to capture both light and shadow, swirling within their depths like ancient glaciers.

As she slowly parts her lips, the movement is cautious yet resolute. I let a dark, satisfied smile curl at the corners of my mouth.

"Good girl," I say, my voice smooth and dripping with smug approval. I realise, in this charged moment, that beneath all the tension and brutality, I am completely, irrevocably in love.

I press the cold metal of the gun barrel against her tongue, feeling the tremor that runs through her. The gun's weight is solid in my hand, and as I slide it slowly in and out of her mouth, the subtle twist of the barrel is intentional, forcing her to feel every inch of it. Each time I withdraw the barrel, I see her breath catch, her throat working involuntarily. As I push it a bit deeper, I can't help but grin as her eyes widen, her mouth struggling to accommodate the intrusion.

"That's it, baby," I encourage her. "Make it nice and wet." I continue to press the barrel further, inch by inch, until she gags, her body jerking against the wall.

I pull the gun out abruptly, the metal slick and shining with her saliva. A glistening trail follows as it slips free from her mouth. She gasps for air, her chest heaving with the effort to steady her breathing. Her lower lip trembles, a result of the force I've been asserting. I allow her a moment to gather herself, observing her with a blend of satisfaction and cold detachment. Her eyes remain wide, shimmering with unshed tears.

After letting her calm as much as she can, I decide it's time to get this torture over and done with. Placing one hand firmly against the wall beside her, I lean in closer, watching her as she struggles. I lower the gun, using it to shift her underwear aside and position the barrel firmly on her clit. Her lower lip trembles as she manages a soft, desperate,

"please." But I cut her off with a harsh command.

"Be quiet."

I move the gun down to her entrance and slowly push it inside, feeling the resistance as her body reluctantly gives way. Looking down at her tiny frame, I can see every shiver, every tense spasm as I slide the barrel deeper. Her whimpers are sharp, her eyes wide with a mix of fear and grudging pleasure. She's trying to stay composed, but her movements betray her discomfort. The way her legs twitch, the way she squeals, it's all raw and real. I relish the sight of her torture, the way she's forced to stretch and adjust to the roughness of the metal.

Each time I push the barrel deeper, her cries grow more strained, and a wicked thrill pulses through me. Her fear, her pain, her desperate attempts to squirm away. I can't help but smirk at the sight of her breaking down, her tears mingling with her cries. The way she looks up at me, so small and vulnerable beneath my imposing presence, making me rock hard.

Once I feel the gun beginning to slide smoother, I begin pumping it into her; harder and slightly faster. Keeping the pace consistent, constant. Intense. Unavoidable. I notice the way her body reacts, how she begins to give in, the agony in her eyes slowly shifting towards an acceptance. As I watch her closely, something changes in her expression. Her breathing, ragged and uneven, starts to sync with the pace of everything happening. Her lips part slightly, and her eyes begin to roll back, softening in a way that catches me off guard. For a moment, I swear I catch a small, fleeting smile; barely there, but enough to make me pause. She bites her lip, and I can't tell if it's from pain.. or pleasure.

I feel the slick warmth on my hand, confirming what I'm starting to suspect. It takes me a second to process, and it twists something in my gut. I lean down to her eye level, searching for any hint of hesitation, but all I see is the strange blend of vulnerability and something more. She's turned on.

A slow, mocking grin spreads across my face.

"Are you having fun too, princess?" I ask.

As she looks at me, her lips part slightly, but she doesn't say a word. The moment her eyes flash with that wicked, daring look, something in me snaps again. It's like the animal inside me takes over, feral and hungry. I feel it in my veins, pulsing with adrenaline. I want to see her break. I want to watch her unravel beneath me, and I'm not stopping until I get that. With that primal switch flipped, I push the barrel deeper, twisting it slightly, feeling her thighs tense.

Her wetness coats the gun as I drive it in further, the disinclination of her tight body sending a dark thrill through me. I start pumping it harder, a brutal rhythm, each twist purposeful. Her back arches as I force her to take more, the tension in that tight little body making it clear she's fighting to keep control.

"Come, Skylar." I order firmly as I straighten up once again, towering over her. "Now."

As I pump faster, the movements become more intense, her wetness soaks everything. With each brutal thrust, tiny droplets flick off, splashing against my hand and her thighs. The slick sounds of it fill the room, mixing with her sharp breaths and quiet whimpers, and I feel her trembling under me, losing the battle against herself.

Tears mix with the sweat on her flushed cheeks, and she can barely hold herself together as the waves of ecstasy crash over her. A choked cry escapes her lips, her eyes squeezing shut as she tries to hold it together, but she's completely unravelling, coming hard.

"Atta girl," I praise, pumping harder, ignoring her adorable, desperate pleas as they spill from her lips in broken sobs,

"Please, Noah. Please.."

I hold the gun still, pressed deep inside her, sensing every quiver and tremor as her body tries to recover from the orgasm. I don't move, just watch her. Tears of mascara streak down her cheeks, mixing with the flush of her skin; her pretty little ass is squished hard against the wall. Her legs are weak, barely holding her up, and I can feel the slick trickle of her come reaching my fingers. She's nothing but a trembling mess, and the wetness coating my hand is proof of how much she's given in, whether she'd admit it or not. I keep the pressure steady, savouring how she's completely fallen apart, undone, and knowing I'm the one who's done it. I press in a little deeper, just to hear that pathetic little whimper once more.

There's no fight left in her at this moment, she's just a used-up, panting princess who's exactly where I fucking want her.

I remove the gun and loosen the rope, watching her collapse as soon as her wrists are free. I let the gun drop to my side and look down at her. Her eyes are glassy, and her body is thoroughly spent. I lean over, grabbing a fistful of her hair and yanking her face up to mine; allowing myself a full view of her dishevelled state.

"Am I still boring, princess?" I ask, my voice icy and mocking. My grip tightens slightly, pulling her face closer to mine. "Or have you changed your mind?"
To my surprise, she meets my gaze with a bratty sparkle.

"No," she says, her voice sassy and firm, "I haven't changed my mind." With a sudden, sharp move, she snatches the gun from my hand, pointing it directly up at me. The dynamic of the moment shifts as she pulls the trigger with a quick, wanton motion. The click of the empty chamber reverberates in the room, and a disturbingly sweet smirk blooms across her plump lips.

"The gun wasn't even loaded," she says, her voice dripping with a smug, seductive edge. I stare her down and smile along, a dark thrill coiling in my gut.

Fuck, she's good.

CHAPTER 19:
PLOT CHANGES

Sienna

The morning light streams through the sheer curtains, illuminating my room with a soft, golden glow that dances across the floor like a warm embrace. I'm sprawled comfortably on my bed, a slight smile curling my lips as I gently cradle Butter in my outstretched hand. She flutters her delicate wings, a mesmerising display of iridescent hues contrasting beautifully against the pleasant yellow of her wings.

My gaze drifts to the dainty gold ring glimmering on my finger; a stunning little diamond that catches the light in a way that feels almost magical. Yesterday, amidst a whirlwind of emotions, I said yes to a future that just days ago I had believed to be out of reach. It's not just a piece of jewellery; it's the embodiment of everything my heart has whispered for so long. Marcus. Peace. A future suffused with the kind of love that feels like home. And as I watch Butter swirl gracefully through the air, I find solace in the knowledge that I am safe, that I am loved, and that Marcus stands beside me; an unwavering pillar in a world that often feels unmanageable.

The door creaks open, and Marcus walks in, the two magical books in hand. He's got that look in his eyes, serious and focused; he's on a mission. Sitting up with an instinctive rush, a smile blossoms across my face. His gaze softens, melting away the seriousness that often cloaks him. With a loving smile breaking through, he approaches me. His glare is soft, full of tenderness. He leans in and places a gentle kiss on my forehead, before moving over to the desk.

"Whatcha doing?" I ask. He picks up Noah's book and starts flipping through its pages carefully; his brow knitting into a frown of concentration.

"His book didn't glow." he says, his voice edged with a hint of frustration.

"That's weird," I say, settling back against the pillows, watching him work. I watch as Marcus picks up his book, his fingers brushing delicately over the latch. For a moment, I become entranced by the rhythm of his movements. His jaw is clenched tight, and his gaze is still. Locked in. Then, the realisation hits me like a bolt. My eyes shift from his fingers to his taut expression, and it sinks in; Oh my god, he's considering opening it again. My heart races wildly, and a wave of anxiety crashes over me.

I can't hold back.

"Don't, Marcus," I urge, my voice tight with worry. He doesn't look at me, nor does he reply. His focus is entirely on the latch, fingers lingering; almost trembling hesitation. The way he's gripping the book, the deep furrows on his brow, it's clear he's wrestling with himself. His jaw is clenched so tightly that it seems he's grappling with an invisible force. Every second feels heavy with his internal struggle, the weight of whatever decision he's about to make pressing down on him.

I get up from the bed, my heart pounding a little. I walk quietly behind Marcus, not wanting to disturb the intense concentration etched on his face. Gently, I wrap my arms around his shoulders, resting my head by his ear. The warmth of my body against his seems to ground him, just a little. I can feel the tension in his muscles.

My voice comes out soft but worried.

"Marcus.. if you open it, we have no way of closing it. Not without Millie here." Marcus hesitates for a long moment, his fingers still brushing the edge of the book's latch. Finally, he exhales sharply and mutters,

"I'm starting to think it doesn't make any difference whether it's open or closed." His words hang heavy in the air, and I feel a knot form in my stomach. Partly because I wasn't expecting that reply, but mostly because I know exactly what he means.. And I fear that he's right.

"What do you mean by that?" I ask softly, even though I already know. The sadness in my voice betraying me. Marcus turns to face me, and I can tell by the way his expression softens that he's seen the anxiety in my eyes. He offers a small, almost apologetic smile before patting his lap, silently inviting me to sit. I nestle into his lap, and he instinctively reaches up to sweep my curls back over my shoulder, his touch delicate. His hand settles on my thigh, warm and solid, anchoring me in the moment. There's something intense about the way he holds me, like he's trying to reassure me, even though his own thoughts seem far away.

Marcus' eyes bore into me with a fierce intensity, their fervour coiling around my heart like a serpent waiting to strike.

"Sweet, if we don't do something, Dean is gonna die." His voice is a low rumble, thick with strain. He takes a breath, as if gathering strength from the air, his grip on my thigh tightening. "I don't think he has much time." He pauses for a moment, swallowing hard, before placing his hand on the book. "And clearly I've missed a piece of the puzzle." The calamity in his tone is undeniable. His frustration is bedlam beneath the surface, like he's bracing for the storm ahead, hand gripping the book like it holds the answers to everything.

Which we know now, *it does*.

I study him, my brows furrowing in uncertainty. My attention drifts to the book, its worn cover obscuring a trove of perilous secrets. *Is Marcus right?* My thoughts whirl, a cacophony of questions colliding, each one more insistent than the last. After a taut moment, I finally whisper,

"Are you sure you wanna do this?" As soon as the words escape my lips, Butter flits from the bed and gracefully settles on the desk beside the book. Marcus and I freeze, our stares colliding in mutual disbelief. We share a look of astonishment that conveys everything. It's like the universe just handed us a sign.

We exchange a resolute nod, our unspoken concord unmistakable. With measured caution, he reaches for the book, his fingertips grazing its timeworn cover.

Gradually, he elevates it from the desk, and an electric tension crackles heavily in the air around us. We both know there's no turning back now.

Marcus's fingers tremble slightly as he pulls open the latch. The room holds its breath, and we exchange a tense glance, bracing ourselves for something; anything. But as the latch clicks open, an unsettling silence falls. There's no explosion, no glowing light, no dramatic noise. Just the quiet, still air and the book lying innocuously in Marcus' hands. We stare at it, our anticipation giving way to bewilderment.

That's a good thing, right?
Is that a good thing?
The absence of any immediate danger is oddly comforting, yet the silence leaves me with a gnawing sense of uncertainty. Marcus and I exchange a look, our expressions a tapestry of relief and mild disappointment. We almost shrug in unison, a shared sense of anticlimax hanging in the air. It's as if we had anticipated something far more dramatic, but instead, we're left with a quiet moment that feels almost underwhelming. Deflating.

Marcus starts flicking through the pages, the faint sound of paper rustling filling the room. We both lean in, carefully reading each line, our eyes scanning assiduously, but nothing jumps out as immediately dangerous. When we reach the last couple of pages, Marcus suddenly pauses, his brow furrowing.

"Hold on," he mutters, his voice low. "It's not the same."
He slams his finger down on the page, his voice sharp with urgency.

"Look," he demands, eyes wide with intensity. I snap to attention, following his finger to the line he's pointing at. As I start to read, my stomach drops. The story, it's different.

'Despite their fear, the animals fought back valiantly, determined to defend their beloved home..

In the midst of the chaos, the Queen left the safety of the castle, determined to protect the village herself. As she moved through the smoke and fire, the battle raged on, with spells and arrows flying.

Then, just as suddenly as it had begun, the Derpy Dragon faltered, its strength drained. With a final, shuddering breath, it collapsed to the ground, lifeless. The village was spared, but something else had been lost that day.

The King emerged from the castle, surveying the battlefield, the smouldering ruins of homes, and the faces of the villagers; those who had fought, and those who had fallen. Among the debris, the Queen was nowhere to be seen.

The villagers, their faces etched with exhaustion, gathered together in a solemn circle. They joined hands, forming a tight-knit ring of solidarity and shared grief.

His heart heavy, the King led the animals back toward the castle, their footsteps slow and quiet. As the rain began to pour heavier on the village, the King whispered a promise to the villagers and the fallen, that they would always be his family.

Once they passed through the great gates, the King turned and ordered his trusted guard to close them. The sound of wood and iron sealing shut echoed through the village like a sigh. The King's final gesture, his reassurance and whispered promise, seemed to bind the gates with more than just physical barriers.

And so the gates remained, never to open again. Though the village had survived, the King stood at the walls, staring out beyond them, knowing deep within that nothing—no spell, no courage—could change the course that had been set that day.'

The changes aren't just small, they're unsettling, like pieces of a puzzle rearranged into something dangerous. I look at Marcus, concern and stress etched into my face. He's still staring at the book, his breathing quick and uneven. His eyes flicker with disbelief, and he's subtly shaking his head, as if trying to deny what we're both reading.

Marcus begins flicking through the following pages, his movements frantic. One after another, the pages turn, but they're all the same as before.. blank. His frustration builds with each turn, his hands trembling slightly as he searches for something, anything, to make sense of it.

"This can't be it," Marcus says, his voice cracking as panic takes over. He flicks through the pages even faster now, his hands shaking. "There has to be something more!"

The implications of the ending, the story's cruel suggestion that Dean's fate is sealed, that there's no way to change it, are sinking in fast. Marcus' eyes dart across the empty pages, as if willing more words to appear, but all that greets him is an endless void.

"We can't let this happen," he whispers, his voice barely holding it together. I watch his panic and try to steady my own racing thoughts.

"Just wait," I say, trying to keep my voice calm. "There has to be a loophole or a hidden message somewhere. A way we can change this."

My eyes stop on a poignant moment right after the battle.

'The villagers, their faces etched with exhaustion, gathered together in a solemn circle. They joined hands, forming a tight-knit ring of solidarity and shared grief.'

"This has to mean something." I say, pointing to the passage. Marcus peers at the text, his brows knitting together in concentration.

"You think it's important?"

"Yes," I insist, my finger tracing the line. "It's right before the gates are closed, and it's a moment of collective action. It might be a clue that we need to do something similar in order to close the book." Marcus squints at the line I'm showing him, not looking totally convinced.

"So.. you're saying we all hold hands in a circle while I close it?"

He's being polite, but it's obvious he thinks it sounds ridiculous. I can't help but roll my eyes a little.

"I'm not sure, sweet. There has to be something else."

"What do we have to lose?" I question. He scratches his head, clearly a little uncomfortable and trying not to shoot me down. I take a few steps closer to him and look into his eyes, hoping to comfort him. "If it doesn't work, we can come back and look for something else."

Marcus takes a huge breath, his chest rising and falling heavily. His face is tight, and when he looks down at me, he tries to force a smile, but it barely holds together. I can see the stress in his eyes, the hopelessness he's trying to hide. He gently cups my face in his hands, leaning in to kiss my forehead, his touch lingering.

"We'll try everything, sweet," he whispers, his voice shaky but filled with forced reassurance. "Everything."

His words are meant to comfort, but the weight of them presses down on both of us. I can see it, he's holding on by a thread; trying to stay strong, even though he's not sure there's anything left to hold onto.

CHAPTER 20:

GIVE IT UP

Noah

There's a certain satisfaction in being alone in the kitchen. Well.. *my* kitchen. State-of-the-art appliances, countertops gleaming, the fridge stocked with anything I could want; and zero interruptions. No chaos, no noise. Just the gentle hiss of butter melting alongside a hefty ribeye that's sizzling away. The enticing aroma of garlic and rosemary fills the air. No bland sandwiches here.

Lunch, done right.

I let it sear undisturbed for a few minutes, the crust forming a rich-brown colour that promises a juicy interior.

As the steak cooks, I prepare the plate. I swipe a small amount of garlic butter over the surface, letting it melt into a slick sheen. I sprinkle a touch of sea salt on the plate, creating a subtle base. When the steak is nearly done, I use tongs to flip it, watching as the other side takes on a deep, caramelised hue. I add a sprig of rosemary and a couple cloves of garlic to the pan, letting their flavours infuse the meat as it finishes cooking.

With the steak cooked to a perfect medium rare, I transfer it carefully onto the prepared plate, drizzling a bit of the pan juices over it.

I reach for the whiskey bottle from the top shelf. It's a familiar weight in my hand. I twist off the cap and pour a generous measure into a glass, the amber liquid flowing smoothly. The sound of it hitting the glass is sharp, distinct. I set the bottle back on the counter with an adept flick of the wrist.

I take a deep, contented breath, letting the rich aroma of the steak mix with the smoky notes of the whiskey. I cut into the perfectly seared ribeye, the meat tender and juicy. As I take a bite, the flavours burst in my mouth; just the way I like it. I follow it with a generous swig of whiskey, feeling the warmth of the alcohol as it settles comfortably in my gut.

Everything's in its right place; the steak is spot-on, the whiskey smooth, and the kitchen blissfully quiet. I'm fully in my element, enjoying this rare moment of peace. I think back to last night, and a slow smirk tugs at the corner of my mouth. Skylar had stepped out of line, pushed things a little too far, so I had to remind her who was in charge. The gun was the lesson. It was punishment, plain and simple. I made her take it, every cold inch and as it spread her, I watched her eyes; the flicker of fear mixed with that twisted, dirty need.

For the first time, she wasn't acting bratty or full of attitude. The cocky confidence she always wears like armour was gone, replaced by something raw and vulnerable. Whether she hated it or secretly loved it, I couldn't be sure, and I didn't give a fuck either way. She needed it, and she had no choice in the matter. It wasn't about pleasure, not for her anyway. It was about control, and I held it tight. I take another bite of steak, washing it down with a heavy swig of whiskey.

Fuck, life is good sometimes.

Then, as if on cue, the pounding footsteps from upstairs rip through my calm. Marcus barrels into the kitchen, clutching that fucking book again like it's about to explode in his hands.

"Hey, I need to show you something." He says, almost breathless, slamming the book onto the counter.

211

I don't even look up. I sigh and stab another bite of steak, chew, but it doesn't taste the same; the satisfaction quickly fading. The flavours that were perfect a moment ago feel dull now.

Marcus doesn't wait for a response. He dives right into it, flipping open the book.

"Look, the story's changed. It wasn't like this before, there's something new here. I'm almost certain we need everyone's help to close it this time." He says. I hear him, but I'm not listening. Not really. I take another swig of whiskey, staring at my plate as he goes on about villagers and loopholes or whatever the fuck he thinks this book is telling him.

But I already know better. Fate's fate. The book's going to do what it wants, and there's no point in trying to fuck with it. You can't change the ending, it's already written.

Marcus starts from the top, reading out the entire story. I don't show it, but I listen to every word, chewing on my steak as he goes on. He flips through the pages, his finger tracing the words like he's cracked some kind of code, before turning back to a specific line.

"Right here," he says, his voice urgent. "The villagers joined hands in a circle before the gates were closed. I think it's symbolic, maybe even literal. If we do the same thing, it'll give us a shot at stopping this before.. before it's too late."

I stand at the counter, chewing on another bite of steak, barely acknowledging him. The silence hangs between us for a second after he finishes. Then I snort, setting my fork down and letting out a low, sarcastic laugh.

"So, let me get this straight," I say, wiping the corner of my mouth. "You want us all to stand around in a circle holding hands?" I raise an eyebrow, waiting for him to hear how ridiculous that sounds.

Marcus hesitates, his eyes darting between the book and me. He knows it sounds crazy, I can see it in his face, but he's desperate, hanging onto any shred of hope he can find.

"I know it sounds.. like a stretch," he admits, scratching the back of his neck, "but what else do we have? This could be something, right?" I take a sip of whiskey, shaking my head.

"You're grasping at straws, man." I lean forward, voice low and blunt. "Fate's already set. This book? It's just playing out the script. You can't fuck with that."

Marcus lets out a frustrated sigh, slamming the book shut but keeping his hands on it.

"Then what, Noah?" he snaps, his voice tight with tension, though it's not directed at me. "What are

we supposed to do? Just let it happen? Let Dean die?"
He questions. I shrug, not flinching.

"Look, I'm sorry to be the bad guy, but you're
searching for answers in a story that's already written."

He stares at me, his frustration simmering beneath the
surface, not at me, but at the situation, the helplessness
of it all.

"I know it's a long shot, man. I know it's fucking
ridiculous. But I don't know what else to do." His voice
cracks slightly.

"Then stop trying to control it," I say, my tone
sharper now. "If you don't have the answer, then maybe
there isn't one."

"But I'm not like you, Noah!" he snaps, his
voice rising. "I can't just switch myself on and off. I
can't act like I don't care. I'm not built that way." I don't
react, just taking another sip of whiskey, my gaze steady
on him. He's worked up, and I know this isn't about me.
He's pissed at the situation, at how powerless he feels.
I've seen it before, in a thousand different ways.

"That's your problem, Marcus," I say, my voice
calm, almost cold. "You think that just because you care
about something, that gives you the power to change it.
It doesn't."

The words strike a chord in him. He freezes, and for a
fleeting moment, our eyes lock. It's a difficult truth, the

kind that stings not merely because it's harsh, but because it's undeniably real. I can tell he's taking it in, even if he doesn't want to admit it. Silence overtakes us. Nothing but that unspoken understanding, a hard, brotherly moment where I'm not saying it to be cruel; I'm saying it because he needs to hear it. He looks at me, and I see it in his eyes. He knows I'm right.

Marcus just stares down at the book, his jaw clenched tight, silent as a statue. The tension in the room lingers, thick and heavy. I sigh, glancing at the whiskey bottle, and figure maybe it'll loosen him up. I pour a glass, sliding it across the counter toward him. He doesn't touch it right away. Just stares at it like it holds something more than liquor, his eyes narrowing slightly. I can tell he's thinking about something, feeling something; though what, I have no idea.

I wait, watching him carefully. He's not saying a thing, but something's clearly off. After a beat, he subtly shakes his head, a motion so slight I almost miss it. Then, out of nowhere, he grabs the glass aggressively, knuckles white as he downs the whole thing in one go, like it's nothing.

It's more than nothing, though.
Something's eating at him.

Before I can even take him up on it, Dean Douglas strolls into the room, hood up, heading straight for the fridge. He clearly didn't expect to find anyone here and looks thoroughly pissed to see the two of us standing around. I lean back against the counter, exhaling through my nose; staring at him as he scowls.

Oh boy, here we go.

CHAPTER 21:
TENSIONS FLARE

Dean

I trudge into the kitchen, hood up, mind set on one thing, the fridge. I just need to grab something and get out. But, of course, as soon as I step in, I'm met with Marcus and Noah, both of them already looking my way.

For fuck's sake. Here we go.

Marcus has that intense look on his face, like something's eating at him, and Noah's leaning against the counter, looking like he's already annoyed before I've even opened my mouth. Perfect. I pretend I don't see either of them and head for the fridge, hoping they'll take the hint and let me be. And, of course, that was a stupid thing to hope. Silly me for thinking the complex task of grabbing a drink could ever be straightforward. Before I even get my hand on the fridge door, Marcus speaks up.

"Dean, I've got an update on the book."

Great. I grip the handle tighter, already feeling the headache coming on. I inhale sharply, yanking the fridge door open and grabbing a drink. I twist the cap off, already feeling my patience wearing thin. Turning back to them, I take a swig before muttering,

"What is it now?"

Marcus dives into his explanation about how the story in the book changed. I listen, but it feels more draining than anything. The book used to mean something, used to offer a sliver of hope. Now? It's just a reminder that things are spiralling, and I've pretty much given up on it. When he finally finishes, I take another swig.

"So you want us all to hold hands in a circle?" I ask, bluntly. Noah snorts.

"Yeah, that was my response too."

I rub a hand down my face, the weight of everything just crashing in. This whole situation is exhausting. Before I can say anything else, Marcus snaps,

"I'm fucking trying, alright?" But to his surprise, I lower my hand and look at him, dead serious.

"Well, stop."

The room goes quiet. I know it's the last thing he expected to hear, considering I'm the one with a death sentence hanging over my head. I look Marcus in the eyes, feeling the weight of every word. He looks stunned, but I don't care.

"Stop," I say again, harsher this time, though my voice cracks just a little. There's a hint of desperation behind the words. I'm tired of the constant fight. I've given up hope and, right now, I would rather just ignore the problem than keep pretending we can fix it. Marcus looks at me, eyes pleading, the kind of look that digs deep.

His voice shakes as he speaks,

"How can I just stop? How can I sit back and watch this happen?" I see the desperation in him, the fear of losing me. I'm just as scared. But I can't give him the answer he wants. I exhale, feeling the weight of everything.

"I don't know, man. But I can't keep getting my hopes up, only to watch them crumble over and over again." Before I can even finish, Marcus steps toward me, quick and determined.

"We already closed it once," he states. I laugh, the sound bitter and hopeless. I throw my hands out to the side, gesturing at everything around us, like it's obvious.

"Yeah, and look where that fucking got us." The frustration bubbling up in me spills out with those words, and I can't help it.

Marcus' voice cuts through my frustration, sharp and laced with anger.

"What is your fucking problem lately?" He starts. "The grumpiness, the isolating yourself, and walking off the other night at the tunnel. What the fuck is going on with you?" I clench my jaw, feeling my pulse quicken. I don't need this right now. Not from him. Not from anyone. But he keeps pushing, his words striking at the raw spots. "What, you think I didn't notice?" He asks. His eyes bore into me, and I can tell he's hurt, frustrated, confused. But it's too much. He's too much.

I grit my teeth, trying to keep my voice steady.

"It's nothing, alright? You're making a big deal out of nothing. I'm just fucking knackered." The words feel hollow even as I say them, and I know Marcus isn't buying it. He's never been one to fall for bullshit, especially mine.

"The Dean I know wouldn't fucking rest until he worked this out," Marcus says, his voice rising. "You've given up."

His words hit harder than I want to admit. My head starts to blur with the weight of everything, his voice becoming more distant as my thoughts spiral. I'm trying so hard not to snap because deep down, I know he's right. I know I'm wrong for keeping the secret, for shutting down, for pushing everybody away. But my mind is so full of stress, tangled up with everything that's been happening. Noah, the book, the fear of what's coming; it's suffocating.

"Marcus, I-" I start, but he keeps going, his words hammering in my skull.

"It's like you've just decided to roll over and die. What the fuck is going on with you?" Marcus' voice doesn't soften; it sharpens, each word hitting like a slap. He slams his fist down on the counter, rattling the glass next to him. "I'm trying to help you, man. Why won't you let me?" he shouts, and the sound echoes in the kitchen. I feel my pulse spike, the tension in the room thickening like smoke. My head is spinning, trying to keep everything together, but Marcus isn't letting up. His anger is raw, cutting through the air, and I can't escape it. He's right there, in my face, pushing me, demanding answers, and all I can think is how much I want him to stop. How much I want to just shut down and forget about all of this. But he's not letting me.

"I didn't ask for your fucking help!" I snap back, my voice harsher than I intended, but I can't stop it.

"I didn't ask for any of this shit!" I shout, the anger burning through me as I throw my hands up. "I didn't ask to be beaten up and tossed away as a kid. I didn't ask to be dealing drugs on the streets by the time I was fourteen. I didn't ask for you to write that stupid fucking book that's ruined everything, and I definitely didn't ask to be stuck here with this cunt!" I point sharply at Noah, who just raises an eyebrow like he couldn't care less. My chest is heaving, and I'm so wound up I can barely see straight. All the shit I've kept locked down just keeps pouring out. "I didn't ask for any of it"

The room falls silent, my heart pounding in my ears.

"I never even wanted to live this long." I say, my voice breaking as the words leave my mouth. The world freezes. Every breath feels heavy, the ambience thick with disbelief. Even Marcus, that ball of frustration, stands frozen, as if my words have knocked the wind out of him. His expression shifts, haunted.

"Are we done?" I ask defensively, my voice rough and strained. Marcus' face tightens with anger and frustration. Without saying a word, he turns and walks over to Noah, who's still standing by the counter. Marcus slams the book down in front of him with a finality that's almost palpable.

"Do whatever you fucking want with it," he says, his voice cold and clipped.

As he storms past me on his way out, he halts just long enough to shoot me a burning glance, fury simmering in his eyes.

"What would Delilah think of you giving up now? Huh?" he asks, each word laced with accusation. "Ever stop to consider what she would want?"

He lets out a short, harsh laugh; more of an angry exhale through his nose; sharp as a blade. It's a sound of disbelief and raw frustration, as if to say he can't believe I'm being this selfish.

The echo of his disbelief carves through me.
I know he's right.
And I can't believe it either.

CHAPTER 22:

INTERESTING

Noah

Dean stays in the room for a second longer, his glare sharp, full of anger and blame. Like he's waiting for me to say something. As if everything that's happening is somehow my fault. I glance over at him and shrug my shoulders, indifferent. What does he expect? A cuddle? A pep talk? I've got nothing for him. He shakes his head, muttering,

"Fuck you," through gritted teeth as he storms out.

I lean back against the counter, letting the significance of the moment settle in the air for a bit. Marcus leaving, all dramatic. Dean, doing his whole emo, tortured-soul act. I'm supposed to care, I guess. But, of course I don't. I've got enough shit of my own. I never thought I'd say it, but I actually agree with Dean Douglas. Marcus is running around like a headless chicken, frantic, desperate. It's like watching a dog chase its own tail. He's not thinking straight, just clinging to this idea that he can somehow fix everything if he just tries hard enough. The guy's lost the plot.

My eyes drift to the book sitting in front of me, and I feel a strange sense of relief. It's here. In my possession. And that's where I like it. It means I've got control, not just over the book but over where it ends up; whose hands it falls into. Everyone's so caught up in what the book might do, but they forget the most important part; who owns it. And right now, that's me.

I slide the book off the counter, tossing it up and catching it almost playfully. The weight of it feels good in my hands; familiar. It's funny when I think about it; Marcus and I, the stories we'd written for ourselves, both literally and figuratively. While Marcus was stuck in the orphanage, lost in his own world of fairytales, scribbling stories about animal characters and dragons, I was already knee-deep in the real world.

From a young age, I was moulded by a world of crime and brutality. By the time I became a teenager, I was already living a life of violence and corruption that no

225

child should ever have to know. My book was not a collection of whimsical tales but a detailed record and wish list of my rise within my father's criminal empire. I wrote wishes of how my mother wasn't dead, and how I'd eventually kill my way to the top of the organisation. I detailed how my father would be murdered, leaving me to take his place. Every page was a blueprint of my rise through the criminal world. And it all came true; murder, corruption, and absolute power became my reality.

It's almost tragic, really. While I was groomed for a life of crime and abuse, Marcus was sheltered in his imagination, thinking his minor rebellions and petty crimes made him something he wasn't. He's got a lot to learn, and he has no idea just how harsh the world can be.

I walk upstairs, the book clutched in my hand. The early evening light filters through the windows, casting a glow on the walls. The idea is to head to my room just to put the book away before diving into some work. I'm not planning on sticking around for anything else.

But when I open the door, I freeze. Skylar is lying on the sofa in my room.. asleep. Her chest rises and falls steadily, her expression peaceful, completely unaware that I've walked in. A slow, smug smile spreads across my face. After last night, I figured she'd be avoiding me, or at least keeping her distance. But here she is, asleep in my space, like she's made herself at home.

The thought amuses me. After what I put her through last night, she should be wary, should be thinking twice before being anywhere near me. Yet here she is, asleep and completely vulnerable, in my room. It's almost too easy. Not the smartest move. I thought my princess would know better. She clearly has no idea how easily that could backfire.

But then I catch myself. Maybe she's not as clueless as she looks. Maybe, on some level, she feels safe around me. I can't help but feel a bit flattered. After all, if she really thought I was a threat, she wouldn't have let her guard down like this.

I toss the book on the table, eyes still on her. The smirk remains still on my face as I prowl toward her. I can't help but take in how beautiful she looks right now. There's a fragility to her that I don't usually get to see, like all the attitude has melted away, leaving just this peaceful, serene version of her behind.

As I stand over her, watching her sleep, something unexpected stirs in me. It's rare that I look at anyone this way, but there's something about Skylar right now that makes it hard to tear my eyes away. Her pink hair, usually wild and untamed, falls perfectly around her face, soft and delicate. It frames her like some kind of halo, the strands resting gently against her skin; skin that looks so smooth, almost porcelain in this light. There isn't a flaw to be found, like she's carved out of something more fragile than the world around her.

Her lips catch my attention, full and plump, parted just slightly as she breathes. They look softer now than they ever have, like she's left all the fight behind. There's a sweetness to her in this moment that almost doesn't fit with the Skylar I've come to know; the one who challenges me at every turn. Right now, she's delicate, peaceful, like something that could break if touched too roughly.

I'm not used to seeing her like this. I'm not used to thinking about anyone like this. I've trained myself to ignore that kind of beauty, to see it as nothing more than a distraction. I've spent my life in a world where humans are just tools, commodities to be used and discarded. I've seen more death than most people can fathom, more abuse, more trafficking, more torture. It's desensitised me, numbed me to the point where I don't view people as human anymore.

I grew up in a world where survival was paramount, where the mantra was kill or be killed, trust no one, and never let your guard down. Emotions were a liability, a weakness to be exploited or, worse, a vulnerability to be eliminated. I learned early on to shut them off, to see people as mere functions in a ruthless game, never allowing myself to connect, to feel. They're just moving parts in a machine I know all too well.

I had always despised when my father's men would drag women in for torture or worse. It wasn't part of the game I ever enjoyed, not like the others did. I'd make it my mission to get them out, find the easiest way to give them an out; no matter how slim the chances were. I'd never let them suffer more than necessary, not if I could help it. But it was never about connection. I never pretended to connect with them. I didn't feel anything for them. It was just a matter of principle.

But I'm realising quickly that Skylar is different.

Looking at her now, asleep on my sofa, I'm confronted with a side of her that I've never allowed myself to see in anyone. I realise that I've grown accustomed to viewing others as robotic entities, devoid of real substance or emotion. It's how I've survived, how I've kept myself from caring too much, from losing control. By keeping my own humanity at arm's length, viewing the world through a lens of cold detachment.

For the first time, I can't do that. For the first time, I'm *feeling*. Really feeling. She looks so human to me. This revelation is terrifying. I'm afraid of what it means to actually care for someone beyond myself. It's as if my control, the very essence of what I've been taught to uphold, is slipping away. I understand that I've been isolated from everything that makes life human. Skylar's presence forces me to confront the depth of that isolation, and the facade I've built around myself. It's a new, frightening frontier; one that threatens to unravel absolutely everything I've ever known, everything drilled into my head from the start, everything I've been told to believe.

And I hate it.

I pull my mind back from the tangled mess of emotions threatening to overtake me. The soft hum of Skylar's breathing is the only sound in the room. I draw in a slow, controlled breath, then gently exhale near Skylar's ear, the warmth of my breath stirring her from sleep. It's a technique I've learned. She stirs, her body tensing as she becomes aware of my presence.

Her eyes snap open, and the shock of waking in such an intimate, unexpected way causes her to gasp. Before she can fully react, I swiftly cover her mouth with my hand. I don't mean to hurt her, but the urgency in my grip is unmistakable. Her eyes widen in alarm, and she tries to wriggle free, but my hold is firm.

I keep my hand over her mouth until her breathing steadies, and the initial panic in her eyes begins to fade. The moment stretches taut with tension, and I watch as her frantic energy calms, her breaths becoming more measured.

"Farmer," I murmur with a chilling calmness. "What are you doing in my room?" I hold her gaze as I slowly lift my hand from her mouth, my fingers brushing against her skin. As if in slow motion, I move a strand of her hair from her face, the gesture almost tender.

I watch as Skylar gulps, trying to steady herself before speaking. Her voice comes out in a hesitant murmur.

"I needed a first aid kit." She says. I raise an eyebrow, my curiosity piqued.

"A first aid kit? Why?" I ask. She meets my gaze steadily, her voice calm.

"I've got an injury. I couldn't find a first aid kit anywhere, so I came here to ask you for one. When you weren't around, I must have fallen asleep waiting."

I scrunch my eyebrows, processing her request. Without a word, I walk into the adjacent box room. The door creaks slightly as I open it, revealing a space cluttered with mundane items; an ironing board, various tools, and the first aid kit I need. The sterile scent of the room mingles with the faint odour of dust. I pull open the cabinet, the rustle of the kit's contents against the plastic is faint but distinct. I grab the first aid kit and head back, the door clicking shut behind me.

When I return, Skylar is sitting up on the sofa, rubbing her eyes. I approach her.

"Where are you hurt?" I ask bluntly. She keeps steady eye contact with me.

"My legs." She says. I nod towards her tracksuit bottoms with a curt gesture.

"Take them off, then." I crouch down to the floor, keeping my eyes on her. Skylar hesitates briefly, but then slowly begins to pull down her tracksuit bottoms. As the fabric slides down, the full extent of her injuries is revealed.

My gaze sharpens as I see the gashes and cuts scattered across her thighs, extending down to just below her knees. Blossoming bruises mar her skin in vivid purples and reds. The sight of these injuries triggers a deep, immediate anger within me. They're reminiscent of knife cuts and marks from a brutal fall, and the thought that someone might have done this to her stirs a surge of fury. My hands clench around the first aid kit, my mind racing as I struggle to keep my cool.

I stare up at Skylar, my anger barely contained.

"Who did this to you?" I ask, my voice strained with concern. Her face briefly registers confusion before shifting to a hint of amusement. She looks at me with a touch of irony in her eyes.

"Nobody, you freak," she says, her tone light and dismissive. "I fell off the roof."

Huh?

I blink, completely thrown off. The absurdity of her explanation hits me, and despite myself, I can't help but let out a short, incredulous laugh. It's somehow such a typical Skylar thing to do, yet still completely unexpected. I'm momentarily stunned.

"You were on my roof?" I ask, the disbelief clear in my voice. She nods in response, as if it's the most normal thing in the world. I let out a weary sigh, rubbing my forehead with disbelief and confusion.

"Skylar, why were you on my roof?" She huffs, clearly annoyed by what she perceives as an obvious question.

"I like to climb onto my roof at home to stargaze," she explains, her tone carrying a hint of irritation. "I was trying to find a good spot here, but I slipped and fell onto the balcony."

I'm still processing her casual tone and the absurdity of the situation. My concern for her well-being remains, but the way she's handling it is almost surreal. I raise an eyebrow, trying to gauge her seriousness. Shaking my head, it's still hard to wrap my mind around this bizarre situation. As I start treating her wounds, my movements are precise, almost mechanical. Antiseptic is applied to the cuts, bandages to the bruises; the clinical routine providing a sense of grounding amid the absurdity.

After a few moments of working in silence, I look up at her, puzzled.

"Why can't you just stargaze on the ground?" I ask. Skylar shrugs, a hint of wistfulness in her voice.

"It's not the same down low," she says softly. "I like looking at the stars from high up." Her words, tinged with a subtle sadness, catch me off guard. It's unexpectedly cute and wholesome. Despite my usual stoicism, I find myself smiling slightly at the sincerity in her voice.

As I finish tending to her wounds, I keep my focus on the bandages, my hands moving with practised efficiency.

"I'll figure something out for you," I promise. I pause briefly, "and Skylar, don't ever climb on my roof again." Only then do I glance up, my eyes meeting hers just before I continue. "That's an order." Skylar looks back at me, her expression softening as she nods in acknowledgment.

I stand up, towering over her as she sits there. I look down at her, and for the first time in my life, my first instinct isn't to be cold. It's something else, something softer, and it startles me. It scares me. I'm losing myself-

Ah, fuck it.

Before I can think, I grab her face, fingers pressing into her skin a little too hard, and pull her towards me, kissing her authentically. I crush my lips against hers with raw intensity, and she gasps, startled. For a split second, I expect her to push me away, to fight back; but then she melts into it, kissing me back. The kiss spirals quickly into something chaotic, frenzied; like we're both starved for it, for each other. Our hands grasp at whatever we can reach, and the air between us thickens with heat. It's reckless, unrestrained, like everything we've kept locked away is erupting all at once. Her breath mingles with mine, and the wildness of it makes me feel like I'm on the edge of losing myself; but I can't bring myself to stop.

And I don't want to.

I lift her off the sofa, my hands gripping her ass, fingers slipping just beneath the edge of her knickers. Her body tenses in my hold, and I push her against the wall, the cool surface a contrast to the heat building between us. Our lips never part, the kiss becoming more frenzied, more desperate, like we're drowning in each other.

I trail my mouth down to her neck, tasting her skin, the soft gasp she lets out driving me further. It's messy, unrelenting, my grip tightening as I press her harder against the wall, completely lost in the intensity of the moment. She lets out a sharp squeal as I kiss and suck on her neck, hard enough to leave marks. My hands dig deeper into her asscheeks, pulling her closer, my grip rough and passionate. Her body squirms against mine, reacting to the intensity, but she doesn't pull away. Instead, she grips onto me tighter, her breath coming in short gasps as I continue my sweet assault on her neck, each sound she makes only spurring me on.

She whimpers my name, a sound that hits me like a spark to gasoline. Before I know it, I spin her around and slam her down onto the bed, her stomach pressed against the mattress. My hand grips the back of her neck, pinning her, but she's not entirely still. She shifts beneath me, her movements hesitant; like she's toying with herself. It's not complete submission, but it's enough to stir that need.

With a rough motion, I rip away her underwear, her cry swallowed by the mattress. I spit onto my fingers, then shove them inside her with a brutal, relentless speed. My movements are chaotic, desperate, as if I'm trying to claw my way back into the familiar coldness I know so well. Each thrust is frenzied, a frantic attempt to drown out the unsettling warmth that's threatening to consume me. Her body jolts, her cries muffled by the bed, and I can barely think straight, lost in the struggle to revert to the monster I'm used to.

As she tries to scream and wriggle, I press her harder into the mattress, the rough fabric biting into her skin. My voice is cold, devoid of any warmth.

"Shut the fuck up," I growl, the words harsh and uncompromising. My grip tightens, my movements relentless, as if trying to suffocate any trace of vulnerability that might linger. "Shut your mouth and fucking take it." I order harshly.

I keep my focus on the task, my fingers moving with a relentless rhythm. The wetness against my fingers increases, her reactions growing more pronounced. I twist my fingers deeper, my gaze locked onto the way her body shifts under me. I watch as her hips squirm, her body arching slightly with each movement. Her gasps are muffled against the mattress, and I see her muscles contract rhythmically. Her body's reactions grow more pronounced, her ass jiggling with every thrust.

"Keep still, baby, or I'll make it worse," I threaten, tightening my grip on her neck.

I keep going, in a trance. I lose myself in the rhythm. Hypnotic. Her body begins to shake under my touch, her reactions almost distant. I keep going. My focus narrows to a single point, and my mind goes blank. I persist, each motion driven by an instinct I can't fully grasp. I keep going. Her screams and cries are there, but they blur into an eerie silence, a world where nothing else exists. The sounds blend into a muted cacophony, like static on an old radio. I keep going, the repetition unending.

Then, without warning, I feel it. Her body convulses violently, a signal that she's reached her peak. She's coming. It jolts me from the trance, dragging me into harsh reality. I realise that I'm sweating, my breath ragged and uneven. The sensation is foreign, a visceral shock to my system. I pull my fingers out abruptly, the brusqueness shocking even me. The slap I deliver to her ass is brutal, and it reverberates with raw energy. It's as if I'm merely a vessel for a violent impulse, my body acting on its own accord.

I stand up straight, my body trembling with an unnerving energy. Adrenaline surges through me, but it's not the kind I'm used to; it's erratic, unsettling. Tingling. My entire being feels charged, electric, like a live wire barely contained. I stare down at her, to my shock, she looks up at me with a flush of obvious pain and subtle satisfaction. Her eyes are half-lidded, her breathing steady, and there's an unsettling calm in her expression, as if the tumult we've just experienced has left her feeling fulfilled. My body feels alien to me. I'm a storm of feelings I don't understand, and I'm desperately trying to shut them down with the only weapon I know..

Cruelty.

I yank open the drawer of the side table, my fingers fumbling slightly as I grab a cigar. I flick open my lighter, the flame hissing to life. The familiar scent of tobacco fills the air as I draw in a long, steadying breath. With the cigar firmly between my lips, I collapse onto the sofa, my body sinking heavily into the cushions. I lean forward, resting my forearms on my knees, my eyes locked on the floor, trying to ground myself. From the outside, I'm sure I look calm and collected. But inside, it's a different story. A tempest of adrenaline and confusion roars through me. Every nerve ending feels alive with a jittery energy.

I draw another puff from the cigar, letting the smoke curl around me, and with a deep breath, I finally force myself to look over at Skylar. She lies there, still and unnervingly silent, her body trembling ever so slightly. The shaking seems approaching deliberate. Her breaths come in uneven gasps, shallow and almost imperceptible, making her seem more like a marionette whose strings have gone slack. I look back to the ground.

We sit in the oppressive silence for nearly twenty minutes, the only sound being the faint crackle of my cigar and the occasional shuffling from Skylar as she tries to find a more comfortable position. The room feels like it's holding its breath, heavy with unspoken words and the residue of what just happened. Finally, breaking the stillness, Skylar whispers, her voice barely above a breath.

"Did I do something to make you angry?" Her tone is laced with the usual sarcasm, a defence mechanism she uses so well. The question hangs in the air, a strange mix of jest and genuine inquiry. It's clear she's trying to keep things light, but there's an undercurrent of real concern.

I can't answer immediately. The question pricks at the edge of my brain. I exhale a cloud of smoke, my gaze still locked on the ground.

"No," I finally say, my voice devoid of emotion. There's a pause, a stretch of silence that seems to stretch on forever. Then, I let out a low, gravelly laugh. "The problem is, I don't think you could ever make me angry, Farmer."

I look up at her then, I don't expect a reply, but she snaps back quickly.

"Why is that a problem?" she asks, her tone moulded with genuine curiosity. I let out a short breath, the cigar smoke curling between us.

"Because that means you're in charge."

CHAPTER 23:
SWEET HEAT
Sienna

It's now 9 p.m., and the tension in this house could cut glass. About an hour and a half ago, Noah ordered pizza; probably his attempt to keep us all grounded in some shred of normalcy. Not that it worked. Everyone ate separately, like we were strangers. We've never been like this before. Fragmented. like a mirror that's shattered but still pretending to hold its shape.

It's ridiculous, really, when I think about it. I was in a basement, practically counting my breaths in the dark, and yet, now? *Now* we're all sulking. And for what? Dean, Marcus, everyone's too wrapped up in their own misery, their own secrets. What are we even doing anymore?

Marcus has been sitting at the window, smoking since dinner. His posture is rigid, a constant cloud of smoke swirling around him, eyes barely open. It frustrates me, more than it should. I get it; he's stressed. Everyone's on edge right now, but the way he just sinks into himself, blocking everything out.. it's making things worse. I cross the room, standing right beside him. He doesn't move or even acknowledge me.

"You've got to get out of this room," I say firmly, but with care.

Marcus exhales a cloud of smoke, barely turning his head as he mutters,

"I'm fine here, sweet." His bluntness stings, but I don't let it show.

"Do you think this is gonna help?" I ask. Marcus just looks at me, his eyes heavy and dark, like he's barely present. He doesn't say a word, but the stress is etched deep into his features; his clenched jaw, the lines on his forehead. I almost back off. But I don't.

"Life is shit, Marcus," I tell him, my voice sharper than I expect it to be. "It's shit, and it's unfair, and it's hard. We all know that better than most." I continue, gesturing to the others in the house. "But I can't keep doing this. I can't keep spending every day in a slump just waiting for the next shitty thing to happen." I pause, hoping something I'm saying is getting through to him.

I'm almost pleading with him now, my usual sunny demeanour replaced with something raw and desperate.

"I owe it to my parents to make something out of this, to live a life that means something, even if it's not the life they wanted for me. I owe them the chance to look down and see me not just surviving, but actually living. To see me not fucking losing anymore." He's listening, really listening now. I take a deep breath, trying to steady my voice.

"If we don't have any unity left in us, if we let this break us, then we're done for." The room is heavy with my words, with the grim reality of our situation. "We owe Dean more than that." He takes a deep breath and gives a slight nod, looking a little more resolute.

"I'll talk to Dean tomorrow," he says, his tone still weighted with stress. I walk over to Marcus, gently leaning in to place a soft kiss on his cheek.

"Do you want to come downstairs with me?" I ask, trying to offer a little warmth despite the chill in the room. He looks at me with tired eyes, shaking his head slightly.

"Maybe in a little while," he replies, his voice quiet. I feel a twinge of disappointment, but I understand.

"Alright."

I head downstairs, hoping that diving into something that brings me joy might also help lift the spirits of everyone else. The clatter of the house is subdued now, but I need a distraction, something grounding. Baking should do the trick. I glance around the foyer, spotting the phone Noah had mentioned earlier. I pick it up, dial, and wait for the line to connect. After a few rings, someone answers with a crisp,

"What do you need?"

"Hi," I say, trying to sound upbeat despite the heaviness of the day. "I need some ingredients."

After a brief exchange, I rattle off my list:

-Butter
-Caster sugar
-Light brown sugar
-Eggs
-Flour
-Chocolate

Not long after, a delivery arrives with all the ingredients neatly crammed. I unpack everything and lay it out on the counter, feeling a bit lighter as I anticipate the scent of freshly baked cookies filling the air. The oven hums to life as I preheat it, and I catch myself softly humming too, my fingers already itching to get started. First, I take the butter and sugars, blending them together until they're a smooth, creamy mixture, like sunshine in a bowl. I tap the egg against the edge of the counter, feeling oddly proud as I crack it perfectly. In it goes, blending in with the sugar and butter like they're meant to be together.

Then comes the flour. It always makes me feel like a little kid, scooping it out carefully and watching it puff in little clouds. As I stir it in, the dough starts to form; thick, golden, and just begging for those chunks of chocolate. I can't help but sneak a taste, grinning as the rich sweetness hits my tongue. Once the chocolate chunks are mixed in, the dough looks absolutely perfect. I grab my spoon and scoop it onto the baking trays, making cute little mounds, all evenly spaced.

I slide the trays into the oven and wipe my hands clean, taking a moment to twirl around the kitchen, feeling lighter than I have all day. The scent of melting chocolate and butter beginning to fill the room, and I can't wait to share this little bit of happiness with everyone else.

I pull the tray out of the oven, the edges of the cookies perfectly set, and the centres just soft enough; exactly how I love them. The kitchen smells incredible, rich with warm chocolate and butter.

Grabbing a spatula, I lift one of the cookies carefully, feeling its warmth through my fingers. I take a bite, the chocolate melting in my mouth, the dough soft and chewy, sweet but not too sweet. It's perfect. A tiny, happy sigh escapes me, and I feel a sense of accomplishment.

As I turn around, still savouring the warmth of the kitchen, I nearly jump out of my skin when I see Marcus standing in the dark doorway, leaning against the frame. His presence, silent and brooding, feels almost spectral, like an apparition that has silently materialised

He's smiling, but not quite. His eyes are locked on me, deeper than usual, like he's seeing me in a way that's both familiar and intense. It's not intimidating, but the atmosphere feels charged, a mix of quiet admiration and that unspoken tension that always lingers between us. I don't say anything. Neither does he. We just stand there, caught in the moment, as if words would break whatever this is.

"How long have you been standing there?" I ask, my voice quiet. Pushing off from the doorway slowly, his eyes never leaving mine, he replies,

"long enough." Marcus walks over, his movements unhurried and knowing. Without saying a word, he places his hands on my waist and lifts me onto the counter with ease. My breath catches as he leans in, pressing soft kisses against my neck, his lips warm against my skin.

"You don't even realise it, do you?" he murmurs against my ear, his voice low and rough. "How much I need you.. how you keep me together when everything else is falling apart." He pulls back just enough to meet my eyes, his gaze intense. I smile softly at him, my heart swelling.

"I love you," I whisper. He doesn't hesitate, his voice deep as he responds,

"I do more than love you, sweet." He pauses, "You're in my blood. Loving you is instinct, but the way I *need* you, that's a hunger I can never satisfy."

Marcus' words hang in the air between us, his voice deep, like a whisper brushing against the heat of my skin. My heart skips, my breath catching as I feel his hands still holding me. I kiss him softly, letting the moment pull me in, but as it starts to heat up, I pull away. I don't want it to end, but at the same time, the cookies are still sitting there, and I can see the flour and sugar scattered across the counter.

"I should probably clean up the mess," I say, feeling a bit breathless. Marcus smirks at me, his eyes dark and teasing.

"Why clean up the mess," he starts, his voice deep and low, "when we could make some more?" I bite my lip, pretending to consider his offer as if I'm weighing the pros and cons. My eyes flicker to the mess on the counter, flour, sugar, chocolate chips scattered everywhere; but in reality, I've already caved. I nod very softly, tilting my head to the side as if I'm still thinking.

But he knows me too well.

And he knows that cookies are the last thing on my mind now.

Before I know it, Marcus' lips find mine again, pulling me into a kiss that quickly deepens. His hands slide up my waist, pulling me closer as I wrap my arms around his neck, letting the moment take me. I feel the heat between us rising, the air thick with everything unspoken, but then, just as things start to get more intense, he pauses.

His breath is warm against my ear as he lingers there for a moment, his hands steady but gentle.

"You're okay with this, right?" His voice is low, careful. I feel a flicker of frustration, not at him but at the situation. I don't want what happened to change this. To change us. I won't let it. I nod against him, closing my eyes for a second.

"Don't be gentle with me," I say, voice firm. His grip stays tense for a moment, like he's still unsure, but I meet his gaze and push harder. "Do what you always do. I'm not fragile, Marcus."

Marcus smiles deeply as his lips brush my ear.

"Anything but," he pulls back slightly to look me in the eyes, his gaze intense and unwavering. "Which is good," he growls, voice rough with satisfaction. "Because gentle isn't really my thing." Before I can respond, his mouth finds mine again, the kiss fierce and demanding. He's unapologetically rough, and I'm more than ready for it.

Without hesitation, he pushes me down onto my back, making me gasp as I find myself splayed out on the cool surface of the counter. His hands are relentless, gripping my thighs tightly as he leans in. His mouth trails fiery kisses up and down my legs, each touch a mix of heat and hunger. I know he can see my scars, but he doesn't comment on them. Doesn't avoid them. He does as I've asked. He sucks and nips at the sensitive skin. I can feel the intensity in every kiss, every touch, as he devours my skin with a fervour that makes my breath catch.

Marcus pulls away slightly, his eyes glinting with a predatory gleam. He looks me over, taking in the contrast between the warm, sugary cookies and the raw desire in his gaze. His voice is low and gritty.

"Looks like I've got more than cookies to feast on tonight," he says, a dark promise in his tone. He maintains a firm grip on my thigh, his fingers pressing in with a possessive urgency. With his other hand, he pushes up my 'nightdress', a simple, oversized t-shirt, exposing my bare skin. His touch is rough,

249

unapologetic, as he grabs my breast, his fingers kneading with a fierce intensity.

Without breaking his gaze, he leans down, biting onto my underwear. The fabric stretches and tears under the pressure of his teeth, and I feel a shiver run through me as he pulls them away. He moves his mouth down, and I shudder as he spits slowly; followed by the sting of his tongue, barely making contact with my clit but sending jolts through me. His touch is calculated, almost cruel in its teasing.

His fingers dig into my flesh, rolling my nipple with a fierce pressure that makes me gasp and whimper; and he begins to feast. Roughly. Passionately. Sucking, licking with raw ferocity. My body responds instinctively. My back arches, lifting me from the counter as if drawn by an invisible thread. Each swipe of his tongue is like a spark that ignites a firestorm within me. The sensation is an electric current coursing through my veins, sending jolts of molten pleasure radiating from my core.

His tongue is a relentless force, tracing patterns that feel like both a caress and a demand. As I arch further, my body responds to his relentless rhythm. My skin feels like it's on fire, each movement a plea for more, my whimpers a soundtrack to the visceral dance we're engaged in.

He suddenly shifts, his demeanour turning fierce and primal. Without warning, he yanks me up, his grip hard and unyielding. I barely have time to react before he drags me toward the stairs in the foyer. The sudden shift sends a jolt through me, my breath catching as he hauls me across the room.

He slams me down onto the steps, my front hitting the cold surface with a harsh thud. I feel his weight press down on me, his hand gripping my neck with a firm, controlling hold.

In a dark, hushed tone, he leans in close, "Now, you have to be quiet, sweet," he orders, the edge in his voice sharp and commanding. "We wouldn't want anyone knowing what a good little slut you are for me. Right?"

He waits for a response, but when I don't immediately reply, he slams his hand down on my ass with a sharp, stinging slap that makes me squeal. The pain is immediate and intense, causing me to squirm. Before I can make another sound, he clamps his hand over my mouth, his grip forceful and unyielding.

"Behave." He warns. I can feel his grip tighten on my waist, his fingers pressing into my skin as if marking his claim. He keeps his hand clamped over my mouth, his fingers pressing hard against my cheek. There's no escape, not that I'd ever try.

I nod quickly this time, not daring to disobey, the tension in the air thick enough to choke on. He positions himself at my entrance, slowly, deliberately, and I can feel the sheer force of his presence. The anticipation claws at me, and then, suddenly, there's nothing soft about it. He presses forward into me, hard and unforgiving, and the sensation tears through me like a shockwave. There's no space left for anything but this moment; raw, consuming, and relentless.

Each thrust is intended, slow but rough, the intensity building with every movement. My body arches instinctively, my senses overwhelmed by the mixture of pain and pleasure, every nerve alight with sensation. The weight of his body, the sound of his breath, the friction; it all blends together, driving deeper and deeper into something primal, something I can't control.

His grip tightens, his fingers digging into my waist, and I can feel him claiming every inch of my body. The rawness of it, the way he commands every part of me, leaves no room for thought; only the burning need that consumes us both. His hand stays firmly over my mouth, silencing the muffled cries that escape as he pushes deeper, rough and relentless.

"Feel that?" He asks quietly. His voice is rough, full of raw possession. "You're mine. Every fucking part of you."

I'm trembling beneath him, caught between wanting to cry out and knowing I can't. His hand presses tighter, stifling the sounds of my struggle, leaving me helpless under his control. The pressure in my body builds, a tension that threatens to break me completely, and he feels it too.

"*God*, you feel so fucking good," he growls. "You're taking it so well, sweet." His hand presses down harder, keeping me silent, while his voice and movements make it clear that he's revelling in how well I'm responding. "So fucking tight. You love this," he breathes, his grip firm. "Don't you?"

I try to nod, my body betraying me, and a muffled moan breaks free from my throat, trembling against his hand. He chuckles darkly, satisfied with the response, and slams harder, his voice thick with authority. The room is filled with the sounds of our movements, the rhythmic pounding punctuated by my soft, muffled gasps as he keeps me pinned in place.

"*Fuck,*" he moans. "Keep taking it like this, and you're gonna make me lose it," he growls, the promise of his own release mingling with his praise.

Every nerve in my body is on high alert as Marcus continues. The relentless rhythm drives me to a breaking point, pushing me past the edge. The intensity builds and builds until I can't hold back any longer. I'm overcome by a powerful release, my body arching and trembling with the force of it. The sensation is overwhelming, a hot, pulsating force that fills me entirely. I feel as though I'm caught in a vortex, being pulled into a whirlpool of intense pleasure that drowns out everything else. The stairs beneath me are cold and hard against my skin. My fingers claw at the steps, gripping desperately.

The pleasure is so powerful it seems to stretch time, each moment dragging out into a prolonged, exquisite agony. My legs tremble, unable to hold me steady as the final waves of release crash over me. My body quivers uncontrollably.

But the pleasure is marred by a sharp, stinging pain. The pain is a fierce, almost unbearable reminder. But I consciously ignore it. The pleasure is what I deserve, what I want to feel, and I concentrate on it with everything I have.

The lingering pain fades into the background as I bask in the aftershocks of pure ecstasy. My body still tingles, every nerve ending alive with the remnants of the experience. The discomfort is just a shadow, an insignificant part of the broader spectrum of what I'm feeling. My focus is entirely on the pleasure, the satisfaction that eclipses the pain, making every ache worthwhile. He leans in, his voice a dark, mocking whisper.

"Already coming, huh? Didn't even wait for permission?" His tone is rough, filled with an edge of satisfaction that makes my skin prickle. "Well, I'm not fucking finished yet."

Before I can even fully process his words, he's moving again, increasing his pace with a relentless drive. The sudden intensity takes me by surprise. Each thrust is harder, faster, and the sensation is beyond anything I could have imagined. My body, already spent and on edge, is thrust into a new realm of sensation. It's as if every nerve is alight, heightened and exposed. Through the haze of sensation, I can distinctly feel his focus and the depth of his enjoyment.

As he reaches his peak, he grips a fistful of my hair, pulling me closer into his rhythm. I can feel the warmth of his release inside me, a powerful and all-encompassing sensation. The moment is a jolt of ardour, spreading through me in waves that mix with the lingering pleasure.

"You feel that?" he growls, his tone cold. "You better take it all, you hear me?"

I whimper his name, a soft, broken sound that escapes my lips as he continues. After a few more intense moments, he pulls out, and I can feel the heat of his come trickle down my thigh, a slow, dripping stream. The sharp edges of the stairs dig into my skin as I collapse onto them, the coarse, unforgiving surface a brutal counterpoint to the intense, throbbing pleasure that still pulses within me.

"Aww," he mocks with a slight chuckle and dirty tone. "Look at all the come dripping from that pretty little cunt." he towers over me, staring down as if to admire his handiwork.

Then, with a swift motion, he picks me up, draping me over his shoulder. He strides confidently into the kitchen, the sound of his footsteps echoing slightly against the crisp floor. The shift from the stairs to the kitchen is jarring, the cool air of the room a stark contrast to the heat we left behind. He sets me down, and I brace against the counter as he grabs a damp cloth.

His hands are steady as he wipes me clean, each motion charged with a dark satisfaction. There's a casual, yet intense pleasure in his gaze, his words a testament to the pride he takes in how well I've handled him. Marcus finishes wiping me clean, his touch lingering for a moment longer before he sets the cloth aside. With a smooth, confident motion, he wraps his arms around me from behind, pulling me close against his chest.

His breath fans against my neck as he begins to press soft, languorous kisses along my skin. Each kiss is purposeful, a feather-light caress. His lips trace a slow, reverent path from the nape of my neck to just below my ear. Each kiss is imbued with a languid sensuality, a blend of devotion and desire that sends shivers cascading down my spine.

"I vow to spend my entire life worshipping you, Sienna." As he finishes speaking, he deepens his attention, his lips now sucking harder on my neck, leaving a trail of heated marks. His touch is insistent, a blend of rough and passionate, as he demonstrates his devotion in the most physical way.

After a moment, he pulls back slightly,

"I should've been your safety," he says, his voice heavy with regret and intensity. "I'll never forgive myself for letting you slip away, my sweet. But I'd die before I let it happen again."

CHAPTER 24:

BAD MOVE

Dean

It's late afternoon, and I traipse into the living room, a quiet sigh escaping me as I notice Delilah, Skylar, and Birdie lounging around. The room feels different, lighter somehow, despite the weight that's been hanging over me. My hood is up as usual, a habit I've fallen into lately, cocooning myself in a shell of solitude.

As I take a seat next to Delilah, I can already feel her eyes on me. She's had enough of my constant gloom, and I know what's coming. Without a word, she reaches over and pushes my hood down, exposing my face to the room's soft light.

I look at her, seeing the mix of frustration and care in her eyes. It's a gesture that cuts through my self-imposed darkness, reminding me of the warmth and support I've been trying to shut out. I manage a small, apologetic smile.

"Sorry," I mumble, the word carrying more weight than I intend. It's an apology for not just being down, but for letting it affect everyone around me. I know Delilah's been trying to pull me out of this, and her action is both a reprimand and a reminder of how much she cares.

But as I sit there, surrounded by their light-heartedness, a grim thought settles in my mind. Death is literally knocking on my door; every step I take feels like a march toward something inevitable. How am I supposed to enjoy life when I'm so clearly running out of time? The heavy knowledge that my days might be numbered makes it hard to fully engage with the small moments of joy around me.

Am I crazy for feeling this way?
Or are they all crazy for not feeling it?
I guess I should take some comfort in the fact that they don't seem overly concerned. Maybe their apparent ease is a sign that they've accepted the uncertainty of life in a way I haven't. Or maybe it's just a smarter way of coping. Delilah gives me a soft, encouraging look, her

touch lingering on my shoulder for a moment before she settles back into her spot.

I glance around at the others, trying to distract myself from the relentless tick of my internal clock.

"So, what's today's conversation, ladies?" I ask with a rasp, as if the words are struggling to escape. Delilah glances up from her spot on the couch.

"We were just talking about Birdie's new lifeguard job," she says. Birdie beams, practically bouncing with excitement.

"So, Dad's rented me a place right by the beachfront. It's pretty sick." She says. Delilah raises an eyebrow, a playful grin tugging at her lips.

"So, does that mean there's room for a sleepover?"

"Sleepover? *Girl*, I plan on throwing parties every weekend. It's gonna be a non-stop scene."
Skylar, sitting with one leg draped over the arm of the opposite couch, perks up.

"But please tell me you're not inviting your snobby private school friends. I don't think I can handle their whole *'I don't do sand'* routine." She pleads, and I agree. Birdie snorts.

"Definitely not. I only plan on inviting people with a personality." I glance over at Skylar, a grin tugging at the corner of my mouth.

"Well, I guess that means Skylar's not invited then." The reaction is instant; Birdie and Delilah both burst into exaggerated gasps, their voices ringing out in unison,

"Ooohhhhh!"

For a second, the tension in me breaks, and I let out a real laugh. It's been a while since I've heard that sound from myself, and it feels.. strange. But good, in a way. The girls are laughing too, the room feeling lighter for a moment. Skylar crosses her arms, shooting me a sharp look.

"I've got more personality than you, Mr. Dodgy Dealer." I let out a low laugh, settling back deeper into the couch, stretching my arms across the back of it.

"Your only personality trait is being a little fucking brat."

She scoffs, rolling her eyes dramatically, but the smirk on her lips betrays her. There's a flicker of something almost like warmth in the room, the kind of energy we used to have when we'd tease each other relentlessly. For a moment, the heaviness that's been clinging to me all week seems to lift, just enough to let me breathe.

It's the first time in days that I've had even an ounce of my usual banter with Skylar, and it feels uncanny, but nice; like I've grabbed onto a piece of normalcy in the middle of the mess my life has become. Skylar smirks, leaning in with a mischievous glint in her eyes.

"How many fingers you got there, Dean?" She starts counting her fingers dramatically, her gaze lingering on my hands. "One, two, three, fo- Oh, shit, I think you're missing a couple. "

I glance down at my hands, feeling the faint sting of her words.

"Yeah, thanks for the reminder." I chuckle. Delilah laughs softly, shaking her head.

"Skylar, you're evil."

Birdie and Skylar's conversation about Birdie's new lifeguard job continues in the background, their voices blending into a low murmur. They're animated, clearly excited about the upcoming changes, and I can't help but overhear snippets about beach parties and new decorations.

My attention, however, is drawn to Delilah. She stands up gracefully and walks over to the other side of the room. Her movements are smooth, almost soothing in their deliberate calm. I watch as she grabs a tupperware container full of cookies. She returns, her movements fluid as she carries the tupperware container like a prized possession. She places it on the coffee table with a soft thud, the lid popping open to reveal a tempting stack of cookies.

"Sienna made these last night," she announces cheerfully. "They're *incredible*."

Skylar's hand shoots out almost instinctively, snagging a cookie with a satisfied grin. Birdie, never one to miss an opportunity, takes three, her expression one of pure indulgence. Skylar can't resist a jab, her tone dripping with playful sarcasm.

"Typical rich kid." She states. Birdie arches an eyebrow, unfazed.

"And *that* attitude is exactly why you're not rich, Sky."

Delilah's laughter is warm, a soft counterpoint to their banter. She turns her gaze to me, her smile inviting.

"Dean, aren't you gonna have one?" She asks. I shake my head, offering a faint smile.

"Nah, I'm good." Skylar's gaze lingers on me with a puzzled frown.

"Why aren't you taking a cookie?" She asks. I glance back at her, feeling a slight tightness in my chest.

"Not really in the mood for one right now," I reply, trying to keep my tone casual. Skylar doesn't let it slide.

"You didn't eat dinner last night either."

"I just wasn't hungry. No big deal."

Skylar tilts her head, then suddenly breaks into an exaggerated, over-the-top tone.

"*Mmm!* Oh my god, this is literally the best cookie in the entire world!" she announces dramatically, waving the cookie in the air. It's clear she's trying to make me feel like I'm missing out, her showy performance a blatant attempt to get a reaction from me.

263

Her efforts are well-intentioned, but they only seem to highlight the chasm between her world and mine. The truth is, sometimes it feels like the end of the world is closer than anyone realises. Everyone's attempts to lighten my mood are earnest, but they miss the mark. Death is knocking on my door, and no amount of cookies or jokes can change that.

I force a chuckle, even as my irritation simmers beneath the surface.

"Very funny." I say. Skylar, still holding her cookie, gives me a sideways look.

"Seriously, what's your deal with not eating? It's just a cookie." Delilah senses the shift in my mood and steps in, her voice calm but firm.

"Skylar, just leave it. Let him be." She says. I glance over at Delilah, her concerned eyes meeting mine. A flicker of gratitude passes through me, and I give her a small, weary smile. I reach out and place my hand gently on her thigh, a silent thank you for stepping in. The warmth of her skin beneath my palm a significant comfort.

Skylar sighs dramatically, clearly annoyed but relenting.

"Fine," she relents. I seize the opportunity to let my irritation surface.

"Thanks for the support, Skylar. Really appreciate the concern." I reply. Skylar's eyes narrow, her tone sharp.

"Oh, don't get all grumpy on *us* now too. Marcus offered to help you, and you wouldn't even let him, so what do you actually fucking want?" Her words hit harder than she realises. My jaw tightens, and I don't reply. I don't have a response. I can feel the anger rising, my patience wearing thin. Delilah notices the change in my demeanour and leans in to whisper softly,

"Skylar shh."

Skylar doesn't relent, her tone growing more insistent.

"No, seriously, what are we supposed to do? Just sit here and mope around? We wanted to help you, but you don't wanna help yourself." The frustration in her voice only fuels my own anger. I feel a surge of heat and the sharp sting of her words. My anger spikes, and I snap,

"Sky, shut the fuck up." She raises an eyebrow, her lips curling into a smirk.

"What happened to tough guy Dean, huh? Can't even finish a game of 'Never Have I Ever' without running off these days." She mocks with a jokey smile. I let out a harsh laugh, the sound almost a growl.

"Yeah, well, believe it or not I'm not exactly in the mood for games right now."

Skylar, undeterred, stands up and shifts closer. Her voice drops into a sarcastic baby tone.

"Aww, is big bad Noah too intimidating for you?" She says. I shoot her a steely look.

"I can assure you, your boyfriend doesn't intimidate me." She smirks, wiggling her fingers in a teasing manner as she edges closer. The playful gesture only heightens my irritation. She inches closer, her grin widening as she continues her relentless teasing.

"Are you *scared?*" As she reaches right in front of me, I bat her hands away, my voice sharp.

"Sky, stop."

She misinterprets my tone and keeps on, her voice dripping with playful mockery.

"Ooo, is Noah *scary?*" I feel my body tensing, my chest tightening with each inch she closes. The space around me feels smaller, as if the room itself is closing in. My skin is crawling, every sound and movement around me amplifying my stress. I'm overwhelmed, overstimulated, my breath coming in short, sharp bursts. I grip the arm of the couch, my knuckles white.

"Seriously, stop," I growl, my voice strained, but Skylar seems to think I'm still playing along. The playful banter, once a welcomed distraction, now feels like an assault. I'm suffocating, each touch and word from her only intensifying the pressure building inside me.

The building tension snaps like a taut wire. I rise abruptly, my movements driven by a storm of pent-up frustration and a suffocating sense of inevitability. With a force I barely comprehend, I shove Skylar. The shove is more than a push; it's a violent expulsion of every suppressed emotion, propelling her backwards onto the unforgiving wooden floor.

The sound of her hitting the floor is like the shattering of glass, a stark and jarring contrast to the otherwise muted room. The impact is immediate, the wind knocked out of her. She's sitting there, her knees drawn up and her arms splayed out, her breath coming in quick, uneven gasps. She looks up at me, eyes wide and brimming with confusion and fear. I stand there, rooted to the spot, as the realisation of what I've done floods over me. My heart pounds like a war drum, each beat echoing the horror and regret crashing through me.

My hands, which moments ago were just extensions of my anger, now feel like foreign entities. They tremble and seem almost translucent, as if they've betrayed me in the most profound way. I feel utterly isolated, trapped in a moment of profound regret, knowing immediately that there's no easy way to undo the damage I've just caused.

"Sky, I'm so sorry-" The words tumble out, but they are abruptly swallowed by a deafening crack. The sharp, clean sound of a gunshot splits the air, and a

267

bullet buries itself into the wall just inches behind my head, leaving a jagged hole and a whiff of burning gunpowder. Dread floods my veins.

I'm fucked.

I turn slowly towards the doorway, my heart hammering in my chest. I know exactly who I'm about to see holding the gun. Noah stands in the doorway, his presence as formidable as a thunderstorm. The gun is lowered but still clutched in his hand, the steel of it cold and unforgiving. His eyes, dark and burning with a righteous fury, fixate on me with an intensity that feels like a physical assault. It's not just anger; it's a tempest of rage and resolve, and it makes my blood run cold.
Noah's voice lacerates through the charged silence, controlled but laced with deadly firmness.

"Put your hands on my girl again, and I'll cut them off," he says, his tone a chilling whisper of menace. Noah's eyes burn. The room falls into a heavy, suffocating silence. I can't breathe. My mind is a whirlwind. Thoughts collide. I'm fucked. I'm so fucked, and rightly so. I can't move. I can't think. Just his gaze is enough to paralyse me. "Is that fucking clear?" Noah's voice rises, sharp and commanding. I inhale sharply, the oxygen burning in my chest. I nod, barely moving.

"Clear."

CHAPTER 25:

RUNNING IN THE RAIN

Noah

The night is still as I mosey down the long stretch of the front drive, my footsteps echoing faintly off the stone beneath me. A low fog blankets the ground, swirling around the edges of the stone path, creeping up the dirt paths and manicured lawns before me. The mansion looms behind, a silent giant, its vastness fading into the murk as I leave it behind. The estate feels endless, the emptiness sprawling out like a ghost town with no life, just shadows and mist. I pull out a cigar, the weight of it familiar between my fingers. I take my time lighting it, watching the orange glow flare up as I inhale the first drag. The smoke curls into the haze, vanishing into the cold air.

The silence is thick. Too thick. The kind of quiet that feels unnatural, like the whole world is holding its breath, waiting for something to break. The stillness presses in on me, heavy, but I welcome it. A chill seeps into the space around me, but it doesn't reach my bones. Not much does anymore. I breathe it in, the smoke mixing with the brume, both lingering in the air like ghosts. I stand there, letting the cigar burn slowly.

Everything's quiet. The trees stand tall and unmoving, shadows cast long and dark across the ground. The wind shifts slightly, carrying the smell of wet earth and old stone, like something ancient, something untouched. The fog rolls across the dirt paths like it's bowing at my feet. There's power in the quiet, in knowing everything around me is under my control. Mine. I don't need to speak or move to prove it.

The silence quickly breaks with the soft sound of footsteps behind me. I don't flinch, but my grip on the cigar tightens slightly. Turning, I catch sight of Skylar, her figure cutting through the mist, her steps light but purposeful as she struts toward me. Or so I think. As she gets right up to me, close enough that I can smell the faint hint of whatever sweet perfume she wears, she gives a slight nod.

"Noah," she says, her voice steady, before continuing past me without breaking stride.

It's calm, almost too casual, like she's acknowledging me without really engaging, as if I'm just part of the scenery. I watch her walk ahead, the fog swallowing her up a little more with each step. I let her have her moment. But as always, I'm never far behind. I fall into a slow, calculated pace, letting the silence stretch for a beat before I speak.

"Going somewhere, princess?" My voice cuts through the stillness, low and smooth, a warning wrapped in calm.

Skylar keeps walking, her back to me as she mutters simply,

"Out." It's enough to make me chuckle, a subtle sound that barely leaves my chest. I take a long, slow puff of my cigar, savouring the taste before crushing it out under my boot. I watch her figure in the mist, each step taking her farther into the night, and my lips curl into a smirk. I take a few steps closer, just enough so she knows I'm right behind her.

"Not at this time of night you're not," I say, my tone smooth but firm, like I've already decided for her. Because I have. She doesn't stop right away, but I know she heard me.

She always hears me.

As she flips her hair with a dramatic sass, her voice dances with defiance.

"I'm not spending another minute locked up in this house. I'll lose my mind." She says. My lip curls into a smirk as I fall into step beside her.

"And where exactly are you planning on going?" I ask, my voice smooth and deliberately casual. My tone is laced with a touch of smugness, knowing full well that the sprawling estate around us is nothing but country lanes and empty fields beyond the gates. She shrugs nonchalantly, her gaze fixed ahead.

"I don't know. Somewhere high up." She says. A flicker of amusement dances across my face as the pieces fall into place. She's looking for a high vantage point to stargaze. It's a small, almost endearing detail; her need to escape the confines of the house and lose herself in the night sky. I find it oddly charming, this simple pursuit of a celestial view.

If stargazing is what she wants, stargazing is what she gets.

I turn slowly, my boots crunching on the gravel as I head back towards my line of sleek, darkened cars parked near the mansion. The haze clings to the polished surfaces, casting an eerie glow that seems to pulse with the subtle movements of the night air. The car I approach is a black silhouette against the mist, its form both imposing and elegant. As I draw closer, the headlights cut through the mist with a sharp brilliance, piercing through the monochromatic gloom.

I slip into the driver's seat with purposive ease, the leather cool beneath my touch. The engine roars to life with a throaty growl that shatters the night's stillness. I rev it with intention, the sound echoing ominously across the vast estate. With a smooth motion, I ease the car out of its spot, the tires gripping the damp gravel as the vehicle glides forward. The headlights cut through the haze in sharp, slitting beams, creating a serpentine path through the swirling mist.

I drive the car smoothly out of the driveway, the engine's purr a steady companion to the night's quiet. As I ease the car alongside Skylar, the vehicle appears to glide like a phantom through the mist, barely making a sound. I lower the passenger window with a soft hiss and lean slightly across the seat.

Skylar glances over at me, her face illuminated by the harsh light of the car. She lets out a weary sigh, clearly irritated. Without a word, she turns away, her steps resolute as she continues traipsing through the night.

"Get in the car, Farmer," I say, my voice low and teasing. Skylar doesn't even break stride. She glances at me again, her brows furrowing, a hint of defiance in her eyes.

"No," she snaps, turning her head away. "I don't need you watching over me. I'm fine on my own."

"You don't even know where you're going." My voice drips with that smug, knowing tone. Skylar quickens her pace, her chin tilted defiantly upward, that familiar stubbornness igniting within her as she strives to prove a point.

"I'll figure it out," she retorts, her voice resolute yet tinged with a trace of uncertainty.

The thing I love is that she genuinely believes that. She has that reckless confidence, the kind that would probably land her somewhere eventually, even if she had no fucking clue where she was going. Odds are, being the obstinate person she is, she'd find a spot; might even be a good one.

But unfortunately for her, there's no way I'm letting her walk out here alone in the middle of the night. Not even on my estate. Not anywhere.

"If you don't get your pretty little ass in the car right now," I say, voice low and steady, "I'll come out there and drag you in myself." Skylar stops, turning to look at me with a raised brow, her face saying *'Really?'*. She thinks I'm being dramatic, but I'm dead serious. "Don't think I won't," I add, not breaking eye contact.

"I'll set your fucking car on fire." She snaps.

Hot.

When she still ignores my instruction, I turn the wheel abruptly, the car lurching forward just enough to cut her off, forcing her to stop. The tires grind against the dirt path, kicking up small stones. She spins around, eyes blazing with anger.

"Are you fucking crazy?" she shouts, fury spilling out as she glares at me. I don't rush. She knows I won't back down. I just let a slow, calculated smile stretch across my lips.

"I think you already know the answer to that." I reply, my voice smooth as glass.

She stands there for a moment, staring at me like she's weighing her options, the defiance still simmering in her eyes. Then, slowly, she does that little move; her tongue sliding across her top teeth in frustration, like she's biting back a string of curses. I just sit there, watching her fight it out with herself. And then, as I knew she would, she turns with a huff and pulls open the passenger door. Without a word, she slips into the seat beside me, the car door shutting with a solid thud.

I settle back into my seat, one hand casually gripping the top of the wheel. The other rests on the gearshift, fingers drumming lightly.

"Good girl," I mock, my tone considered, almost purring. "See, baby? That wasn't so hard." I let the words linger in the air, the smirk on my face barely visible but unmistakable. Skylar doesn't say a word. She just shoots me a look of pure annoyance before turning her attention to the window.

I flick the car back into gear, my fingers barely touching the steering wheel as I guide it with a smooth, practised roll of my palm. The wheels hum against the gravel, the sound slicing through the night.

As the car lurches forward, I glance over at my princess, her profile illuminated by the headlights. A sliver of moonlight catches her face, revealing her tight-lipped irritation. I can't help but chuckle softly, the sound blending with the growl of the engine. With a final roll of the wheel, I turn the car onto the darkened road, the landscape outside merging into a blur of shadow and fog. The night stretches out ahead, and I drive into it.

I cruise in silence for a while, the roar of the engine slicing through the stillness of the night. The road unfurls ahead, and I press the pedal, pushing the car into a blur of speed. The headlights cut through the dense mist, illuminating the path with a stark, penetrating glow. Skylar's presence beside me is a mix of calm defiance and quiet amusement. She occasionally grabs the side handles, her fingers gripping them tightly during sharper turns or sudden accelerations.

After about ten minutes, she breaks the quiet.

"So, where exactly are you taking me, anyway? Or is this some sort of kidnapping plot?" Her voice is light, laced with playful sarcasm. I cast a sidelong glance at her, a smirk tugging at the corners of my lips.

"You wanna stargaze, we stargaze." I say, matter of fact. Skylar's eyes dart to me for a moment, and I catch a glimmer of a cheeky smile tugging at her lips. She tries to mask it, but I can see the satisfaction in her expression. She leans back in her seat, her posture relaxing slightly as if my words have validated her desire.

After almost two hours of driving through quiet roads and dense trees, the road begins to open up. I ease the car to a halt in a large, secluded clearing right at the edge of a cliff. The forest encircles the space like a protective barrier, the trees towering high and casting deep shadows around us. The cliff drops sharply beyond the clearing, offering an unobstructed view of the night sky, where stars are scattered like diamonds across a velvet canvas.

I shift the gear into neutral and kill the engine, the sudden silence contrasting sharply with the previous roar. The only light comes from the moon, which bathes the clearing in a soft, eerie glow. I step out of the car, my movements smooth and headstrong, and look back at Skylar.

She exits the vehicle, her eyes scanning the vast, open space before her. The edge of the cliff looms ahead, but the forest provides a natural barrier, keeping the view both stunning and secure. I lean against the car, watching as Skylar takes in the scene. Her expression shifts from curiosity to something softer; a mix of appreciation and contentment.

Her eyes widen slightly, reflecting the myriad of stars above. She looks up at the sky, a gentle, almost breathless awe in her gaze. The glow from the distant stars casts a delicate sheen on her face, highlighting her piercing, ice-blue eyes that are now softened by the night's splendour.

Her usual careless attitude seems to melt away in the presence of such beauty. It's as if she's momentarily lost in a world far removed from the one we've been navigating. The way she stands, with her head tilted back slightly and her eyes locked on the vast, glittering expanse, speaks volumes. For a moment, she's just a girl, spellbound by the sheer magnificence of the universe.

I remain still, observing her with a quiet fascination. There's something enchanting about watching her like this.

"Is this to your liking, princess?" I ask. She turns her gaze away from the heavens and looks at me. Her eyes, though still shimmering with starlight, carry a subtle smile.

"It'll do," she replies, her tone carrying that familiar sarcastic edge but tempered by the quiet wonder that still lingers in her voice. She doesn't need to say more. The way her eyes instantly dart back to the sky, the way her body seems to relax in this place, tells me all I need to know. This moment, this place; it's exactly what she was looking for.

Skylar slowly lowers herself to the ground, lying flat on her back in the middle of the open space. Her eyes stay fixed on the sky as if she's trying to memorise each star. I stand there, hands in my pockets, watching her; content in her own little world. She turns her head slightly, glancing over at me.

"So, are you gonna join me," she says with a hint of playful teasing in her voice, "or just watch over me like a creep?"

A low chuckle escapes my lips, but I don't move. I just keep staring down at her, a calm admiration flickering in my chest. She rolls her eyes and looks back up at the sky, her lips curling into a half-smile.

"Ahh, I get it," she sighs, shaking her head slightly. "You're too cool for fun." I let out a loud, exaggerated sigh, playing along with her little jab, before stepping toward her. It's not that I mind, but I like making her think it's more of a hassle than it is.

I settle down beside her, the ground solid beneath me. The world feels still, untouched, save for the faint rustling of trees swaying in the breeze, the distant call of an owl, and the rhythmic chirping of crickets. The quiet presses in, the kind that's thick with space; where the silence speaks louder than words.

Above, the sky is a jagged expanse of obsidian, dotted with fractured shards of starlight. Each one pulses faintly, distant but alive, shimmering through the fog that clings to the edges of the horizon. The stars provide little respite from the void that seems to swallow everything. It's the kind of night sky that makes you feel small, insignificant under its vastness, like you're standing on the edge of something unfathomable.

The moon hangs, not just in the sky, but like a weight pressing on the world; an ancient eye, cold and watchful. Its light dominates the night, washing the landscape in pale luminescence, sharp and cold like the gleam of steel. The stars struggle to compete. It's sharp, cutting through the darkness like truth slicing through lies; yet so soft, so lenient. There's something unnerving about it tonight, something eternal, like it's seen a thousand lives begin and end and will see a thousand more. It hangs there, full and unapologetic, as if daring the night to swallow it. But the night can't. No matter how thick the dark, the moon pierces through, exposing everything. Bone-deep. a ghost's caress; soft, but full of weight, carrying every secret ever whispered under its watch, every glance exchanged in the shadows. And tonight, it feels personal, as if it knows.

The moon doesn't hide.
It bares all.

I point up at the sky.

"See that?" I start, cutting through the quiet. She follows my finger.

"Yeah," she answers, her voice soft beneath the moonlight.

"That's Saturn," I share. Her laughter bubbles up, light and genuine.

"Nerd." The word dances across the silence, a playful jab that catches me off guard, a smile tugging at my lips. She turns her head, curiosity glinting in her eyes. "How do you know that?" She asks.

I shrug, my gaze still fixed on the sky.

"I don't know. I've always quite liked astronomy." It's a simple truth, but in the moon's harsh light, it feels like more than that. To me, it feels almost monumental, sharing something so trivial about myself. I've never had anyone in my life who knew me on any kind of a personal level; not even my father. It's like I'm revealing a deep, dark secret. It's strange because, in reality, it's just a hobby. Something pretty mundane.

"Well, you learn something new everyday."

As I watch her, taking in the night's spectacle, I'm struck by a sudden clarity. This is real. I'm here. Down on the grass, looking at the stars with a girl who's quickly woven herself into the fabric of my existence. So unexpectedly important to me. Sharing something so simple and human, yet so profoundly different from anything I've ever known.

"Skylar," I start. "Why don't you hate me?" The question escapes my lips before I can second-guess it. Skylar turns to me, her pale blue eyes reflecting the soft luminescence of the moon. There's a genuine tenderness in her gaze, something that catches me off guard. A gentle smile curves her lips, and she says,

"I do," her tone light and teasing. For a moment, we both laugh. Genuinely laugh.

As the laughter fades, we turn to face each other once more.

"I mean it," I say. "After all the things I've done, why don't you hate me?" Her eyes hold a quiet vulnerability, and her smile is timid, small but sincere. The soft moonlight highlights the delicate curve of her lips as she answers,

"Because I'm broken too." The words linger in the night, a fragile confession that deepens the stillness around us. She pauses, then continues, "because I've also gone through life playing a role I never really wanted to play." There's a delicate pause as we both absorb her words.

282

"You make it really fucking hard to stay in character, Farmer." I admit, my voice a low growl, laced with frustration and something like reluctant admiration. I can see the way my admission affects her, a flicker of joy crossing her features. It's not just that she's unsettled my carefully maintained facade; it's that she's done it with an unexpected ease, peeling back layers I thought were impenetrable. The night feels charged with a raw honesty, the distance between us shrinking with every breath. She glances away, her eyes shifting back up to the star-studded sky. There's a moment of silence as she absorbs my words, her posture relaxing slightly. I see a new edge in her expression; contentment, or maybe even relief.

We lie there, side by side, lost in conversation as the stars shift subtly across the sky. Our talk drifts from light-hearted banter to deeper revelations, the line between flirting and genuine connection blurring effortlessly. Her laughter punctuates the night air, and each shared glance feels like a thread weaving us closer together.

Hours pass in this intimate dance, our words and touches blending with the tranquil backdrop of the universe. After a while, I notice a change in the sky. The stars that once twinkled brightly are gradually obscured by a blanket of clouds, their dark mass creeping in from the horizon. The atmosphere grows heavier, and the once-clear expanse begins to take on a greyish hue. Skylar, too, seems to sense the shift. She glances up, as the first wisps of clouds drift across the sky.

"Looks like we've got company," she says.

Tiny droplets start to fall, the first hints of rain catching the edge of the moonlight. I feel the light patter against my skin, and then a few more drops hit, quickly turning into a steady drizzle. I sit up and stretch, my clothes beginning to cling uncomfortably to my skin. I glance over at Skylar, who's still seated now too; her head tilted back, letting the raindrops cascade over her.

"Come on, let's get going," I say, standing up and offering my hand to her. She stays put, her eyes closed as she revels in the sensation of the rain.

"But this is fun," she replies, her voice light and carefree. I shake my head with a wry smile,

"You'll catch a cold if you stay out here like this." She looks up at me, her eyes reflecting the raindrops, but she doesn't move; almost captivated by the rain.

"That's a myth," she says with a small, defiant smile. I shake my head, half-amused and half-exasperated.

"Come on, princess." I say, trying to keep my tone firm.

"No," she replies, disobediently.

I step closer and gently but insistently pull her to her feet. I start striding towards the car, rain dripping from the tips of my hair and soaking through my clothes. She resists, her feet stubbornly planted.

"I'm not moving," she declares, crossing her arms, her voice resolute even as the rain grows heavier; droplets cascading down her face and shoulders.

I halt and turn back, the rain now pouring down steadily, creating a curtain of droplets around us. I can see the raindrops clinging to her lashes and the soft, defiant smile playing on her lips.

"We can't stand here all night" I insist, my voice raised to cut through the relentless sound of the rain. "Get in the car."

We stand there, locked in a silent standoff, our gazes holding each other's despite the downpour. The rain coming down in a torrential cascade that blurs the world around us. The sky is an expanse of relentless grey, and each drop feels like it's racing to join the flood gathering around our feet.

Her pastel-pink hair is plastered to her forehead, and water streams down her cheeks, but the playful smile never fades. There's a spark of challenge in her eyes, as though she's daring me to do something about it. I can't help but be impressed by her stubbornness, even as the rain soaks through.

The torrential rain continues its unrelenting descent, drumming loudly against the roof of the car and the ground beneath us. I realise that if I want to get her into the car, I'm going to have to take matters into my own hands. I take a few intentional, yet subtly quiet steps toward her, trying to close the distance without startling her.

Just as I'm close enough to reach out and grab her, Skylar takes one large, premeditated step backward, her eyes still locked on mine, her mischievous grin widening as she dances just out of my reach. I feel a laugh bubbling but keep my expression firm.

"Alright, that's enough." As I hold my ground, her gaze drifts momentarily toward the dense forest beside us. Before she can make a move, I catch her intent and cut in sharply, "Don't even think about it, Farmer."

Her eyes flicker back to me, the playful challenge momentarily replaced by a flash of contemplation. I step closer, letting the weight of my warning hang heavy in the air.

"If you try to run, there will be consequences. I'm not playing games anymore."

The rain pelts down with increasing intensity, the droplets blurring the edges of the world around us. The forest stands in stark contrast to the storm, a tempting escape, but I'm resolute. My tone is firm and unyielding, making it clear that there's no room for negotiation. Skylar's smile fades slightly, but her eyes still hold a glint of mischief, tempered by the seriousness of my warning.

She doesn't obey.
She runs.

I stretch out a hand, trying to catch her, but she's already out of reach, her laughter mingling with the roar of the rain. She disappears into the dense undergrowth, leaving me standing in the storm, drenched and momentarily stunned. I pause for a moment, rubbing my jaw with a mixture of frustration and intrigue. The rain continues to hammer down around me, a relentless downpour that soaks me through.

Okay, princess.
You run, I hunt.

I take a deep breath, shaking off the water, and start moving toward the forest. The rain splashes around me, a veil of atmosphere, but I maintain a steady pace, my movements deliberate against the storm's fury. My eyes lock on the dark silhouette of the trees, which seem to swallow her presence whole. The forest's shadows deepen, becoming an ominous labyrinth where she's chosen to hide.

There's no rush in my approach. I walk steadily, the rain cascading off my shoulders and dripping from the strands of hair, hanging in front of my eyeline. The forest looms ahead, its dark, tangled branches reaching out like twisted fingers, beckoning me into its depths. I hear her footsteps, a distant echo through the dense foliage. The sound is faint but clear. A mere whisper compared to the storm's roar, but it's enough to guide me.

I move through the rain, my face set in a focused expression, every muscle in my body attuned to the hunt. The air is cool and thick with moisture, each breath I take mingling with the midnight chill. My eyes are sharp, scanning the shadows for any hint of her presence; the rain lashing against my skin. I catch glimpses of movement in the periphery; quick flashes of her silhouette darting between the trees. Her flight is desperate, but the darkness and the downpour make her elusive. Every now and then, a splash of water or a snapped twig betrays her position, but I only quicken my pace slightly, never breaking my steady, calculated stride.

The forest grows denser as I push deeper. My senses are heightened, attuned to every sound, every shift in the shadows. She's moving faster now, but so am I, the thrill of the pursuit sharpening my focus. Suddenly, I catch a clearer sight of her; a fleeting shadow against the dark green of the trees. I adjust my path, drawing closer, the distance between us narrowing.

I stop next to a particular tree, its gnarled trunk slick with rain. The forest around me is a dark, rain-soaked expanse, but In the darkness, I notice a stray, pink hair. She's hiding behind this very tree, her breath a faint shudder. A slow, dark smirk curls on my lips as I stand facing the trunk, my body casting a looming shadow. The rain hisses around me.

"I know you're there, my princess." I say, my voice low and smooth, dripping with a predatory edge. "I can hear your heartbeat."

I shift slightly, my face close to the rough bark. My voice is a whisper, intentionally distorted by the wood between us, creating an eerie, intimate proximity.

"Come out and face me," I taunt, my voice a velvety purr that slashes through the storm. "Or should I come around and pull you out?" I continue, my voice dripping with a cruel, seductive promise. I pause, letting the words linger in the rain-soaked air, relishing in the silence that follows. The anticipation crackles like electricity between us, and I can almost feel her trembling just out of sight. I smile, savouring the thrill of knowing she's so close, so vulnerable.

"Are you scared, Skylar?" I ask, my voice a low, predatory whisper. No reply. "Do you want to know what I'm gonna do to you when you finally come out of your little hiding spot?" I wait, the darkness and the storm swirling around us, my eyes fixed on the wet strands of pink hair creeping around the tree trunk.

I lean in, pressing my face close to the rough bark, the cold, wet air mixing with my breath.

"I'll make sure every second of your fear is stretched out until you're begging for it to stop." I let my fingers trace the grooves of the tree, the sensation cold and almost comforting against the dark intent simmering beneath. "I'm going to savour every fucking moment of this," I continue, my voice now a cold whisper that wraps around her like a noose.

My hand grips the tree tighter, as if holding onto the thrill of the hunt.

"You're hiding now, but soon, I'll have you right where I want you," I say, my voice a dangerous, dark caress. "And when I do get my hands on you..." I let the words hang, dripping with malevolent intent. "I'll make sure you never forget what it means to run from me."

I press against the tree, the rain streaming down in relentless sheets, drenching everything around us. The storm's fury is nothing compared to the dark anticipation crackling in the night. Her fear is a tangible thing, seeping through the rain, guiding me.

"So what's it gonna be, baby?" I growl, my voice a low, dangerous rumble. "Are you going to come out and face me, or am I going to have to drag you from your little sanctuary?"

The sky is a roiling, black sea, unleashing its fury. It pours from the heavens like a thousand vengeful eyes, watching, waiting. I clench my jaw, the tension in my muscles mirroring the storm's ferocity. My patience is wearing thin, the seconds stretching like a taut wire.

"You have five seconds, Farmer." I say, my voice harsh and edged with a dangerous finality. "I'm starting to lose my patience."

I count down, my tone dropping to a low, threatening whisper.

"Five.. four.. three.." The rain continues its relentless assault, each drop a small, insistent drumbeat, driving the tension higher. "Two... one..."

At the final count, her tiny figure emerges from behind the tree, stepping into the open, drenched. I let my eyes rake over her, noting how her soaked top clings to every curve with a transparency that leaves little to the imagination. Her eyes lift to meet mine, wide and glistening, the storm's reflection dancing in their depths. There's a mixture of guilt and resignation in her stare.

I take a slow, menacing step toward her, the mud squelching underneath me. As I take a step closer, I notice her shuffling back, trying to put some distance between us. Not happening. My reaction is immediate and ruthless. I close the distance in an instant, my hand shooting out and grabbing her by the throat. The grip is ironclad, merciless. I slam her against the tree, the rough bark biting into her back as the impact jolts through her. Her eyes widen in shock and fear, her breath coming in shallow, ragged gasps.

"You think I'm gonna let you keep running from me?" I hiss, leaning in close. "You should be begging for fucking mercy right now." I feel her chest heaving against my grip, her breaths coming in strained gasps. "Does it make you wet, knowing that I control your breath, your life?" I can feel her struggling, her body pressing harder against the tree as she tries to pull away.

"Be a good little girl, Skylar." I continue, my fingers digging deeper into her flesh, restricting her airflow. "Beg me to stop."

Her eyes are wide, pleading, but the words she wants to scream are choked off by my unyielding grip. I can feel her desperation, her inability to beg me as I've commanded. The realisation only deepens the cruel satisfaction I find in her helplessness.

"Look at you," I say, my voice dripping with disdain and mockery. "You can't even beg, can you? Too weak to even form the words. And I haven't even fucking started." I maintain my grip a moment longer, savouring her futile struggles and the shiver that runs through her. "You might think you're a big girl with that sharp mouth of yours when you're out there, showing off in front of everyone else. But I'm not everyone else, princess."

Then, without warning, I release her throat with a rough shove, watching as she gasps for air, her breath coming in ragged, uneven bursts. In one fluid motion, I haul her up over my shoulder. Her body shifts and adjusts, the wet fabric of her clothes clinging to me. With her draped across my shoulder, I begin to walk back towards the car, the rain slashing against us in a relentless cascade.

As she struggles on my shoulder, her movements are fierce and driven by desperation. She pounds my back with surprising force, her kicks and wriggles intense enough to make me feel her frustration. Despite the strength and energy she puts into her attempts to break free, her resistance is nothing compared to the iron grip I have on her. A wild storm against an immovable mountain.

With a cold smirk, I decide to make her discomfort even more palpable. I lean in and sink my teeth into her exposed thigh, the bite sharp and unmistakable. Her body tenses and jolts, and I relish the way she reacts to the sudden, intense sensation.

"Keep it up." I threaten.

I reach the car, the open space around it now drenched through by the relentless downpour. The rain cascades off the edges of the car, pooling into muddy puddles beneath it. With her still draped over my shoulder, her struggles having subsided to occasional, exhausted twitches, I stop beside the car. The water running in rivulets off the roof.

"Now, let's see how much you can really endure." I say, my tone a menacing promise.

With a swift, forceful movement, I slam her down onto the car's bonnet. The metal is slick and cold beneath her. Her body hits with a sharp thud, and the sound of her startled yell pierces through the storm. The impact reverberates up my arm, but her reaction, pure, unfiltered, sends a thrill through me. The rain pours over us, relentless, soaking into her skin, her clothes translucent and plastered to her body. I keep her pinned there, one hand pressing down hard on the back of her neck, forcing her to stay face down against the car.

"Scream all you want," I growl, leaning over her, my mouth close to her ear. "No one's gonna hear you, sweetheart. Not out here." The scream that tore from her lips was satisfying, but it's her silence now, her stunned, breathless surrender, that really does it. "Go on, scream louder for me."

I press down harder, feeling her body tense beneath me. With a chilling calm, I grip the waistband of her shorts, ripping them down with disturbing ease. The sound of fabric tearing is sharp in the air, and her body jolts in shock. I let out a dark chuckle, my hand grazing her exposed skin as I toss the scraps of clothing aside like they're nothing.

"You fucking prick!" she spits, her breath ragged as she tries to push back against the fear tightening in her chest.

"That's not very polite, princess." I reply coolly, my voice dripping with dark amusement. "You should know by now that I'm not one to tolerate disrespect."

I look down at her, my gaze sweeping over her drenched, vulnerable form. The rain cascades relentlessly, soaking her to the bone, each drop clinging to her curves and tracing a path down her body. Her hair, once perfectly styled, now falls in wet, tangled curls, sticking to her back and shoulders. The rain trickles down from her body, streaking down the car bonnet. Her skin glistens under the downpour, each droplet accentuating the curve of her spine and the swell of her hips. The car bonnet beneath her is slick with rain, making her every movement a slippery, tantalising sight.

I spread her legs apart, the wet fabric of her clothing now discarded on the ground, leaving her exposed to the elements and to me. I position myself at the entrance of her pussy. Leaning in close, my voice drops to a low, sinister murmur, meant only for her ears.

"Any last words?" I ask, my breath warm against her cold skin.

"Fuck you." She whispers.

With that, I begin to ravage her.

I thrust into her forcefully. Her tight cunt stretching around my length. Her body tenses and she lets out a strangled gasp, her fingers scrabbling for purchase on the slick metal of the car hood. I give her no time to adjust, setting a punishing pace as I slam into her again and again. The rain lashes down around us, each droplet stinging against my skin as I drive into her mercilessly. I can feel her resistance, her muscles clenching around me as if trying to push me out. But I'm unyielding, my pace brutal and unforgiving. The car rocks beneath us, creaking in protest with each forceful thrust.

Her screams pierce through the night air, mingling with the storm, a haunting symphony of pain and surrender. My hands roam with a dark satisfaction, feeling her shudder with every powerful movement before I pin her face against the car with a bruising force.

"Try to run now, princess." I taunt. I let a stream of spit fall onto her back, the warmth mingling with the rain. The act is intentional, meant to further degrade and break her down.

I drive deep, each thrust calculated, slow, a haunting rhythm in the night. I'm relentless, carving my path with a measured intensity. Her gasps, raw and fragmented, dance in the dark. The downpour slicks her skin, a translucent sheen that glistens under the dim moonlight, each droplet cascading down her spine like a cruel, mocking caress.

"Keep struggling if you want," I taunt softly. "It'll give me a reason to push harder." My hands grip her with an almost reverent force, fingers digging into her flesh as if to imprint my mark, to brand her with my presence.

Leaning in close, I murmur in a low, menacing tone,

"How's this feel, princess? You like that?" I pull back slightly, teasing her before plunging back in with a fierce, almost cruel intensity. I grab a fistful of her hair and pull her head back, her back arching uncomfortably.

"Think you're ready to be full of my come? Are you going to beg for it like a good little girl?" I smack her hard, the sound sharp and biting against the roar of the rain. Her head jerks with the impact, and I yank roughly on her hair, pulling her back against me. "Come on, baby," I growl, my voice thick with dark satisfaction. "Let me hear you say it." Her voice comes out in a desperate plea, barely audible over the storm.

"Please, Noah. *Oh God*, please." She manages to utter, her voice trembling with vulnerability and need. I lean in closer, my voice a dark murmur in her ear.

"Yes, atta girl," I rasp, my tone laden with malicious approval. "I am your fucking God."

With a fierce, almost savage delight, I slam into her again, my movements now frantic and wild. I press deeper, pushing through her, feeling the intense heat and tightness around me. As I reach the deepest point, I stay there, unloading inside her pretty cunt. Her body quivers uncontrollably, her screams slicing through my eardrums.

"*Fuck*, princess." I moan as I throb inside her, my body pulsing with intense release. Each spasm is a testament to the raw, consuming pleasure that grips me.

After emptying myself deep inside her, I pull out and immediately yank her up from the car hood. I crush against her, my hands grabbing her face, holding it with a desperate, hungry intensity; as if she's my last tether to sanity. Our lips meet in a fierce, passionate kiss. The kiss is a savage reckoning, a collision of need and possession. The rain continues to pour, relentless, drowning us. Our breaths mix, heavy and laboured.
I'm in love.
I'm so in love it hurts.

I'm terrified.

I pull back, my breath coming hard and heavy. I grip her face, forcing her to look at me.

"I claimed you, Farmer. You fucking belong to me. Understand?" I rasp.

She nods, gently.

"And I'm fucking in love with you." I growl, my voice rough and unrelenting. Her eyes widen, the fierce light in them matching the storm's fury.

"I love you too," she breathes, her voice trembling yet sure. Her smile is sharp; hitting me like a punch to the gut. My own smile is jagged, a blend of triumph and disbelief. I've been holding my breath for so long, finally exhaling. It's like peeling away layers of steel and ice to find a beating heart. A recognition of the fact that, despite all my attempts to stay detached,

I've let someone in.

I can't help it. A low, genuine laugh escapes me. Skylar's laugh follows, a light, infectious giggle that makes the ambience between us feel lighter, more open. They mingle. And then, she says the most Skylar Farmer thing she could possibly say.

"So.." she starts. "Round two?"

CHAPTER 26:
BLOOD

Marcus

11:27p.m. The storm outside mirrors the tension I've been feeling all day. Thunder rumbles in the distance, and the rain's been relentless, drenching everything in sight. I need to talk to Dean, and I know exactly where to find him. I always do.

I don't even have to think about it. The moment I heard the rain slamming against the windows, heavy and relentless, I knew exactly where he'd go. Dean has always loved storms. While most people run inside, he thrives in them. There's something about the chaos, the unpredictability of it all; he always says it makes him feel alive. So when I hear the downpour, I already know

I'll find him outside, under some half-assed shelter, using the storm as an excuse to light up a blunt and disappear into his own head.

I throw on a plain, black hoodie and head for the front door. The mansion feels empty as I move through it, the sound of the rain drowning out any noise inside. But I can feel the tension hanging in the air, thick and heavy like the storm itself. Everyone's on edge, and I know Dean's no different. He's been avoiding me, avoiding all of us, sinking deeper into the dark place he's been living in lately.

The moment I step outside, cold raindrops pelt my skin, but I barely register it. Dean's right where I knew he'd be, huddled on the front step, blunt pinched between his fingers, smoke curling up into the dark air. His hood's pulled low over his face, but I can still see his eyes, sharp and distant, staring out at the storm like it's got answers.

He looks up when I walk out, our eyes catching for the briefest second. Then, just as quickly, he looks away, taking a long, slow drag like he didn't see me at all. He doesn't say anything. Neither do I. I sit down next to him, the step cold and slick beneath me, the rain coming down so hard it's bouncing off the concrete. The space between us is thick; years of knowing each other too well, of seeing too much, and yet probably not saying enough.

I pull a pack of papers and some weed from my pocket, the familiar motions grounding me as I start to roll my own blunt. The sound of the rain hitting the porch blends with the subtle crinkle of paper in my hands, a rhythm I've known for years. It's easy, automatic, something to do with my hands. He doesn't look at me, still lost in the storm, his own blunt burning down to a slow ember. I lick the paper, seal the blunt with precision, and spark it up. The flame catches instantly, glowing bright for a second before it dulls into a slow burn. I inhale deeply, the smoke filling my lungs, harsh but welcome.

I glance at Dean out of the corner of my eye. His face is set, jaw clenched, staring straight ahead like if he stares hard enough, something out there in the rain might fix what's broken. The silence stretches out, thick and unbroken, but somehow there's no edge to it, no awkwardness. It's like we've settled into a space where words aren't needed.

I break the silence, my voice rough from the chill and the smoke.

"I'm sorry, man," I say, the words feeling heavy as they leave my mouth. The sound of the rain almost swallows them, but I know he heard. He doesn't respond. His eyes stay locked on the storm, his profile unmoving. I let out a slow breath, the smoke curling lazily around me. "I didn't mean to get so angry with you," I continue, trying to keep my voice steady. "I'm just scared."

Dean's silence is heavy, but it's not hostile.

"I'm scared too," he says, his tone raw. "Terrified, actually." He pauses, his shoulders tightening as he clears his throat, a gesture that seems to strain against the dam of emotion he's fighting to control. "You were trying to help and I-" he pauses, the words coming out in a low murmur, almost swallowed by the storm. He clenches his jaw, as if to keep his emotions from spilling over. His gaze remains fixed ahead, not meeting mine.

I watch him struggle with his words, my own breath hanging heavy in the air.

"It's okay," I say, my voice soft. Dean finally turns to face me, his eyes glistening with a mix of rain and unspoken emotion.

"I just wanted to avoid it altogether, you know?" he says, his voice carrying a tremor of regret. "Pretend it wasn't real."

He looks down, the weight of his words settling between us.

"But you were right. I should've accepted your help. If not for me, then for Delilah." He drags his hand

303

across his face, as if trying to wipe away the heavy truth. The lines on his face deepen. The blunt between his fingers is almost forgotten, the smoke curling aimlessly in the air. The silence stretches for a beat longer, until I can't fight the urge to ask him the question on my mind any longer.

"Did you mean what you said?" I ask, my voice barely above a whisper. The question hangs in the air, loaded with the gravity of our shared pain. "About not wanting to live this long?" Dean's jaw tightens, a muscle in his cheek twitching. He looks away, struggling with the turmoil in his mind. The weight of his words is too much for him to bear alone. His hand clenches the blunt so tightly I can see the strain in his knuckles.

"I don't know," he says finally, but the way he says it, I can tell there's more tangled in those words than he's letting on. "I've been through hell, bro. I'm fucking tired. I thought I'd be gone by now, you know? I figured if someone hadn't taken me out by now, the drugs surely would've." He looks up at me, his gaze weary and haunted.

"I didn't think I'd have anything worth fighting for," he says, his voice rough but tinged with a strange clarity. "I figured, why bother? Nothing mattered much. But now," he pauses, looking deep into my eyes with an earnest intensity; raw and unguarded. "Now I've got

Delilah, and I've got you. And I uh.. I'm realising that having nothing to lose was a lot easier than having everything to lose. But now you have Noah and I-"

"Dean." I take a deep breath, the cold air sharp against my lungs as I cut him off.

"You'll never lose me, man. Just like I'm never gonna lose you." I'm watching him, my eyes starting to burn. My voice shakes a little as I continue. "We might not share blood, but our lives have bled into each other. We're carved into each other's flesh." My throat tightens, and I blink rapidly, trying to hold back the tears. "Our bond is stitched into the very marrow of who we are. Not even death can erase this. If we lose each other in this lifetime, I'll find you in another." A single tear escapes, rolling down my cheek, as I finish with a raw, trembling voice. "And I'll still annoy the fuck out of you."

Dean lets out a shaky laugh, and it's like a sudden crack in the dam. Tears cut paths down our faces, mixing with the rain, forming rivulets of our shared pain. It's a messy, beautiful collision of the storm and our sorrow, as if the universe itself is weeping and laughing with us. Our laughter is an uneven cadence, punctuated by the tremors of our breath and the raw honesty of the moment. I see his eyes, those deep pools of emotion, glistening with a vulnerability that lays everything bare.

He wipes his face with a grimy sleeve, attempting to regain a semblance of composure. Through his tears, he smirks, a bittersweet glint in his eyes.

"*Fuck*, bro. Look at us," he says, his voice thick with emotion yet trying to carry a hint of his old defiant humour. "A couple of pussies, crying in the fucking rain." I chuckle through my tears, shaking my head.

"Yeah, who woulda thought," I reply, my voice rough but steady. He takes a puff of his joint, looking up at the sky.

"You know," he begins, his voice cracking slightly, "for the longest time, I really felt like the world owed me something. I used to think if I held on long enough, if I fought hard enough, it'd all pay off. Like, someday, the universe would hand me some kind of fucking trophy for just surviving." He lets out a thoughtful, almost rueful laugh. "But the stupid part is, my trophies were already on the shelf."

He shakes his head, another chuckle escaping him even through the tears. "Delilah, you, everyone who's stuck around. I was so busy looking for some grand prize that meant fuck all, that I missed what was standing right in front of me." He says. I let the words settle between us, my voice soft but filled with sincerity.

"I love you, bro." I tell him, "you'll always be my family."

His eyes glimmer with something close to relief as he smiles, a simple,

"I know" slipping from his lips. With a shared glance, we tap the ends of our blunts together; a silent toast to our brotherhood. The quiet gesture feeling like a promise.

There's no one like Dean. He's the brother fate forgot to name but the universe delivered anyway.

And I'm gonna save him.

CHAPTER 27:
SURPRISE!

Noah

We're trampling through the woods, branches snapping under our feet; the usual banter bouncing between the group. It's normal. There's a buzz of curiosity hanging between them; they're all wondering what the fuck I've dragged them out here for. Except for Dean. He hasn't looked me in the eye once, and I don't blame him.

The way he shoved Skylar, her body hitting the floor like she was nothing. My blood boiled the second it happened. It took every ounce of control not to put a bullet in his skull right there and then. I fired that shot as close as I could, I wanted him to feel it. To let him know what I could've done. I wanted to see him flinch.

Killing him then would've been the easiest thing I've ever done. But easy wasn't what he deserved.

And now, I've got a surprise up my sleeve.

We're getting closer to the tunnel now. I can feel it. The trees are thinning out, and the air's shifting, getting cooler as we near the entrance. Every step brings us closer, and my pulse picks up. I'm trying to keep my face neutral, but there's this buzz under my skin, this electric hum that only gets louder the closer we get. The tunnel's just a few yards away, the mouth of it dark and yawning, like it's been waiting for us. I stop short, turning to face them.

"Alright," I say, holding up a hand. "Everybody close your eyes." Skylar's the first to speak, her voice tinged with suspicion.

"Noah, what's going on-"

"Shh," I cut her off, giving her a look that tells her to trust me. "Eyes closed." They hesitate, but one by one, they close or cover their eyes. Dean, well, he's still not looking at me, but he closes his eyes too, his jaw tight, hands shoved into his pockets like he's bracing himself. "Keep 'em closed," I say, walking backward toward the tunnel, guiding them.

"I'll cut to the chase," I begin, "I couldn't help but notice that Miss Sienna has been sporting a new little ring on her finger." I say, letting a hint of satisfaction creep into my voice. I've always had a sharp eye for detail, and I spotted the ring immediately. It was the sort of thing that didn't escape me; subtle changes, small shifts. It's in my nature to notice these things.

The reaction is almost instantaneous. Skylar's eyebrows knit together in confusion, followed by a sharp,

"What?" Her voice carries an undertone of curiosity mixed with surprise. Birdie's soft,

"Wait, what?" follows, and the excitement is palpable even through their muffled responses. Sienna's face flushes with a mix of embarrassment and excitement.

"Oh my God, Noah," she protests. Marcus, predictably, has a proud smirk on his face. I let the anticipation build, savouring the way the atmosphere is thick with expectation.

"So," I say, the corners of my mouth lifting slightly, "to mark this occasion, I've got a little surprise." A genuine yet menacing grin stretches across my face as I watch them. "On the count of three," I say, my voice smooth but carrying a dark undertone. "Open your eyes."

Here we go.

"One.." I draw out, letting the word hang in the dense, expectant silence. "Two.." I let the pause linger.

"Three."

When they open their eyes, the silence that follows is heavy, weighted with disbelief. The tunnel, once marked by years of Dean's graffiti, has been transformed into something completely unrecognisable. It's beautiful. Dominating the wall, stretching across one side of the concrete, I've painted a massive mural; Butter, Sienna's pet butterfly, rendered in painstaking, vivid detail. Her bright yellow wings painted with an almost ethereal glow, so vivid they seem to flutter against the background.

She soars through the air, delicately carrying two intertwined wedding rings. The whole piece radiates a sense of beauty, almost innocence. It's deceptively sweet.

But sweet, it's anything but.

I watch as the reactions unfold. Sienna is first, of course; her eyes widen with pure astonishment, her hands covering her mouth as a breathy,

"Oh my God.." escapes her. She steps closer, her voice catching. "Noah! This is beautiful. It's Butter."

"Yeah," I say, my voice smooth, almost casual, watching her eyes light up. "Thought she deserved some attention."

Her eyes are wet now, clearly touched by the gesture. She doesn't know. She doesn't know that this wasn't just for her.

Dean knows.

I can feel the heat coming off him. His eyes are locked on the mural, and I can see the recognition hit; this was *his* tunnel. His canvas. Years of his own work, his art, layered in spray paint across that wall, and now? Gone. Erased. His years of expression, pride, and escape wiped clean beneath a yellow butterfly. And I did it with precision. I see it; how his chest rises with a sharp breath, how his teeth clench. But he holds it in. He's good at that.

Skylar steps closer to the mural, brushing her fingers lightly over the painted surface.

"It's amazing," she whispers. "Butter looks so real!"

"Thank you, princess." I reply. Delilah stands a few feet away from Dean, her eyes lingering on him, filled with concern. She knows him better than anyone, knows exactly what's boiling beneath his silent exterior. Her hand hovers near his arm, like she wants to comfort him but isn't sure it's the right time. She's waiting for him to crack, to say something.

But Dean just stands there, stiff, his gaze locked on the mural like it's mocking him. Delilah bites her lip, her brow furrowing with worry. Marcus steps up to Dean, clapping a hand on his shoulder in what's meant to be a comforting gesture.

"You okay, bro?" His voice is casual, but there's an edge to it, a knowing look in his eyes as he peers at Dean. Marcus can sense the tension too, even if he doesn't fully understand the layers underneath it.

Dean doesn't answer. He just nods, barely a movement, more like a twitch. His jaw is tight, and he keeps his hands shoved deep in his pockets. His eyes never leave the butterfly, never leave the rings that dangle beneath it like an insult, a claim to something sacred. Marcus looks between us for a moment longer, clearly confused, before he steps over to me. Closer now, his voice dropping as he leans in, speaking low enough for only me to hear.

"It looks great, man. Really. Thank you." I flash him a small smile; just enough to keep him satisfied.

"No problem," I say, my voice cool and collected. "Sienna deserved something special."

And that part's true. I'm not lying. Sienna does deserve something special, something that shows I care. She's been through hell, and even if she despises me, which she should, I want her to have this. It's *her* butterfly, *her* symbol, something light and beautiful amidst all the darkness.

313

I'm killing two birds with one stone. Sienna gets her sweet gesture, something that'll make her smile, something light and beautiful in a world that's anything but. And Dean? Dean gets his punishment, handed to him in broad daylight, with everyone thinking I did it out of the goodness of my heart. I get to watch him burn, and no one's the wiser.

The sun is dipping low, casting a golden glow that's just warm enough to be comfortable but with a chill starting to creep in. The group is animated, the girls chattering excitedly about Sienna's engagement, their laughter ringing through the clearing. It's a pleasant scene for once. Dean is sitting alone on one of the logs, his posture slouched, his hood up. He's a shadow on the edge of the celebration, and I can see the tension radiating off him. He's clearly trying to distance himself from the group, the cheerfulness of the moment seemingly just out of reach for him.

I watch him for a moment, letting the silence stretch between us. The sounds of laughter and conversation filter through, almost mockingly, as I push off from where I was standing and make my way over to him. My boots crunch softly on the underbrush, breaking the silence just enough to announce my approach.

I sit down next to him on the log, keeping my distance but close enough to make my presence known. The warmth from the fire does nothing to touch the cold, deliberate edge in the air between us. Dean doesn't look at me, his gaze fixed somewhere beyond the trees. His shoulders are tight, and I can see the way his hands are clenched into fists.

Dean's gaze stays fixed ahead. To my surprise, he speaks first, his voice barely above a whisper.

"So, is this your way of apologising to Sienna?" He asks. Brave, but not very smart. I let a thin, almost imperceptible smile curl my lips. I let out a slow breath, my voice steady and cold.

"This is me letting you know I'm still on your fucking back, Douglas. Especially now," I start, "You fucked with my girl and I don't take that lightly."

"I never meant to shove her like that. It was wrong." He admits immediately. Too little too late.

"I should've fucking killed you."

"I agree, I'm sorry." he murmurs. "If anybody pushed Delilah like that, I'd have killed them too."

Dean finally turns his head, his eyes locking onto mine. The air between us thickens, tension rising with every second of silence. His jaw clenches as if he's weighing his next words carefully, knowing anything he says could push me further. He's saying all the right things, so far. But unfortunately, I don't give a fuck.

"You think a quick apology means shit to me?" I ask with a laugh.

"Then what do you want?" he asks. His lip curls slightly, a flicker of anger, but he keeps his voice level controlled. "You just waiting for me to fuck up again?"

"That's exactly what I'm doing." I nod, not bothering to hide the cold truth in my eyes.

For a moment, neither of us says anything, the silence thick and heavy, like the calm before a storm. Dean shifts on the log, and I can see the decision form in his mind before he even speaks.

"Well, you don't have to worry." He says quietly, his voice carrying a finality that catches me off guard. "I'm off." I raise an eyebrow.

"Off?" I repeat. He stands up slowly, brushing the dirt off his hands; his eyes drift back to the tunnel, then to the group laughing around the fire. His jaw tightens, and he looks back at me, a grim sort of resignation in his eyes.

"Yeah, I'm leaving. Going home." For a second, I'm thrown. He's really leaving? I didn't think it would be this easy. My surprise fades quickly though, replaced by a cold satisfaction. Maybe I've actually gotten rid of him.

"Smart move, Douglas." I say, my voice cold. "But don't think for a second that this means you're off my radar," I continue, standing up, lowering my voice. "I'll still be watching,"

"I figured as much," he says, voice steady. He gives me one last look before turning away, walking toward the edge of the clearing. I watch him go, my eyes narrowing as he disappears into the trees.

As Dean trudges off, I can't help but feel a flicker of confusion beneath the surface. I mean, don't get me wrong, I'm over the fucking moon. He's leaving. That's what I wanted. But still, this? This was all it took? The tunnel was nothing compared to what I should've done to him, and yet here he is, walking away like some wounded animal, tail tucked between his legs.

I expected more from him. I expected a fight, some kind of pushback, something that made this feel like it was worth the effort. Instead, he's going home in a sulk, like a kid who just lost a playground scrap. It's almost.. anticlimactic. Well, whatever the reason for his sudden retreat, it doesn't matter.

Mission accomplished.
Dean's gone.

Well, that was easier than expected.

CHAPTER 28:

BARBED WORDS

Dean

I've had enough of Noah's place. The hours here are dragging by like I'm in some kind of purgatory. I've spent the last couple of hours with Delilah, who decided she wants to spend one more night here with Birdie. For her, this whole mess has been like one big sleepover. I get it, she's trying to stay positive, trying to hold onto whatever normalcy she can find. But I can't do it. Not anymore.

I grab my stuff, shoving everything into my duffel bag, and head out. The stairs creak beneath me as I head down; every step feels heavier than the last, like the air in this house is weighing me down. When I reach the front door, I drop my bag beside me and bend down to pull on my shoes; the soles worn and the laces fraying. I'm halfway through tying the second shoe when I sense movement behind me.

"Where are you going?" Her voice catches me off guard, but I don't let it show. I finish tying the knot, then stand up, dusting off my jeans. I take a slow breath, steeling myself as I turn to face her. She's standing in the doorway to the kitchen, arms crossed, looking at me like I'm some kind of alien.

"Home, Skylar." I say, flat and final; the word *'home'* feeling strangely foreign on my tongue. I had almost forgotten my shitty little flat had even existed.

"Now?"

"Yeah." I reply, keeping my gaze fixed on the floor, trying to muster the energy for another conversation.

"Does Delilah know?"

"Yeah, she knows," I say, my tone clipped. I'm not in the mood for small talk. "Where's Marcus?"

"Why are you leaving?" She asks, ignoring me completely.

"I just wanna leave, Skylar. Where's Marcus?" I press, trying to keep my frustration in check.

"He went over to his mum's new place. Now you answer *my* question. Why are you leaving?" She repeats, her eyes narrowing.

I let out a long sigh, running a hand through my hair, feeling the messy strands beneath my fingers.

"I can't be here, Sky. I can't deal with all of this right now."

"*Ahh*, so you're running away?" She mocks. I'm feeling the weight of her words. She has a right to be annoyed at me. I know I should probably be apologising after shoving her, but my frustration and need to escape are overpowering me.

"Look, Marcus is gonna start working on the book again. He'll text me any updates." I explain, my voice a low murmur, every syllable laced with resignation. "Until then, I need to be alone, okay?"

"What's your problem with Noah?" She asks, her voice laced with challenge. I huff, feeling my irritation spike even more. Of course she's bringing him up.

"I'm not getting into this," I state, attempting to deflect.

"Why not?"

"I said I don't wanna talk about it, alright? Can you stop fucking grilling me?" I say, my voice harsher than I intended. Skylar's tone hardens, the weight of her frustration matching mine.

"You can't keep giving all of us the silent treatment," she counters. "Clearly Noah's winding you up."

"Why do you even care?" I snap back, anger pulsing through me like a live wire. I can feel my temper fraying at the edges, but I'm too wrapped up in my own chaos to care enough to rein it in. All I want is to get out of here. Away from her questions, away from everything. She glares at me, her eyes darkening as she takes a step closer, refusing to let this go.

"I care because you, of all people, should be happy for me," she says. It catches me off guard. I feel my breath catch in my chest, like an unseen hand squeezing my heart.

"What do you mean?" My reply comes out quieter than I wanted, a threadbare whisper that betrays just how cornered I feel.

"You told me I deserved to find someone," she presses, her voice tight with emotion, her eyes searching mine for something I can't give her right now. She's right, I did tell her that.

I swallow hard, trying to keep my voice level, but all I manage is a rough,

"I don't know what you want me to say."

"Something.. anything," she pleads, desperation lacing her voice like an urgent melody. I can feel the intensity of her gaze bearing down on me. My chest tightens, and I'm seconds away from just walking out without another word, but the frustration spills over.

"I just don't like him, Sky," I finally say, my voice flat. "It's as simple as that." She scoffs, shaking her head in disbelief. Skylar's voice rises, her words tumbling out in a rush.

"You told me I should find someone who doesn't care about my past, who likes me the way I am.. Someone who's a good guy-" I bite down, hard. My jaw tightens, and before I can stop myself, the words spill out, sharp and biting.

"He's not a good guy!" I yell, my voice reverberating. Her eyes flare with emotion, a wildfire of hurt and defiance igniting within them. She snaps back immediately, the vulnerability in her voice cracking like fragile glass.

"He's good to *me*!"

Her eyes are wide, brimming with tears, and for a second, I just freeze. I stare into her eyes, unable to move, unable to speak. My chest tightens. I'm dying to explain everything, but I know she's too far in. She's in love. Deeply. She wipes at her face, frustration building as her voice cracks.

"He doesn't make me cry, Dean. He makes me feel like I'm enough." She continues, her voice rising slightly with the intensity of her emotions. "Noah is the first person who's *ever* looked at me and didn't just see some broken girl from an orphanage. He doesn't treat me like I'm damaged goods, like someone too messed up to ever be loved properly."

Her eyes fill with tears again, and she doesn't bother wiping them this time.

"You have no idea what it's like, Dean. Every guy I've ever been with, they either pity me or try to 'fix' me. Nobody wants anything fucking real with me. Like I've got too much trauma to be worth any actual effort."

Her voice cracks, and I feel like someone's twisting a knife in my gut. She's never been this vulnerable, not with me, not with anyone. I can't look away from her, but I still can't bring myself to say anything. Her words hit me hard, and guilt seeps in deeper, because I know she's right. She deserves to feel the way Noah makes her feel. I should be glad for her. I should be happy she's finally found someone who sees her for more than her scars, more than her trauma.

But I know Noah. I know the kind of man he is, the things he's capable of.

"I don't understand why you can't be happy for me. Why can't you just let me have this?"

"Skylar, I really have to go," I mutter, my voice low and strained as I turn towards the door. I can't stay here, not with her looking at me like that.

"Fine. Go." Her words tremble, but there's something sharp in her tone, something bitter. "It's easier for you, right? To walk away."

"Because there's shit you don't know, Sky!" I snap, the raw edge to my voice catching her off guard.

"Then fucking tell me!"

323

And then I feel it; this terrible guilt creeping up on me, twisting everything in my chest. My throat tightens, and I can't keep it in any longer. I'm breaking right in front of her, the pressure too much, the weight unbearable.

"I've seen the way he looks at Sienna, okay?!" I blurt out, my voice shaking with emotion. My chest heaves with the lie, the guilt immediately eating at me. I see Skylar's face crumble, her eyes widening as if I've just torn her heart in two. Which I have. Yet I keep going. "He fancies her, alright? He flirts with her all the time. It's fucking obvious."

It's a lie. It's all a lie.
But I can't tell Skylar the real reason.
It's not my story to tell.

If Noah was involved in Sienna's abduction as I suspect, then Sienna is the only one who deserves to share that. So I let this lie, this twisted half-truth, fall between us, hoping it'll keep her safe. Hoping it'll be enough to push her away from him. The silence is deafening, her lips trembling as she tries to process what I've just said.

"What?" she whispers, barely audible. I can't bring myself to say anything else. I'm already too far gone, choking on the regret, watching her fall apart. It's killing her. And I'm the one who's doing it. "Are you sure?" She asks, almost begging me to change my story.

Her tears spill over, and I feel something in me crumble at the sight.

"Sky, I'm sorry." I say. My voice is hoarse, almost pleading. She's searching for something, anything to hold onto. But I've just ripped it all away. Her sobs fill the room, quiet but sharp, like they're stabbing into me with every breath she takes. "I have to go." The words barely make it out of my throat, low and broken.

I turn away, moving toward the door, my shoes scuffing against the wooden floor. Each step feels like I'm dragging a lead weight behind me. As I reach for the handle, Sienna's voice suddenly echoes from upstairs.

"Butter!" The shout reverberates off the walls, and in an instant, the familiar fluttering of wings fills the air. Butter zooms down the staircase, her vibrant yellow wings catching the light peaking through from the kitchen. She begins to flutter around the door handle. My heart sinks. The last time she appeared like this, it was chaos; a moment that nearly cost me everything.

"Please," I mutter, freezing mid-motion. The instinct to flee wrestles with the memory of Butter's chaotic energy, and I tug the handle. In a flurry of frantic movement, Butter begins to batter herself against the door, her tiny frame colliding with the sturdy wood. I wrench the door open wider, and Butter is knocked back momentarily, but she doesn't give up. I make it out of the door and she hurls herself right in front of me, her wings beating wildly a blur of colour and fervour. With relentless zeal, she thumps against my chest again and again, as if trying to force me back into the house.

"What the fuck are you doing?" I growl, my frustration spiking again. She keeps at it, relentless, and I grab her, holding her tiny body in my hands.

For a moment, I just stare at her.

Thoughts whirl chaotically in my mind, a turbulent storm of emotions that refuses to settle. There's an overwhelming weight of expectations, but at the core, it's a void; an aching emptiness that clings to me like a shadow. I know I should feel something profound at this moment, a surge of longing or perhaps regret, but instead, I'm met with silence; a dissonant echo of feelings that should be there but aren't.

I slowly release my grip, letting her slip from my fingers, like a feather drifting back into the confines of the house. Butter flutters backward, confused, but I don't turn.

I walk away.

CHAPTER 29:

BEYOND SALVATION

Noah

I pull into the driveway just after eleven, rain pouring down in relentless sheets; the sound of it drums against the roof of my car. The window wipers struggle to keep pace, smearing the world outside into a blurred canvas. I had a few jobs to wrap up; deals to finalise and a couple of threats to manage. The headlights cut through the darkness, illuminating the slick gravel, where puddles shimmer like scattered silver coins under the faint glow.

As I step out, the chill in the air seeps through my clothes, wrapping around me like a damp shroud. I make my way to the front door, each footfall muffled by the rain-soaked ground. There's a lightness in my chest tonight, knowing Dean isn't here. I head straight to Skylar's room.

I knock on her door, the sound nearly drowned by the storm outside. No answer. I knock again, louder this time, my knuckles rapping against the wood. Silence hangs heavy. So I go in. Inside, the dim light casts long shadows. There she is, sitting on the bed, her back to me, engrossed in her phone. The glow of the screen illuminates her silhouette, but she doesn't turn to acknowledge me. I take a step forward.

"Before you shout at me, I knocked twice," I say, trying to keep my tone firm yet playful, ready to disarm her usual sassy retorts.

Still, she doesn't move. Something feels off. I reach the side of the bed, and she's still glued to her phone, her fingers scrolling with focused determination. Confusion prickles at the back of my mind, but I suppose it's typical for her to pull this kind of silent treatment.

"Farmer," I say. No reaction. I bend down, fingers sliding under her chin, forcing her to look at me. Her eyes finally meet mine, but they're distant; hollow. A cold, unsettling emptiness that gnaws at me in a way I can't ignore. "What's going on?" I ask, the lightness in my voice fading, replaced by a thread of concern. She swats my hand away, the defiance in her voice sharp.

"Don't touch me."

What the fuck?

I step closer, trying to bridge the gap between us.

"Who do you think you're talking to?" I ask, forcing a smirk, hoping to lighten the moment. But instead, she whips her head around to glare at me, and the intensity in her eyes makes my chest tighten.

"You!" she spits, her voice brittle, cracking like something shattered beyond repair. The hurt is so thick it clings to every syllable, and I see the glimmer of unshed tears pooling in her eyes. My heart sinks as I realise this isn't just a passing annoyance; she's genuinely upset.

I take a step back, my playfulness evaporating into thin air.

"What's wrong?" I push gently, my voice low and steady, hoping to draw her out. Skylar doesn't reply, her silence heavy in the air. I narrow my eyes. "What have I done?" I ask, my voice low and incredulous.

She finally looks at me, eyes clouded with confusion and raw hurt.

"Leave me alone. You're a fucking liar." She swallows hard, and I can see the fight in her fading. Her words slam into me, and I blink, caught completely off guard.

"What?"

Skylar pushes off the bed, pacing like she's trying to outrun the mess between us. Her body's shaking, fury rolling off her in waves, but I'm left standing here, clueless; no idea what the hell I did. She won't even look at me, like the very sight of me turns her stomach.

"Sky, what the fuck are you talking about?"

"You're just like everyone else! You pretend you care, pretend you're different, but you're fucking not." A cold feeling settles in my gut.

"Of course I fucking care." I say.

She keeps pacing, her steps frantic, like she's trying to burn off the anger, but the storm in her eyes just keeps getting worse.

"Bullshit." Her voice cracks, betraying the real pain underneath the rage. I step toward her, but she whirls around, throwing up her hands again as if to block me out.

"I haven't lied about anything."

"You think I don't know what's going on? You think I'm fucking stupid?" My head's spinning. I rack my brain, trying to piece together what's gotten her so worked up. But nothing makes sense.

"Sky, I don't know what you think I've done, but I haven't lied to you."

She stops, her lip quivering, biting it down like she's struggling to hold back a flood. I can see her walls crumbling, the tears she's so desperately trying not to let fall. Her fists are clenched at her sides, shaking with the effort of keeping it all together. And then, finally, her voice breaks, barely above a whisper, but filled with the kind of pain that cuts straight through me.

"You've been flirting with Sienna."

The words hit like a sledgehammer, and I just stand there, frozen. For a second, I'm too stunned to even react. But as fast as the shock hits, it's gone, replaced with a searing rage that almost knocks the wind out of me. Dean fucking Douglas.

"Dean told you that, didn't he?" My voice is tight, but the anger simmers just beneath the surface. I'm barely holding it back. She doesn't speak, but she nods, her lips pressed together. She wipes at her eyes like it's taking everything not to fall apart in front of me. But I already know. It's written all over her face.

She looks destroyed.
And that rips me apart.

"Farmer, listen to me." I say, stepping toward her slowly, like I'm trying not to spook her.
"There's nothing to say."
"He's lying to you." My voice is low, strained. The anger boiling inside me is begging to be let out, but not now. Not with her. I swallow it down, keeping it in

331

check, because right now, she's breaking in front of me, and she needs to be reassured. The rage can wait.

She laughs, sharp and bitter, and it tears at me more than I'd ever admit.

"Why the fuck would he lie, Noah?" She asks. I step closer, keeping my voice steady, calm, like I'm trying to soothe a cornered animal.

"Because I know some shit he doesn't want getting out." I tell her, genuinely. I watch her carefully, and I can see the shift in her demeanour almost in an instant. That harsh, defensive edge softens, just slightly, and there's something in her eyes, like a hint of belief. Or maybe it's just that she wants to believe me. Would prefer to believe me.

I can work with that.

She shakes her head, her confusion clear as she whispers,

"I don't believe you." I watch as a single tear finally slips free, tracing a path down her flushed cheek, and for a second, everything else fades. That tear hits harder than any bullet, harder than anything I've felt before.

"Look at me." My fingers twitch, wanting to wipe that tear away, but I hold back. "Now." Her lips part, the confusion still clouding her eyes as she stares at me, searching for something to hold onto.

"Dean's been keeping a secret for a long time," I say, voice steady, low, because I know she'll hear every word. "He knows I know, and he's scared." Her eyes widen a little, the disbelief softening around the edges. I can see her mind working, trying to process it, to fit the pieces together; but it's not enough. She's not fully convinced. I see that flicker of doubt, that hesitation in her eyes. She wants to believe me. I just need to push a little harder.

"But why would he lie? Why would he ever want to hurt me like that?" She chops in. Her voice trembles, her brows furrowing as she tries to make sense of it all. Her eyes search mine, desperate for answers.

"Because he doesn't want me around, Farmer." I say slowly, forcing the calm in my voice despite the fire threatening to break loose. "I know too much. I'm too big of a threat to him."

Her breath hitches, a spark of hope flickering in her eyes for a second, like maybe, just maybe, this could be true. She's clinging to it, desperate to believe me, and I see the crack in her defences, the way her lips part as if she's about to speak; but she doesn't. Instead, her face crumples, and she shakes her head, trying to reject what I'm telling her, like she's terrified of trusting it. But then, Skylar freezes, her eyes narrowing slightly as if her mind is piecing together something monumental. I can practically see her brain ticking, the gears turning slowly.

"Never have I ever kept a secret that could've changed everything." She mumbles. I can't help it; my smile is small, but it's genuine. That's my smart girl.

"Yes, princess," I say softly, the words coming out low, calm, and steady. "You got it." Her expression shifts, and though there's still confusion, there's also a flicker of something else; maybe clarity, maybe disbelief. It's like a veil's been lifted, and she's standing at the edge, ready to see things as they really are.

"What is he hiding?" She asks, with a shred of anger and hesitation; as if unsure of whether or not she actually wants the answer.

I pause, staring at her. The question hangs heavy in the air, and I can feel her eyes drilling into me; and for a second, I debate whether or not I should even tell her. It would put Marcus in the crossfire. But at this point.. fuck it. Fuck Dean. He made his bed. He's the one who pushed this, crossed lines he knew better than to touch.

I never would've gone here.

The silence between us stretches tight, and I can feel her anxiety building with every second that ticks by.

"Dean knew Marcus had a brother," I start, my voice low but steady. "He knew my name. He knew everything. He found my file." Skylar's eyes go wide, her whole body tensing. She looks like I just told her the world was ending.

"What? H-how do you know Dean found it?" Her voice trembles, the disbelief and shock swirling together, fighting to make sense of what I'm saying.

I stare at her, my pulse picking up, trying to keep my frustration buried for her sake.

"*Someone* had to find it, baby," I mutter. "And it sure as hell wasn't Marcus."

"But.. Oh my God.. But," she stammers, completely thrown. "That makes no sense. Why wouldn't you go back for him? For Marcus? If you knew he existed-"

"I didn't," I cut her off, sharp. I let out a breath, trying to pull it back, trying not to let my anger leak out. "I was a kid." I say, my voice steady but tinged with memory. "My father had me almost entirely convinced that Marcus was all in my head. I couldn't even leave his side to find out," I share. "By the time I was old enough to start questioning things again, Marcus had been picked up. Now, of course, I know it was my father who had him at that point." Her expression falters, her lips parting slightly as she stares at me. It's a lot. I know it is. The way she looks at me, so much confusion, pain, disbelief; I can feel it cutting me too.

"And.. Dean knew?"

"Yes. For a long time."

Skylar just stares at me, speechless. Her eyes, wide and stormy, search mine for answers I don't think she's fully ready for. Another tear falls from her eye, rolling slowly down her cheek. The room feels heavy; so heavy it's sinking into my stomach, twisting everything inside me. I take a breath, fighting back the strange ache building up inside me.

"Skylar," I start, my voice quieter than usual, rougher, the words slipping out before I can second guess them. "You think I'd ever look at someone else? Flirt with someone else?" I let out a harsh laugh, the kind that comes from somewhere deep. "I don't even fucking *see* anyone else. No one exists for me but you. You're the only thing I feel, the only thing I've ever felt." Her lips tremble, but she still doesn't speak. She doesn't have to. My voice is low, dark, like the truth clawing its way out of me.

I move closer, my eyes locked on her.

"It's not some passing obsession. You're in my blood. You're in every fucking breath I take." I reach for her, cupping her chin with more force than I probably should, but I need her to see this in my eyes. To *feel* it. She has to see what she's done to me. "It's not something I can turn off, Farmer. You own me. Every part of me. Body, mind, soul, whatever the fuck is left of it, it's all yours."

I hold her face in my hands, hard, pulling her closer so there's barely an inch of space between us. Her breath hitches, but she doesn't move, doesn't resist. I need her to hear every fucking word.

Because it's the truth.
Every single word.

I run my thumb along her jaw, softer now, but my grip stays firm.

"Do you understand?" I whisper, my voice still laced with that dark, consuming edge. "I don't just love you. I'm ruined by you." Her lips part, but no words come out, just shallow breaths. I can feel her trembling, can see the cracks forming in her walls. Good. Let them break. "You've hollowed me out. Crawled into the darkest parts of me, and now you live there. There's no way out." Her lips tremble as another tear falls, and I swipe it away with my thumb, softer now, but my eyes are still locked on hers, still burning with that obsession that she's unleashed in me.

The silence stretches between us, thick and suffocating, like the room can't hold the weight of everything unsaid. She's crying, tears slipping down her face like they're falling from somewhere deeper, somewhere even she can't reach. I watch her shatter, piece by piece, and I stand there, letting it happen.

I don't say anything. I just let it sit, let her absorb every single word, every piece of the obsession I've just laid bare. Her chest rises and falls, her breath shaky, eyes glassy with the weight of it all. I lean in, my voice low and cold.

"Do you understand?" I repeat. I'm not asking. I'm demanding. Her silence isn't enough.

She nods, shaky and fragile, like one wrong move might break her for good. Then, without warning, she throws herself into my arms. The impact of her body against mine sends a ripple through me, but I don't flinch. I hold her, feel the way she clings to me like I'm the only thing keeping her from drowning. And maybe I am.

Her sobs are soft, muffled against my chest, but I feel them. Every tremor, every jagged breath. It echoes through me, stirs something dark, something primal. This is what I wanted; to be her everything. To be the one she runs to, no matter what. The only one who can piece her back together. I tighten my arms around her, pulling her closer, feeling her pulse against mine, syncing. Becoming one.

She's mine. She's always been mine.
And now, she's sure of it too.

I hold her, just feeling the weight of her in my arms as her sobs slowly fade. Time blurs, the world outside this room disappearing into nothing. It's just us. Just her heartbeat against mine, her breath steadying as she calms. She looks up at me, something raw and quiet burning in her gaze. Her voice is barely above a whisper, but every word sinks into me.

"I should be terrified of you," she says, "but I'm not. In fact, this is the first time I've ever felt secure. The first time I'd ever trust someone else to control me. A power I never thought I'd crave." I laugh softly,

"Nobody can control you, Skylar Farmer," I say with a smile. "But I can protect you."

The words slip out, heavy with meaning. I watch her eyes flicker with understanding. It's not about control; it's about survival, about keeping her safe in a world that's anything but. I'm offering her a shield, a promise wrapped in shadows.

"I feel lost," she says suddenly, her voice shaky. "I finally found the one thing I wanted more than anything. And the person who's supposed to be my best friend would rather destroy it than face his fucking secrets."

"I'm sorry," I murmur.

"It's okay." she replies, but I see the hurt in her eyes. "And.. how could he do that to Marcus?" she mumbles, the disbelief clear in her voice. It's a rhetorical question, but one I'd also like an answer to. I look at her, the softness in her voice catching me off guard.

339

"I think I'm gonna get some sleep."

"Good idea, baby," I reply, keeping my tone steady.

I step toward the door, the tension from our conversation still crackling in the air. Just as my fingers brush the handle, her voice pulls me back.

"Noah," she calls, and I pause, turning back to face her. "Goodnight," she whispers. I'm struck by the vulnerability in her eyes. It's a mix of hope and sadness, and I can feel the weight of her unguarded heart in that single word. She looks so small, so delicate, like a candle's fragile flame flickering against the dark.

In that moment, everything sharpens into focus. My world, filled with chaos and shadows, narrows down to her. She's what I want. My life revolves around this tiny pink-haired girl standing before me, the one who makes me feel something I thought I'd lost forever.

"Let's go somewhere," I suggest, the words tumbling out before I can second-guess myself. "I have other estates. We can get away from all this shit. Just for a while." She pauses, her brow knitting as she considers the offer. Then, that smile, a radiant spark breaking through the gloom, lights up her face.

"I'd like that." She says softly, an edge of relief in her tone. A wicked grin spreads across my lips, something dark and possessive swelling within me.

"Pack a bag, princess. I'll be back."

I step out and ease the door shut behind me, the soft click resonating like a heartbeat in the heavy stillness. But the moment it closes, my smirk evaporates, leaving a tightness in my chest. My jaw clenches involuntarily, anger coiling within me like a serpent ready to strike. Concentration floods my senses, sharpening every sound, every flicker of movement in the shadows.
I have one more thing to deal with.

I stride into my bedroom, the dim light casting jagged silhouettes across the walls. My gaze sweeps the room, finally landing on two vital objects that lie on my desk. The book.. and my handgun.

I slide into the car, the door slamming shut like a declaration. Every movement is tight, precise; like a wound spring ready to snap. I crank the key, the engine roaring to life, a beast awakened. With a growl, I floor the gas; the tires screaming like a banshee wail that shatters the night, while the downpour transforms the roads into slick, shimmering ribbons.

The city unfurls before me, a sprawling maze of shadows and flickering lights. I cut through the streets at 100 mph, the world outside dissolving into a blur; just noise, just chaos. My focus is razor-sharp, every heartbeat synchronised with the thrum of the engine. I'm not driving; I'm stalking my fucking prey.

341

I cut the engine and step out into the downpour, the rain drenching me instantly. It's a cold slap against my skin, but I welcome it. My gaze fixes on the rundown block of flats ahead, a crumbling monument to despair and decay. It looms like a grave, each cracked window a hollow eye. The rain drips from the eaves, each drop echoing like a countdown in my skull, relentless. The world around me is silent, eerily still, as if holding its breath. The only sound piercing the quiet is the furious thrum of my blood in my ears.

I stride toward the entrance, the flickering light above sputtering, casting grotesque shapes on the walls. I step inside, the door groaning like a wounded beast. The air is heavy, saturated with mildew and despair. A chill snakes down my spine. The hallway stretches ahead, long and narrow, like a throat waiting to be cut. The stairs creak beneath my feet. The wood groans, whispering secrets to the silence around me. I let it speak. Let it fill the space, stretch it out. The railing brushes my fingers, cold as death. I grip it once, hard, then let go. Let it breathe. I reach the top.

Flat number 2. Faded numbers, paint peeling away, like this place forgot what it was a long time ago. I stand there, just staring at the door. Flat number 2. I trace the edges of the doorframe with my eyes. There's nothing special about it. Just another door in a rundown block of forgotten lives. Flat number 2. I whisper it under my breath, just to hear how it sounds. Just to feel it on my tongue.

I slam my fist against the door. Hard. It echoes down the empty stairwell, rattling in the silence like a warning. I take a step back, just far enough. The door creaks open. For a second, he looks normal. A split second. But then our eyes lock, and the light drains from his face, replaced by a cold, hollow emptiness. His pupils widen, reflecting nothing but black. There's a flicker of realisation, a flash of fear that he can't hide, but it's swallowed by a void. It's the look of a man who knows he's cornered, a recognition.

"Don't say I didn't fucking warn you, Douglas."

"Look, man. I can explain-"

I raise the gun.
I pull the trigger.
Then.. I close the book.

After all,
I am the trusted guard.

CHAPTER 30:

GOODBYE,
FOREVERMORE

Marcus

The shovel hits the dirt, a hollow thud. The sun hangs low, bleeding into the sky, drowning the field in gold and fire.

Dean's dead.

Two days, and it still feels like a lie. Murdered. A word that burns every time it crosses my mind. I never thought this moment would come, not like this. Not standing in this forgotten, unkempt field.
I never imagined I'd be the one to bury him.

But here I am.

I stare at the freshly turned earth, my body heavy, my heart hollow. The grave is raw, a gaping wound in the middle of nowhere. It feels wrong. No flowers. No words. Just a rough, ugly hole, because that's all we could manage. Because he's gone, and there's no way to make sense of it.

No tears. I've cried them all. My chest aches, but there's nothing left to spill. Not here. Not now. Dean wouldn't want it. He didn't believe in tears. He believed in moving forward, even when everything felt like it was crumbling around us.

Now look where we are, brother.

The sky is a palette of bruised colours; deep pinks, orange streaks, as if the world is mourning with me. The sun slips further, casting long shadows over the grass, the light barely touching the grave. But he's not here to see it. I swallow hard, the lump in my throat refusing to budge. My hands shake, but not from the cold. It's a strange kind of numbness, something that creeps into my bones and sits there, heavy and unmoving. It settles in, and I let it.

I wish I could say I'm angry, but I'm not. Not anymore. That fire burned out the moment I saw his body, lifeless

345

and cold, when everything went still inside me. Now, all that's left is this void where he used to be. We were supposed to grow old together. All of us. That was the plan. A bunch of screw-ups from a children's home who made it out. We were gonna make it, no matter what the world threw at us.

But the world threw more than we could catch.

I exhale, my breath shaky. I should say something; some final words, some kind of closure. But everything feels too big for words, too tangled to unravel. What do you say? I don't know. I'm not sure I ever will.

The sunset blurs, the edges of the world softening, the darkness creeping in slowly. My hands are filthy, covered in earth, sweat and death. I step back from the grave, the hole now just another part of the landscape. I feel like I'm floating, like nothing's real. It's too quiet here. Too peaceful. Dean would hate it. I hate it.

"I'm sorry," I whisper, the words barely audible. Maybe he can hear me. Maybe he can't. I don't know if I believe in any of that anymore. But I still say it. Somehow, it still feels like he's standing right behind me. Like I'll turn around and see him there, grinning that reckless grin of his, ready for the next disaster. But I won't. Because he's not here. He's buried underneath my feet.

I turn around, and there they stand. Sienna, Birdie, and.. Delilah. *Oh God*, Delilah.

Her face is gaunt, eyes vacant, like the life's been drained out of her, like she's buried too. She loved him- *loves* him- and now she's here, staring at the same grave, the same patch of dirt, and all I can think is how much more she has to lose. How much death can a person take before they just fucking break?

She's trembling, her lips quivering like she's about to say something, but there are no words. There never were. She looks at me for a second, and I feel it; the weight of her grief, her confusion. And all I can do is stand there, just as lost, just as broken, with nothing to offer her. No comfort. No answers.

Sienna's eyes are red-rimmed, her hands stuffed deep into her jacket pockets, like if she just keeps them there, keeps them still, maybe the world will stop spinning for a second. Maybe she'll stop feeling like everything's falling apart. Birdie's standing beside her. Her sobs break through the silence, sharp and raw. Her cheeks are a burned red, streaked with tears. That perfect, prided hair of hers now lies dishevelled, flat.

But there's one face missing.

No Skylar.

She should be here. She was the light in all this darkness. Dean's best friend, his sister in every way that

347

mattered. Always loud, always laughing, filling the room with her chaotic energy. She would've thrown her arms around Delilah right now, whispered something stupid, something only Skylar could get away with saying that'd somehow make you want to laugh even in the middle of this hell.

But she's not here. She and Noah disappeared without a trace. Gone. Like smoke in the wind. Noah. My brother. My blood. The one who tore into my life like a hurricane, and now he's left just as suddenly. Leaving a trail of death and sorrow in his wake. I'll never get to ask him why. Why he did it.

I wonder if that was always the plan. For him to tear through everything, to rip apart what was already fragile, and then vanish, leaving me to clean up the mess. The deaths. The grief. The emptiness.

He left, just like he came.
And I don't know if I'll ever see him again.

The wind picks up again, cold and biting, as if the earth itself is reminding me that nothing stays, that everything slips away sooner or later. I close my eyes for a second, trying to breathe, trying to steady the storm brewing inside me. But it's no use. I open them and see Delilah again. Her eyes filled with unshed tears, staring at the place where Dean's body lies, and I know there's no peace to be found. Not here.

Not anymore.

I glance over at Sienna. Her butterfly, that fragile little thing she's carried through so much, is perched on her shoulder, wings still, unmoving. Just like her. We lock eyes, and there's a quiet knowing. My sweet, broken yet again, shattered by this life we've been forced to endure. Her strength cracks, but it doesn't crumble; Sienna always finds a way to hold on, even when the world rips her apart piece by piece. I walk to her, wrapping her in my arms. Keeping her.

Delilah takes a step forward, her body moving on instinct, like she's walking through a dream she can't wake up from. She kneels at the patch where Dean's buried, and places down a note, written in her delicate handwriting, along with a single flower. A rock goes on top to keep it all in place, like she's trying to hold onto something, anything, that won't be taken by the wind.

Then she stands, slowly, and turns back to us, her face a blank slate, her eyes distant.

"I can't believe this is real," she whispers, and her voice trembles like a leaf caught in a storm. Then it steadies, and she looks up, eyes burning with something darker. Something that hurts to look at. "He's gone.

Actually gone. And now.. now I have to carry him with me. Not in some sweet memory. Not in some photo I can look at when I miss him. No. I have to carry him like a fucking wound. An open wound that will never close. I have to carry his death with me, every single day." She pauses, wipes a tear from her cheek, but it's like trying to stop the rain. It just keeps coming. "And I don't know how to do it. I don't know how to live in a world where he doesn't exist."

Her words crack like thunder in the stillness, shaking the ground beneath us. My chest tightens, and I can't breathe, but I still can't cry. I'm too far gone for that.

"The last thing I told him was *'Be safe'*." She says. "*'Always'* he told me. Always." The irony twists like a knife, and her breath catches. Her eyes blaze with sorrow, reflecting the dying sun.

I wish I could turn back time, erase the moment he walked away. I want to scream his name, to shake the universe until it gives him back. But all I have are memories; flashes of a boy who was fierce and loving, a brother who deserved more than this cruel end.

I close my eyes, and the memories flood back; those golden moments that feel like they belong to someone else, another life. Riding bikes down cracked pavement, the wind whipping through our hair as we raced under the sun, laughter echoing like a song of freedom.

Playing pranks. Running. Jumping. Scratches and doodles on the peeling walls, our fingerprints marking a chaotic canvas, proof of our innocence, proof we existed.

Sneaking out under a blanket of stars, hearts racing, shadows dancing in the dark. The thrill of rebellion, tiptoeing past creaky floorboards, bursting into the cool night air; stealing sweets, drinks, freedom on our tongues. We thought we were invincible, a force of nature, untouchable.

Those memories soon shifted. Smoking together in the stillness of midnight, clouds swirling like the secrets we kept. Stored, for each other. Those endless conversations, the world dissolving, every whispered hope, a promise, a bond forged in smoke and laughter. Stealing cars, adrenaline pumping. Fights that left us bruised, bloodied, but laughing. Those moments, woven tightly, the fabric of who we were, now frayed at the edges, unravelling before my eyes.

But those are the only memories I'll ever have. That's it. There will never be a new one. This is the end of our story, the last chapter unwritten, and it crushes me. The memories wrap around me like barbed wire, each one a reminder of a bond severed too soon. No more adventures. No more anything.

The world keeps spinning, but I'm standing still.

I shift my gaze to the left, and something catches my eye; a flash of vibrant blue against the muted backdrop of grief. A butterfly, beautiful and serene. A butterfly, suspended in the air, not fluttering aimlessly but hovering, poised as if the universe itself has held its breath, watching us.

I extend my hand, palm open, an invitation wrapped in thick hesitation. To my surprise, the delicate creature alights on my skin, a featherweight against the weight of everything I've lost. It feels like a whisper, a secret, a connection that transcends this world. Then it lifts. A spirit set free. It drifts toward Delilah. Dances around her head, a soft glow.

Her eyes widen, captivated. The atmosphere thickens with magic; fragile yet potent. The butterfly flutters gently, lingering deliberately near her stomach, before landing on the rock she placed. The world falls away, leaving only this sacred exchange. A spirit, dancing through the air. It transforms. Transcends. Becomes something eternal.

In that instant, I'm reminded,
    not even death can erase this.

Fate may carve its path,
but what we've built endures,
for fate intended this as well.
Goodbye, forevermore.

THE END.

Playlist

Chapter 1 :

Welcome Home, Son - Radical Face

Chapter 2 :

When Was That - Angus & Julia Stone

Chapter 3 :

Brother (Stripped Back) - Kodaline

Chapter 4 :

Sarcophagus III - $uicideboy$, Ramirez

Chapter 5 :

Mind Games - Sickick

Chapter 6 :

Skydive - Astronauts

Chapter 7 :

Big city blues - Lil Peep, Cold Hart

Chapter 8 :

From A Dream - Angus & Julia Stone

Chapter 9 :

To All Of You - Syd Matters

Chapter 10 :

Shadow - Chromatics

:(

ABOUT THE AUTHOR

Amber Fawn, born 2002, is a Cornwall-based indie author, specialising in Romance & Dark romance. Her passion for reading and writing began as early as 3 years old when she forced herself to learn how to read. Her preferred writing style is often on the darker side, experimenting with elements of gore and psychological trauma.

Website: amberfawnwrites.com
Instagram: @amberfawnauthor